John Heermans

Nuggets of Gold

John Heermans

Nuggets of Gold

ISBN/EAN: 9783337310257

Printed in Europe, USA, Canada, Australia, Japan

Cover: Foto ©Andreas Hilbeck / pixelio.de

More available books at **www.hansebooks.com**

NUGGETS OF GOLD;

OR, THE

LAWS OF SUCCESS IN LIFE,

IN BRIEF AND PUNGENT LECTURES TO YOUNG MEN;
TO WHICH IS ADDED THE SCIENCE OF ALCO-
HOLIC MEDICATION; ALSO THE PHIL-
OSOPHY OF LABOR, WAGES,
CAPITAL, MONEY AND
WEALTH.

BY JOHN HEERMANS.

The finest writing is that which says the most in the smallest space.

- - - - -

CORNING, N. Y.:
PUBLISHED BY THE AUTHOR.
1880.

TO THE

YOUNG MEN OF THE UNITED STATES,

ON WHOM, IN RAPID SUCCESSION, THE

DESTINIES OF THIS GREAT NATION ARE DEVOLVING

AND ON WHOSE

PRACTICAL EDUCATION AND HABITS OF LIFE

ITS SUCCESS

MUST ALWAYS DEPEND,

THIS WORK IS MOST RESPECTFULLY DEDICATED, BY

THE AUTHOR.

WHAT IS THIS BOOK FOR?

Whoever writes a book is presumed to have a reason for writing it, and such reason is looked for at this end of the book. I will therefore tell the reader how the matter of this book came to be written, and why it is presented to the public in this form.

I am not an author by profession. My writings for the press, for forty years, on various subjects, have been chiefly amateur. I have written because I thought somebody ought to write such things as I have written.

A call came to me to write a series of brief articles for publication in a local paper of large circulation, for the benefit of the young men of my locality. Looking out upon the condition and habits of a large majority of the young men of the time, and looking back over my experience and observation of fifty years of a laborious life, I thought I might offer some suggestions useful to all well-disposed young men striving to get on in the world.

I had not gone far in the work before the subject seemed to open up before me in much greater proportions, and involving a much greater labor than I had anticipated, to do it reasonable justice. But having entered upon it, I persevered until I had discussed most prominent subjects in the practical affairs of life. And long before I got through, compliments and encomiums came to me from many sources entitled to respect, as to the value of the articles; and numerous calls have been made upon me for their publication in book form, for preservation, and for general circulation; for the principles embodied in them are applicable to civilized society everywhere and for all time.

I have read many excellent books of advice to young men; but I do not remember one that comes down to the pith of practical life with economy of words. They contain too much elocutionary fine writing, too much elaborate discussion too far away from the heart of the subject in hand, too little in much, and involve too much reading to find what a busy young man wants to know. Whatever of valuable matter there is in these litt'e discourses is set out in plain and direct language, and not hidden away in ornamental circumlocution. This is said to be my forte.

I have named the book *The Laws of Success in Life*, because success can only be achieved by observing the eternal principles therein laid down. I call it, also, *Nuggets of Gold*, because I am not too modest to accept the verdict of my readers that it contains large value in small space.

SECONDLY.

A second object of this book is to correct the fallacy that alcohol is good for sick people. It is difficult to convince the generality of medical practitioners that they have no science for the practice of alcoholic medication ; but I boldly assert here, that in the second part of this book I have clearly demonstrated that the last word of medical science is that alcohol in the human body is never useful, but always bad—sick or well.

In view of the notorious fact that by the use of alcohol for medicine by the doctors, the drug shop is largely the parent of the dram shop, and of the fact that its use is always damaging to the sick, it is of vital importance to the temperance cause, as well as to suffering humanity, that the errors of the common medical profession in this behalf should be everywhere promulgated so as to get the barbarous practice in a course of ultimate extinction. To this end I have taken great care to set out the exact state of medical science on the subject.

THIRDLY.

I have long seen the need of a compact and comprehensive work on the common, everyday principles of political economy, especially adapted to the instruction of working men, and to correct the fallacies by which they are often misled by political demagogues. And as I have not been able to find any such work, I have undertaken it in part third of this book.

Altogether, I present three books in one. And if my readers shall be by them in any degree instructed and improved, my object will be accomplished.

J. HEERMANS,

Corning, N. Y., Dec., 1879.

TABLE OF CONTENTS.

PART THIRD.

LABOR, CAPITAL, MONEY AND WEALTH.

PART FIRST.

LECTURES TO YOUNG MEN.

LECTURE I.

PRELIMINARY AND GENERAL.

I have seen the model young man of the period, with his pretty cane, his ten-cent cigar, his kid gloves, and all his other popinjay embellishments, all of which has seemed to ask me: What more is wanted for a perfect young man? Yes, I have seen that kind of young men all my life; and I have seen another kind also. And I have noticed, in going along, the outcome of each in all that we call success or failure in life.

What is success in life? Not the amassing of wealth simply. I have seen men eminently successful in that, all through life, who were only miserable failures. It is not a conscientious and religious life simply. I have seen many men of that kind who were miserable failures in comparison with what they might and ought to have been.

What I take to be success in life, for the purposes of this discussion, is to make an honest livelihood as we go along, with reasonable investments in all meritorious benefactions, with steady accumulations sufficient for reasonable independence all along life's journey, and a competence for old age, if we reach it, and a conscience void of offense toward God. The opposite of this, *i. e.* to drag along through life the slave of others because always behind hand and under the pressure of want, and to land in the poor house, or some other charity, at last, or to acquire money riches merely, is failure.

When I was young my grandfather gave me this history of himself. In his young days he was of a roving disposition—thoughtless of the future—spending his earnings as he went along—having a good time generally, in all the frivolities and dissipations of the time. But in his travels he had many a time met with paupers upon the public charity—sometimes farmed out to the lowest bidder, as we see them sometimes now-days. Noticing, as we may always notice, that those people were often badly used, and had no rights that their superiors were bound to respect; looking upon those pictures of wasted life, as our young men may look upon the same to-day, he discovered the road that he was traveling. "What," he said to himself, "Must I come to that some day? If I should live to be old and unable to work must I be domineered and driven about by the merest child of the household where public charity would place me? Certainly, all this, unless I call a halt. That shall not be. These strong arms, with health and the blessing of God, can procure for me a competence for old age, and it shall be so."

And so it was. He put his new philosophy into immediate execution. He settled down to work and saved his earnings. Commencing as a farm laborer at the scantiest wages, he so prospered that at the age of fifty he owned a farm that made him independent. All through life I have seen some of that kind of men in all the pursuits of life; but I have seen more of the other kind—those who, whatever their income may be, spend it as they go along. I have seen them drag along through hard working lives, always on a strain, always "under the harrow," "clever fellows," perhaps, but always on the down hill side and more or less a burden upon their friends; and not because they do not earn money enough, but only because they have not the self-denial to save some of it. For it is not the money that a man earns that makes him rich, but what he saves.

I have noticed that class of people, too, when they come to old age—dependent upon public charity. I have heard them assert their *claims* upon the public bounty. They have done so much. They have always been industrious and have been of great value to the community, and the world owes them a living; when the fact is that the world does not owe them a cent. If they have labored hard and long they have consumed all the fruits of that labor and more. Whatever value they have been of to the world, they have received value for value as they went along.

These two classes of people that I have tried to describe comprise the bulk of mankind. Young man, if you are destined to be one of the world's producers—if your good fortune is to do something for the privilege of being in the world—and if you are doing ever so much, or ever so little, you are starting out in the road of one or the other of these classes. And as your choice of these roads is, so will be your success or failure. Extraordinaries excepted, every man with ordinary health through life can raise a family, keep himself above board all along, and accumulate a competence for old age. The lowest-priced men usually earn enough for this. And on the other hand, any man can keep himself in distress all his life with the largest income; for it is not so much the amount of money that a man handles that makes him comfortable, as it is the fact that he has enough at all times to meet all his wants, and more.

I do not think that the accumulation of property is the chief end of man; but I do say that any man that has not the fortitude and self-denial to save something is generally a *failure*. He has never much of anything to contribute for the benefit of humanity—all must go to gratify his own morbid tastes. And his tastes are not half as well gratified as is his who spends not half as much, but is always saving something. Money is not to be worshiped and not to be despised. I have always noticed that those who sneer at the provident as money worshipers, while they themselves never keep any of it long enough to pay it the slightest devotion, are the most eager to clutch the savings of others whenever the law will let them.

We sometimes hear about bad financiering. "So and so is a bad financier and so he fails in everything." The fact is that financiering, on a small or large scale, is usually very simple and easy. It is only to not waste your money. A man makes $50 a month, for instance, and he is fool enough to pay out $25 or $30 of it for nonsense; and you call it bad financiering. It is not financiering at all. It is dissipation. Financiering is to take that money and put it where it will earn something. There is no mystery about that—anybody can do it. The financiering of large business establishments of any kind is all about as simple as that. When the money is allowed to be stolen or wasted in any way, failure ensues; when saved and put to good uses, the financial part is a success. That is all there is of it.

In future numbers I shall try to show, more in detail, how it is that men succeed or fail in their life work.

––––––

II.

THE FALSE AND THE TRUE—IN WORK.

"Honor and Shame from no condition rise,
Act well your part; there all the honor lies."

Before entering further into the merits of this discussion, I must say to you, young man, that in starting out upon the journey of life, there are some things of infinitely more importance to you than this one matter of pecuniary success. There are a hundred ways to make money, or to *get* it rather, by which success in accumulation is the most miserable failure. Better, a thousand times better, to fill a pauper's grave than that of a millionaire from such pursuits. And some of them are called respectable, and bear the sanction of law. "Life is more than meat." A true life is something beyond the mere supplying of our daily wants, and any amount of accumulation. It is to do that in such a way as to do some good to somebody else; to contribute to the common good of the community, so that the world will be the better for our having lived in it; and not by hook or crook so that it will be really all, or some part of it, at other people's expense.

If I cultivate the earth, and add my produce to the stocks in the market, or build a house that may shelter my fellow beings for a hundred years or so, or build a ship that transports surplus productions to distant climes, for suitable compensation, I contribute my quota to the common stock of wealth. We may say, in general, that the true life is,

1st, To do something that will be of benefit to somebody.

And what is this? Not to concoct some scheme or ingenious device by which the unwary can be induced to part with values for your benefit, whether lawful or not, if it does not, somehow, contribute to the sum of human comfort; but it is something that does so contribute. For instance, to cultivate the earth—producing the material of food and raiment; to delve in the mines—dragging out the minerals needful for our civilization; the thousand manufacturing industries that produce the innumerable commodities for the comfort and the rational enjoyment of mankind; the merchant who brings producer and consumer together; the learned professions—the gospel ministry, with its potent influence for the good order of society, to say nothing of its spirituality : the profession of the law, as the foundation of all civilization, with the officers of government as its corner-stone; the medical profession with its healing arts; the public educators, training up the young in the learning of the times; all these and any other vocations that go to make up the sum of human civilization and comfort, I need not say, are of the true and not the false. But the innumerable devices by which people are induced to part with values for no value, or the production or sale of any commodities that are not only useless to the consumer, but tend to his injury and to the general injury of the community; it is self-evident that all such employments are not of the true life, but of the false. Better that a millstone be hung about your neck and cast into the sea than engage in any of them.

And then, secondly, there is a true and a false life in the pursuit of legitimate occupations. We must do our work faithfully, efficiently, honestly.

"Act well your part: there all honor lies," the poet says; and there the profit lies, too, I will add. When I was a blacksmith I took a great deal of pride in having it said that my work was better done than that of my competitors. And so, I may be permitted to say, all along through life, I have tried to do faithfully and well whatever I have undertaken. If I have succeeded in this, my life work has been true and not false, in this one respect, whether otherwise successful or not; other people are the better for their dealings with me, and I know I am the better for my efforts to excel.

Young men and boys are too apt to be heedless of these principles. They do not seem to know that honesty is the best policy in the relations of life, or else they do not know that it is dishonest to be unfaithful in whatever service they are engaged.

I see apprentices and other young men employed by others for hire. Too often it is the case that their ambition is to be as unprofitable as possible to their employers without losing place. A young man who starts out on that principle will always be a fraud and must necessarily stay at the bottom —a failure.

But take a boy of the other make-up; one who starts out with the ambition to excel in whatever he undertakes, be it ever so humble or ever so cheap, he cannot be kept down; that kind of people are too scarce in the world, and they are wanted. The world will find them out, sooner or later, and promote them, just as surely as it finds out the other sort and leaves them where they are. Or at the very least: all promotions and all real successes are of this class. In the one case the life is true; in the other false. All through life I have seen and watched these two phases of life in work, and always seen the fruits of each to be as above stated.

Young reader, the lesson to be drawn from all this is that if you would be anybody, or attain to any success in life, you must train yourself to act well your part in whatever your work is. Make yourself so necessary to your employer that he cannot afford to dispense with you, and you will be sure to be the gainer by it in the long run; but if you start out critical and crotchety—doing as little as possible—working for your wages merely, without an eye to your employer's interest, he will very soon find it out and will be on the lookout for a better man. Business laws are inexorable. A man who hires labor of any kind must have honest work for honest pay. If he has not the brains and the energy to get this he must sooner or later go under and be succeeded by one who has. And this is the reason why shiftless workmen cannot succeed. Sooner or later every man is sure to find his proper level. It is an economic as well as a moral law that you must not cheat your employer. Honesty is always the best policy; and every young man may as well start out with the conviction that this is the rule that God has fixed over him, and it is as irrevocable as is the law of gravitation.

Of course I am not to be understood that shiftless, lazy, time-serving, unprofitable men cannot find anything to do as hirelings; there is generally something for everybody—good, bad, and indifferent—to do. But what I do say is this: that class of men are always at a disadvantage. They must always work at the lowest wages. They are always under suspicion. In times of depression they are the first to be out of work. And in general they never amount to anything but "hewers of wood and drawers of water." And on the whole they cheat themselves the worst, and only amount to miserable failures. This is all there is of it.

III.

THE FALSE AND THE TRUE—IN BUSINESS.

The same rules as to the false and the true life apply to business that apply to work, as I tried to illustrate them in my last number.

As the laws of nature cannot be ignored without incurring their penalties, so the laws of morals are inexorable. To say nothing of Divine retributive justice, or the Word of God, there is an economic penalty to the violation of these laws that we cannot escape.

A miller cannot afford to take too much toll; he is sure to be found out sometime, and lose more in custom than he makes by the stealings. A merchant cannot afford to misrepresent his goods or to cheat his customers in any way; in the long run it will injure his trade more than the amount of wrongful gains, and that diverted trade will gravitate to the honest dealer.

I once knew a sprightly young man in this county, a very competent business man, employed at a good salary in an important business establishment, entirely faithful and satisfactory in his work, and in a fair way to succeed to the position of his aged principal. He proved dishonest in money transactions, lost his place and died a miserable inebriate. Pure selfishness should have kept him honest. He could not afford to steal. The righteous law of economic retribution extinguished him as it is pretty sure to all such fools, sooner or later.

I knew a young man of fine business attainments —educated to business by his friends, and promoted from point to point, until he had attained to a position of great responsibility, honor and emolument. He could not afford to steal, but he did, and he is an outcast from all respectable associations, and degraded from all respectable business. Tweed's millions of stealings turned out to be unprofitable as a business venture; and his *confreres* have all turned out in like manner.

The city of Scranton had been afflicted with a

political leader who plundered her treasury at will, and for years he had been supposed to be invincible. One day I saw him start for the State Prison. His confederates came to their grief before him. And so all the big and little bank thieves and defaulters are coming to justice as we may see in the papers every day.

These few instances are only samples of what I have seen and treasured up in my memory all my life. In all the multifarious transactions between man and man, my testimony and my admonition are that dishonesty in any of its phases never pays. True, I have seen it prosper for a season—sometimes for a pretty long season, seemingly—but I have seen many notable cases where the penalty came at last with severity. Somehow it is so fixed in economic law, as well as in the moral law, that " honesty is always the best policy," and it is not worth while for any man, young or old, to try to get around that law. The smaller cheats and frauds do not meet so conspicuous retribution; but it is sure to come; commensurate to the offenses; for " what a man soweth that shall he also reap." Nobody knows how many business bankruptcies are caused by violations of this inexorable law.

I do not say that dishonest business men always fail in business, but I do say that where one of that class keeps above board through life, his success is attained *in spite of the incumbrance* of his dishonest practices. Without them his success would have been vastly greater. I think the uniform testimony of all intelligent and impartial observers of business and business men is that all *highly* successful business men have been scrupulously honest in their business.

In view of all this, my young friends, and in view of the uniform denunciations of Holy Writ upon all forms and all degrees of rapacity and wrong, I do not see how such a thing as even temptation to wrong in business can ever get a lodgment in your minds, if you will only take a thought on the subject. All species of wrong being inimical to your interest, your comfort and your eternal well-being, you never can entertain a thought of any such thing if you will study out the subject for yourselves, and look about you and observe the practical proofs of these theories. When we once come to understand that wrong to others is sure to recoil, and the severest of the injury will be upon ourselves, it is impossible to entertain the idea of any dishonesty in business.

There is one other principle of business ethics that is, perhaps, worthy of consideration in this connection. When a young man starts out in business he never should undertake to build himself up by unwarrantably pulling others down. To build up your own business by your own real merit —by the excellence of your wares or of your work, whatever it may be, by their reasonable price, by your fair dealing and promptness in execution; in short by your general skill, facilities, and faithfulness to your customers, is all legitimate, and any competitors who cannot survive such competition must and should retire from the contest. But a direct onslaught upon the business of a competitor —by detraction, slander, inuendo, or any other direct interference, is in the highest degree reprehensible, and in the long run never can be successful. It is sure to recoil sooner or later.

There is room enough in the world for everybody. If two of a trade happen to get too close together, so that there is not room for both, the weaker must retire to some more suitable locality, and there is no occasion for them to quarrel, or to try to injure each other's business. And it has always been a puzzle to me why it is that two of a trade cannot agree. Reader, never engage in that kind of competition. You cannot afford it.

I can illustrate this by an incident of my own life. I was once employed in an office, where a fellow clerk, somehow, imbibed the idea that I was in his way and he in my way. I had not thought of such a thing, for I thought there was room enough for both of us. And while I was trying to get him promoted to the place he wanted, he was scheming to get me out of my place. The result was that I was considerably injured for the time, but I came out all right finally; and in schemes to supplant his principal, the individual in question lost his own place, irrevocably, to his great damage for the rest of his life.   And this is no uncommon case.   Any elderly man who has gone through the world with his eyes open can recall numerous instances of attempted overreaching, in various phases, of larger or smaller proportions, with similar ending.

Never think of pulling somebody down for the purpose of building yourselves up, my friends. Success never comes of that sort of effort.   Build up yourselves by your own brains, industry, push and honesty, and let other people alone to do the same if they will.   If you have no merit of your own, the demerits of others, whatever they may be, cannot make you a success.

IV.

ACCUMULATION—GENERAL CONSIDERATIONS.

There are but very few men who have the peculiar ability to amass large wealth, whatever their opportunities may be.   Large pecuniary success requires extraordinary talent in that particular direction, as well as the industry and economy to utilize them.   But for the reasonable and sufficient accumulation of property, it is not the best brains that are the most successful.   It does not require much talent to do that.   I have noticed all along through life that very frequently mediocre and illiterate men are more successful in money matters .

than others with brilliant talents and high education. Henry Clay and Daniel Webster, with all their powers for earning money, would have died entirely poor but for the large donations made them by political friends. And I have seen men, unable to read or write, and scarcely able to count their own money, and with brains not much more than sufficient to shovel dirt, accumulate respectable properties. We say of such men, usually, that they know just enough to make money; but the fact is that they know a good deal more than that —they know enough to save some of it; and any body with better brains can learn that if they will.

I am not sure that *excessive* accumulations are desirable. No man has need of as much as a hundred thousand dollars. And I am sure that it is not well for young people to have very rich fathers. Now and then we hear of a rich man's son who is good for something, but in a general way, to bring up a boy to understand that he is to be rich when his father dies, is to spoil him. Notoriously, rich men's sons are usually good for nothing. They go to ruin themselves, and waste their patrimony very briskly when they get control of it. And all this is easily accounted for on common principles of human nature. Work of any kind is not attractive. People do not take to it from choice. And so when a young man is trained to think that he is to have money enough to carry him through, it is contrary to nature for him to put forth much exertion of any kind.   In his educational course he will depend on his money and his social standing chiefly, and do as little work as possible; and in anything that he undertakes he is pretty sure to amount to nothing.   On the other hand, luxury, dissipation and licentiousness are naturally attractive to the young; and so it is nothing more than human nature that rich young men go to ruin.

But take a boy unencumbered by wealth—knowing that he must make his own way in the world—must do something; if he has the elements of manhood in him, it is only human nature that he should put forth all there is in him to make his mark and be somebody.   A parent can safely aid such a boy to a reasonable extent, in the way of education, or otherwise.

On the whole, therefore, the very worst thing that a man can do for his children, is to make them rich with money in their young days, or to make them think that they are to be rich.

And here, I may as well say, once for all, that whatever I shall say, in these papers, about economy and accumulation, I do not object to the use of the luxuries, the elegancies, or even the baubles of life, by those who can afford them.   To cultivate the beautiful and the refined is only to copy after the work of God in nature.   The landscape of green and fruitful fields, the grandeur of the forest, the rolling rivers, the gigantic waterfalls, the starry heavens, the magnificent sunset, the gorgeous rainbow, the golden corn, the blade of grass, the flowers of the field, all, all invite the development of whatever there is of beauty in the capacities of man.

But what I do insist upon is this : the necessaries of life are first; and every man's duty, and his real comfort and peace of mind require that he shall make adequate provision for these, not only for the time being, but for all contingencies through life, before dissipating his earnings upon mere luxuries. We see men sixty, seventy, eighty years old, working for wages for their daily bread, and go to the poor house when no longer able to earn a miserable pittance by the torturing physical exertion of bone and muscle, becoming paralyzed by age and needing leisure and repose. It is pitiable. Young man, you cannot afford to come to that.

But I see young men in unknown numbers traveling in that road as fast as the wheels of time can carry them. We have had great railroad and other labor strikes; and in looking over the accounts of them, there is one point that everywhere stands out in bold relief, that is mournfully, not to say *fearfully*, apropos to this phase of my subject. It is that the masses of laboring people are destitute of the common necessaries of life, whenever their work is suspended; and there is a general clamor for public provision of food for the people out of work. No matter that they have been receiving extravagant, unprecedented wages, the moment that they are out of work, either by their own act or otherwise, we begin to hear the cry of starvation.   And it is not a false alarm.   I have no idea that one-fourth of all the men who are in the service of others for hire, in all vocations—railroads, manufactories, shops, stores, offices and everything else—in a suspension of work, could pay their *necessary* expenses for ninety days without running in debt.   And by running in debt I mean that they are not worth enough to buy food and raiment for ninety days.   Look around among your acquaintances and see whether this is so.   The stereotyped excuse is that wages are too low, and the appeal is to the public to provide for the breadless in times of depression—provide for able-bodied paupers caused by a brief suspension of employment, when every man, in flush times, spends enough money for cigars, beer, and other needless extravagance to make him comfortably rich at sixty, if saved.   It is an outrage upon civilization.

But what of the other side?   For that state of things is not universal.   There is another way— a better road to travel.   Here and there may be seen a young man who is not spending all his earnings, but economizes and accumulates, so that he is always in easy circumstances and "above board." These may be found in all the trades and occupations of the world of production.   And they are not always the highest priced men.   I have often seen men working for the lowest wages, commencing in their young days to save up, little by little, putting those savings to good use to help to earn something more, and so going on, in ease and independence through life, and finding themselves comfortably rich in old age. These are not the men that are always grumbling at low wages, and hard times, and organize strikes and mobs. And I see men side by side with these, receiving twice, three, four times the wages of the former, and never quite up even; always on a strain; their wages never high enough to support them; times are always hard; and they are always looking for something to turn up to help them out.

Such, in a general way, are the two ways for people to go through life. And as a man starts in his young days, so he will usually go through to the end.

V.

ACCUMULATION—SPECIFIC.

A large majority of young men, earning wages all the way from a dollar a day to a hundred dollars a month, do not save anything. They think they cannot. Approach one of this class on the subject—say a $75 a month man—and he will say: " It is impossible for me to save anything out of my little salary; it is too small; I have tried and it is out of the question; I am not very extravagant, and it will no more than pay my necessary expenses."

Then, my young friend, you never can save anything out of any other sum. No difference what position you ever attain to, or what amount of money you earn, your expenses will always be up to your income, unless you can learn to lay up something out of $75 a month or a good deal less. Then you are to be a poverty stricken subject of want and distress through life; for I have always noticed that your class of people—those who spend all they earn—never earn quite enough to meet their wants. No matter how much their income is, and how high their style of living is, they are always on a strain for something higher. Somebody is a little ahead of them, and are they not just as good as that somebody? And their distress for the want of that higher notch is as poignant as is that of those who have only potatoes to eat and are looking for something else. And they are apt to get in the habit of running in debt—spending their money before it is earned—with all the harassing and embarrassments that that implies, and not infrequently are led into crooked ways and crime to keep up their supplies; examples of which we may read of nearly every day in the papers. Such are the treasures that you are laying up for yourselves, my young friends, for your comfort through life.

It is a great mistake. You *can* save something. It is a notorious fact that a large majority of the large and small fortunes that are originally accumulated in this country have originated from the small savings from small incomes of their owners in early life. Specifically: I can point you to numerous men of my acquaintance, and of about my age, who started out upon hard work upon less than one-third of $75 a month ; and from the savings of such meagre wages, as the foundation, they are now comfortably rich. And I can also point you to others who commenced life with much better prospects, larger incomes, who, like you, thought they could not save anything, and have punished along through life in poverty, genteel poverty, some of them, but none the less distressing to them, for never quite genteel enough for their cravings—and now in old age helpless, only as " hewers of wood and drawers of water."

When John Magee, the millionaire, was doing farm labor in this town at eight dollars a month, and saved his money and put it to profitable use— never indulging in any avoidable expense—he planted the seeds of capital, and established the habits of economy and thrift that made him what he was in after life. And John Magee was a man that all young men can well afford to pattern after in all the relations of life.

I might write down the name of a Corning man who commenced life by blacking boots and selling papers, saving his money instead of wasting it for pleasant indulgences that he could do without, and going on, step by step, into business larger and still larger, not indulging in any needless expense until his accumulations were such that he could really afford it; and to-day he is one of the rich business men of Corning, and the same plain unostentatious, sensible man that he was thirty-five years ago when he was poor.

And I know another Corning man who commenced here in Corning's early days. He earned high wages for the times; but he was a "clever fellow," as the saying is; he thought he must maintain a position up high in young people's fashionable society, indulging in all the costly frivolities of the times. Ostentation, glitter and spread were with him the chief end of man. And he could not save anything. Of course not. On that theory of life, expenses can only be limited by ability to pay. Saving is out of the question. Those habits became chronic, as they usually do by a few years of their indulgence. They have not been cured; he is now an old man—a subject of servitude for the rest of his life. And this is what you are sure to come to, young men of to-day, if you persevere in your unthrifty habits, unless you have the luck to die before you come to it.

I know a man who came to Corning twelve years ago, with a good-sized family on his hands. His wages have not averaged more than $1.50 per day. With that small income in ten years he had a home of his own, worth $1,000—free and clear.

A young business man of Corning, that I know, left his father's house at fourteen years of age; worked for merchants for a series of years, at such wages as boys were able to get—always low—at the last only $18 a month and board ; but he always saved something from his wages. And when he had arrived at a suitable age, his habits of industry, economy and integrity had won for him a name that enabled him to start out in business on his own account. Then, while paying up the debt for his original stock of goods, his personal expenses were $300 a year only. He has been in business ten years, and has accumulated a capital that, with a continuance of reasonable prudence, assures him sufficient wealth. What is noteworthy in this case is : It happens to be known to a certainty that but for that young man's habits of economy, and his *tried* integrity during his apprenticeship, he could not have started in that business at all, which is now making him independent. He was watched when he knew not of it, and found not wanting. He had the groundwork of honest manhood in him, and it mattered not to him who was on his track, or when, or where. And this is another proof of what I tried to inculcate in a former paper, that aside from any higher motive, honesty always pays.

And I know another case of a youngerly successful Corning business man, who started when a boy, with the capital of honesty, industry, fidelity to his employer, and rigid economy. He adopted the policy of *doing all he could* for his employer, instead of as *little* as he could, as is the case with too many boys and young men. He was always on hand and always reliable, never exhausted by any sort of licentiousness or dissipation, and as a matter of course he soon became so necessary to his employer as to command the highest wages that the service would admit of. He began at $6 a month and board, and at the end of six years he was getting $500 a year and board, and had saved a thousand dollars. It is simply a natural result that he is now a prosperous and reasonably wealthy merchant.

What has been done can be done; and from all these examples it is clear enough that almost any young man can save something of his earnings if he will. And it may be taken for granted that pecuniary success is well nigh impossible, in any business, with those who have not learned to save something in early life.

But the answer to all this is: " Well, all this may be true, but I cannot cut down my expenses so as to save anything, without giving up what I consider really necessary to maintain my standing with my associates." I was told the other day, by a man of about my age, as the result of his life's experience, that from the wages of labor—high wages even—a man cannot live respectably and save enough in his life time of vigor to support him in his old age.

Now, it is clear enough that both of these propositions are true. The young man admits that he must spend all his earnings; the old man admits that he *has* spent all his. I am not assuming to *make* a law by which people may get rich, but only *expounding* the laws in this respect that all must be governed by. And it is so fixed, somehow, that wealth is not produced by indulgence. You cannot eat your cake, and keep it. You cannot spend your money, and save it. You cannot use up all your income, and grow rich. You must save something, or not have anything. You must forego some indulgences that may be deemed necessary to a respectable standing in your set, while young, or suffer the penalties of violated economic law all through life, with multiplying intensity, as old age creeps on. This is just the way it is, and you or I cannot help it. The choice is for you to make, and at sixty-five or seventy years of age you will have no right to quarrel with the social fabric, or the laws of the land, or the fortunes of provident people, who are now laying the foundations for future opulence, while you waste your opportunity—as we often hear old people quarrel—if you prefer present indulgence to future fortune.

Our real wants are very few and quite easily supplied. And it is a great mistake to suppose that there is any pressure, worthy of note, upon any young man for spending all his income. You do not need any diamond pins, or other jewelry, or gold watches, or kid gloves, or pretty canes, or ten dollar shoes, or high priced suits, or any of the expensive frivolities that come along, or cigars, or beer, or any other poisons. You do not need any of these for a respectable appearance in your business, whatever it may be. You do not need them to secure the respect of the really high-toned and substantial people of your acquaintance. Without the baubles and the glitter, and with an accumulating bank account, you will be esteemed the more highly by all whose good opinion is worth anything.

The conclusion of the whole matter is that there are two roads open to the free choice of all young men—one leading to competence, and the other through all the distress of continual poverty, and to the poor house at last.

VI.

DO SOMETHING.

There is a class of young men who have qualified themselves—or they think they have—for work that they think more genteel and respectable than farm or mechanic work. They have been educated, or have educated themselves, it may be, in the kid glove way of life, and they think themselves too good to endure the vulgar sunshine without an umbrella, or to do anything to harden up their delicate muscles, to disfigure their pretty hands, or mar their elegant rings. And as with the miners, who think they cannot do any thing else but delve in the mines, and the mechanics who think they cannot do any thing outside of a shop, they think they cannot do anything that is not genteel. The market is always overstocked with that kind of workers, so that many of them are out of employment. They are mistaken. There is nothing about them to disable them from doing any useful labor. They only lack the will and the practice. There is no such thing in physical nature as gentility. If humanity were not all fit for hard work, some of it would not have the same organization, or the same physical needs. " In the sweat of thy face shalt thou eat bread," means that the physical wants of the race shall be produced by physical labor ; and all ordinary developed manhood—womanhood too —is adapted to that labor.

When a thrifty farmer's or mechanic's boy imbibes an ambition to do something other than what his father has made his money at, that ambition may be very well, and when his father strains a point to educate him for that something else, the education is surely very well, for it will qualify him for a better farmer or mechanic in case he does not succeed in the other thing. But when duly qualified for that higher calling, as he thinks it is, and when, wherever he goes for a situation, he finds a dozen applications for every vacant place that occurs, he should remember that his education has not necessarily unfitted him for the work that he has been trained to, or any other that he can get to do, and also that his life mission is to *do something*, and not to be wasting his time in an unavailing hunt for something that he thinks genteel and agreeable. And so of all the hordes of idle young men, who throng, all the towns and cities vainly looking for certain classes of employment, I say retire from such unequal contest; start out: go somewhere and *do something.* There is something for you to do somewhere; go and find it. If you are not too good to do the work that you are looking for and cannot get, you are not too good to do the next best thing that you can get. There is no honest work that is not really respectable. Most of the wealthy men of this country commenced life upon work that you are in the habit of thinking too low for you to begin on. I could mention a prominent and able Corning lawyer who commenced life by chopping cord wood. Another who commenced by teaching district schools when he could get them, and at other times by common carpenter work, and painting, and whatever he could get to do. It is quite likely that these men are the better lawyers for their rough beginning. I think it is generally the case that those who are too good to do the work that comes along, and seems to be necessary for them to do, are never good for much of anything.

The inexorable law is, young man, that if you would succeed in life you must utilize your time by always doing something, and never feel above that which comes along for you to do.

And after all there is not so much difference in

the hardship of employments, if a man's heart is in his work.　Every trade has its pleasures and its pains ; and on the whole I think the enjoyment of the life-work depends more upon the man than upon the vocation.　While what we call hard work, *per se*, is not agreeable, its results may make it very comfortable and easy.　I know how this is by experience.　Not many years ago, when I commenced to build up a new manufacturing industry here in Corning, with my own hands digging foundations, laying stone walls, putting up machinery and then running it, month after month laboring so severely that it was all I could do to climb the hill to my house at night, I can truly say that I never enjoyed myself better in any other occupation.　I enjoyed it, because I thought I was planting the seeds of a business that in other hands might grow into importance.　Again : to go back to my young days, when I was improving a little farm, making acre by acre a continuous source of income, with my own hands building a habitation and a home, in winter time hammering in a blacksmith shop, altogether going to make a homestead and a living for the future ; that kind of work is what we call hard, but I enjoyed it in view of the fruits that were coming all along, and that were in future prospect.　It was really easier than my later, and so-called more genteel work—of the brains, with its responsibilities, its anxious days and sleepless nights, and its premature gray hairs.

No, my friends, the difference is not so much in
the work as in the spirit with which you go into it.
Anything will be irksome and hard that you accept as a mere necessity and a task. But with
your heart in your work, whatever it is, determined to act well your part, with an ambition to succeed in life and be of some service in the world, so
that somebody will be the better for your having
lived in it, you will extract from your vocation as
much comfort as there is for any of us in this imperfect state of existence.

Another class of young men may, if they will,
profit by a word of caution. It is so arranged in
nature that every body is the better for doing something in the way of work. God has not provided
any place for idlers. It is a mistake to suppose
that it is necessary for a part of the population to
be idle to make employment for another part.
There is room enough and work enough for all.
Some parents are so imprudent as to make their
children rich without any effort on their part. And
a great many young men somehow imbibe the idea
that they are to be rich when their fathers die,
without any very good grounds for such an expectancy. Many a man has the reputation of being
wealthy when not worth a dollar, and riches have
a habit of taking to themselves wings and flying
away; so that any young man who relies on his
father's money to carry him through, is quite as
likely to be disappointed as otherwise. In a former

paper (IV.) I have explained how it is that rich young men are usually good for nothing, and go to ruin. The only salvation for them is to commence in early life to train themselves to some useful vocation in the battle of life. Anticipated riches, or riches in hand even, should not debar them from this. A young man is not *necessarily* ruined by riches, or by hopes of them. There is a way of escape. WM. II. VANDERBILT followed in the footsteps of his father in the way of work, and he is a success. I know a young man in the city of Scranton, an only child of a reputed rich father— petted and indulged, and left to himself to lead a life of idleness and dissipation if he would. By his own ambition and energy he pushed himself into a learned profession; so that when his father's riches went down to zero, he was well qualified by habits and acquirements to enter upon his life-work with all the elements of success. Occasional examples of this kind are to be met with, but it may always be noticed that rich men's sons who do not go to ruin are those who engage in some kind of work.

So, young man, if you are rich, your case is not hopeless. Your wealth is not really a disability after all. You can be somebody if you will adopt some useful work and do it. Then, if your riches fail you, you will be prepared to face the calamity with equanimity; if not, I can assure you, from the experience of a busy life, that to a well-disposed ambitious man, the most satisfactory life is to always be doing something useful.

VII.

EDUCATION.

The subject of education is, of course, an important factor in the make-up of young men for their life-work. I think the bearing of what is called education is a good deal misapprehended in this behalf. I have frequently observed, however, that persons of deficient school education are apt to depreciate the value of any higher attainments in that respect than they themselves possess. And this may be what's the matter with me in my estimate of the real value of school education and its province in the labor of life.

Nevertheless I will venture to say that from my observation through life I think the power of mere school education as an element of success in life is often greatly overrated; and when this is the case the education itself may be positively injurious. When I hear a parent say: " I will send my boy to school—to college—I will give him an education, and if everything else fails him that cannot be taken away, that will carry him through; his education will always afford him a support;" when I hear that kind of philosophy, I think that man is mistaken. School education cannot do any such thing. I have seen young men come out of college with parchment all right—certifying to abundant proficiency in all that colleges pretend to do for a man, and so ignorant of the practical affairs of life as to be about as helpless and inefficient as a baby. When I was a young man I met a man of about my age just out of college. He boasted a familiarity with seven or eight languages; and I don't know how many other accomplishments. I thought he was a wonderful man. Horseback riding was quite common, and he did not know which end foremost to put a saddle on a horse. All his other practical knowledge was ditto. I never heard of his amounting to anything.

I have often met with monomaniacs on the subject of college education—men and women run wild with the notion that what they call education is about all that they will ever need in this world. They want an education; they are determined to have an education. Education, education, is the continual burden of their song, but with no definite idea of what it is for; as if education were the the chief end of man. They are mistaken. They greatly overrate the value of school education, and mistake its office. And when it is taken as an *end*, instead of a *means;* when it is substituted for the real knowledge of the practical affairs of life, it is a positive damage.

After having written the foregoing, I met with the following complaint from the New York *Tribune*

The following inquiry comes to us from a city clergyman :

"To the Editor—*Sir :*—How can our young men find employment? This city and other cities are full, and I know not what to advise our young men to do to make their living. Particularly am I interested in a young man who has been to college, is willing to take hold of any kind of work, and is withal of fine personal appearance, and yet can find no employment which will give him his bread. If he wants to emigrate to the West or South, I would gladly pay his expenses and give him an outfit. I venture to ask you for light on a matter beset, as far as I know, with some difficulty. I am, sir, respectfully," R.

Colleges do not pretend to teach a man how to earn his living ; but a large proportion of college students go to school without any definite idea of what for, only under the popular idea before alluded to, that somehow their education is to carry them through ; and after they graduate they find, as in the case of the *Tribune* man, that their education is not available as a bread-producing power. Having all along cultivated the idea that their education must support them, they cannot think of going down, as they call it, to any ordinary work—vulgar work that uneducated men are capable of doing. Oh, no. Their education would be wasted. That is not what they went to college for. And the market for that kind of genteel work being always overstocked, the college education is a positive damage to this class of young men. A four-years apprenticeship in a blacksmith shop, or on a farm, or any other trade that would not cultivate this aversion to what is called hard work, would be of much more value to them.

Well, what then? Is college education altogether useless ? Not at all. It does not disqualify a man for the active duties of life. It does not *necessarily* exalt him above his own plane, so as to spoil him. If a young man goes to college with so much of education on the brain as to depend on the college, in some mysterious way, to turn him out a giant, fit to battle successfully in the brisk competitions for the big prizes of life, it is not the fault of his *alma mater* that he flattens out in a reasonable time. If rich men's brainless sons, with their college parchments in their pockets fall behind poor men's uneducated boys in the race of life, that is not the fault of the colleges. I have known a Corning boy who went from the carpenter's bench to college, graduated and came home with all the usual accomplishments of college graduates, but with the same old spirit of doing something—anything that is necessary for him to do; he is not spoiled. He did not go to college with the expectation that the college would make him, but only that what he could acquire there would help him to make himself. And there are many such.

No. I would not detract an iota from the importance of collegiate education; but I would put it upon its proper footing. I would not ask of it more than it pretends to do. While it does not directly fit a man for the battles of life, while it does not make brains, or work any miracles upon the habits of its subjects, while it does not make fortunes or business for them, and does not do any other miraculous things, it is of great value to any energetic, industrious, go-ahead young man who is determined to push things and be somebody. No matter what occupation he may find it necessary to go down to after he graduates. It will make him the better farmer, or mechanic, or professional man. The discipline, the actual knowledge, and the intercourse with high-toned men, that a college course confers, can hardly ever be wasted on such a man.

So, young man, if you are of that kind of make-up, and if you have a hankering for a college education, go ; go if you can, and you can without an if, whether you have a father to pay your way or not. In an Eastern college there are always not less than twenty men in every class who work their own way through in one way and another. But they are not the dolts and the laggards. They are men of push who will amount to something any how, and of the class that college education is good for. Of course they are not the men who cannot save anything out of six hundred to a thousand dollars a year at home. They do not smoke cigars, or drink any intoxicating beverages, or pay ten cents for every frivolous indulgence that they meet with. Their educational work is primary with them, and they leave it with class-mates with more money and less brains to spread themselves as thinly as they please.

And then, in this matter of education, I think there is a good deal of misapprehension in respect to what are called " self-made men ;" as if a man ever amounts to anything without making himself what he is ; as if there is some other way to success than by his own indefatigable industry ; as if money can make a man. The boy who goes to college to get an education without making it for himself will never get it. The college cannot make it for him— his money cannot. There is no royal road to knowledge. He that expects his school, or his teacher, or his money to make him, will surely not be a self-made man, but he will not be a man at all. He will always be a failure. If, by hook or crook, he smuggles himself through, so as to get the name of a college graduate, so much the worse for him, for, when he comes into the actual competitions of life, his dependence upon his shams will only make his failure the more disastrous. No, my friends, it will not do. Honest work, with the natural powers that God has made for you, is the only way to real manhood. And yet it is convenient and proper for a young man to have a reasonable amount of money furnished him to pay his college expenses. Those who have not that must work the harder or longer than they of equal powers who have. For a father who can afford it, this is the best investment he can make for the right kind of a boy.

Then, again, as I have already said : the power of education is too commonly overrated ; as if it were a substantive thing that will produce something for a man, or do something for him of its own inherent power, without an effort on his part; whereas at the most it is only a slight auxiliary to his own powers to aid him to work out his own destiny. Too much is expected of it. Even the superficial college graduate, who went in with the idea that the college was to make him, comes out with the idea that his sheep-skin certificate is to carry him through, while his self-sufficiency and gasconade are about all that there is of him. Outsiders are apt to expect too much. Somehow they get an idea that there is some mysterious power in a college to work over any ordinary boy and make a prodigy of him in four or five years, so that he shall know everything, and be able to accomplish wonderful things in any literary way. He is expected to astonish all ordinary mortals with his profundity, and to always be ready to deal out the highest grade of literary wisdom on demand: whereas the really successful college graduate, he who has gained all there is in a college course, and knows what there is of it, always appreciates more the paucity of his own knowledge than the amount of it; having learned all along, more and more, as he has advanced in his studies, the littleness of his own knowledge in comparison with what is beyond. Taking his acquirements at their value only, he is prepared to make the most of them, by utilizing them as an aid in his life-work.

After all, a collegiate education is not indispensable to success, even in professional life; or rather, perhaps I should say that a college is not indispensable for the essentials of college education. We cannot know how much better Patrick Henry or Henry Clay would have been with college parchments, but we do know that they were sufficiently successful without them. And we see a good many men rise to eminence without them. But I think it is to be noted that all those successful men are those who get all the substantials of education somehow, outside of college walls. They might get them to better advantage, perhaps, at college, but any other way serves a very good purpose. My own limited common school education for instance, with the private study of the more common sciences, and a persistent and continuous general reading, has probably been as valuable to me as would have been a college course without the subsequent systematic study. At any rate there is an available substitute for college, for any young man who thirsts for knowledge—in the books and the study, *anywhere.* If, as I have tried to show, a man must make himself; if the college cannot do it, it does not make so much difference where he does it, after all. Of course the facilities are better in a college, but the principal difference is that out of college the work is not so likely to be done.

On the whole, therefore, we conclude that book learning is not the chief end of man; that there is no mysterious power in colleges to make men; that college education is an important element in a man's intellectual capital with which to enter into the sharp competition for the prizes of life; and that no young man of brains, industry, and energy need despair of securing all the advantages of such education.

VIII.

TO DRINK OR LET IT ALONE.

It is not necessary to spend any time to prove that intemperance is incompatible with success in life. The inevitable ruin of the inebriate, every-where seen and understood, is conclusive. Young men do not start out in life with the purpose of being drunkards. They know that the drunkard's life cannot be a successful one.

Not long ago I heard a sharp business man, a moderate drinker, and an able advocate of the liquor trade, say that about one out of fifteen can drink occasionally without being materially injured by it—that is, without becoming drunkards. My observation through life corroborates that opinion; so that when a young man begins life by taking an occasional drink, he takes fourteen chances, to one, to be ruined by that habit, if he persists in it.

Forty years ago the temperance question was agitated in my neighborhood. Young men said then, as young men say now, that they could drink or let it alone. They could. Some of them

4

drank on. Some of us let it alone. Of those who drank I have seen a large proportion go down to drunkard's graves; others are living monuments of the folly of young men's not letting it alone when they can; while of those who let it alone through life, I never have known one to be a drunkard. And I think not more than one in fifteen of those who continued to drink failed to be drunkards.

So, young men of to-day, you say you can drink or let it alone. You can. And the very best thing you can do is to let it alone. I can assure you, from my life long experience and observation that your only safety is to let it alone. If what you mean when you say that you can drink or let it alone, is that you can continue to drink indefinitely and retain this power to drink or let it alone, you are making a great, and probably fatal mistake. Oh, how many of those who started out in life with me, who said they could drink or let it alone, but did not choose to let it alone, how many of them I have seen pass along heedlessly, to the point where they could drink but could *not* let it alone. One case I will mention. Nearly forty years ago a man of about my own age was a fellow workman with me in a blacksmith shop. He imbibed the habit of going occasionally to the tavern near by and taking a drink. To my remonstrances he had the ready reply, "I can drink or let it alone," which was true then, but long years ago he resigned that power, he has spent a fortune, and is now a bloated inebriate. And he is a prohibitionist. Yes, a drunkard and a prohibitionist. He is an earnest pleader with temperance men to vote the liquor shops away because he says he cannot refrain from drink when he comes in contact with it, but is always anxious to reform. Ask this class of men— those who have gone through all the phases of the drink habit—how it is about drinking or letting it alone. They know all about it, not by hearsay, not by sight, not by any speculative philosophy, but by its bitterness ground into their very souls, by the slavery in which it holds them. Ask them whether to drink or let it alone while you can do either. Ask them if you can continue to drink with impunity. And if they tell you to drink, drink on.

If my own personal experience in any phase of life is of any value to the young, it is especially so in this matter of temperance; for I know that the temperance pledge has been of as much value to me as to any living man. Not that I was ever a drunkard, or even a moderate drinking man; for I never was; but by that pledge I have been saved from all that. All that I am or ever hope to be I owe, under God, to the temperance pledge, and I am not ashamed to say so. When about fifteen years of age I was so situated as to come in contact with a good deal of drinking and drunkenness; so that I could not but observe much of their consequences. It was very disagreeable to me, and I then concluded firmly that I would never be a drunkard; and secondly, that the only sure way to save myself from being a drunkard was to refrain from strong drink. Such was my pledge, and I have kept it substantially, from that day till now. And from my experience and observation through life, in looking back over what I have passed through since then, reverting to the great numbers of stronger men of my acquaintance who have fallen because they did not take such a pledge, it is no humiliation for me to say that without that pledge in early life, I, too, would have gone down the drunkard's road. I have been probably, as firm in purpose, as stubborn and persevering as most of men, but not more so than was ex-Governor Yates, the great war Governor of Illinois, Senator Saulsbury, of Delaware, and hosts of other distinguished and strong men of the nation, who have been ruined by drink; and I say to you now, young men of to-day, that from fifty years' experience and observation of this matter of temperance, could I go back to youth again, I would not even *dare* to trust myself to the habit of taking an occasional drink. That pledge, and that alone, under God, is all that I would dare rely on to go through all the risks and incitements to dissipation that I must come in contact with. It is the only possible thing that you, my young friends, can depend on to carry you safely through.

And for your encouragement I can assure you that abstinence is one of the easiest things to do: that is to say, for you who can drink or let it alone; and it is to such that this discourse is chiefly directed. Not having acquired the appetite for drink so as to hanker for it, it is no self-denial to refrain, only so far as what is supposed to be the social demand upon you to indulge with your friends and companions who are in the habit. If there ever was any difficulty in this respect, I presume there was much more of it in my young days, when it was not held to be at all disreputable to drink, than now, when most of the better classes of people look upon the habit with horror. I heard a minister of the gospel say, in the pulpit, not long ago, that a boy takes his first drink with a trembling hand—his conscience smites him. Fifty years ago it was not so. Children were trained to drink, and there was no disgrace in moderate drinking, and very little in drunkenness. And yet I can say to you now, that I never have met with the slightest difficulty in carrying out my pledge. In all these years I do not remember any occasion, in any presence, where I have been subject to any insult, rebuff, or embarrassment because of declining to drink with friends. Somehow it has always seemed to me that the modest, unostentatious declination of the proffered glass has endowed the offerer with respect for my principles, and distrust of his own.

Thus far I have assumed that a time comes to men who indulge in drink when they cannot let it alone. This is not strictly true, but so nearly true that it is the only safe theory for a young man to act upon while he can easily let it alone. When we see the victim of an appetite that is ground into the very physical and moral being, that drives a man through all that enures to the drunkard's life, drives him through fire or water to appease it ; yea, when we see a man so enslaved that he would take a drink if he knew it would kill him in five minutes—as I think I have seen—it is not very much at random to say that such men cannot let it alone. But they can. So long as a man is conscious of what he is doing, he is a free moral agent, and his acts are of his own free will. Whatever his appetite or his impulses may be, though he had rather die than refrain from drink, and though the coveted potion be at his lips, yet he is the master of himself, and he can dash it away. Drunkards can reform—sometimes they do. If drunkenness is a disease, it is one that they deliberately bring upon themselves, and one that they can as deliberately cure if they will. They are not heroes or martyrs. They are the victims of their own sin and folly ; and however much we commiserate their condition and whatever we may do to raise them from their degradation, and however guilty the liquor traders or others may be as accessories to their ruin, they themselves are accountable for it all. They have no reason to complain of anybody else. They can reform, and on their own heads is the guilt every day that they neglect it.

But though all drunkards can reform yet they don't. Some people are getting very enthusiastic just now, and think the millennium is pretty nearly here, and all the drunkards are going to sign the pledge and keep it, and all this liquor curse will be out of the way in a few years. But so long as human nature is as it is, so long as the power of the liquor appetite is as it is, and so long as the State employs men to cultivate that appetite and to decoy its victims on and on to their ruin, it is only a question of time and circumstance for most of reformed drunkards to relapse. So it has been, and I cannot see anything in the Murphy movement to change all the laws by which this subject has hitherto been governed.

I do not say this to discourage the many worthy men who have taken the pledge because they needed it ; rather to arm them for the great battle that they have so earnestly engaged in. *They can conquer*—every one of them. This Murphy movement is a grand work—worthy of the support and encouragement of everybody, as one of the agencies for the overthrow of the liquor power in this country ; but it will be found, in the sequel, that its utility will be much more in saving people from acquiring the appetite for drink, than in saving the drunkards. And I would not depreciate the value of the work in this behalf. Oh, how my heart has rejoiced to see its effect on a good many valuable men—any one of whom, arrested in their downward way, and raised to manhood again, to stay, is worth more than all the cost of all Corning's temperance work. All of which goes to show that all young men should let the drink alone while they can without inconvenience.

On the whole, my young friends, this matter of drinking or letting it alone, when we come right down to the essence of it, is a question of only one side. There is nothing in favor of drink. The idea that formerly prevailed that intoxicating beverages are in any case necessary or useful, is extinguished. Nobody now but a small fraction of drinking men themselves pretends that they are ever useful. There is no redeeming quality in them. They are an unmitigated evil. All the terrible consequences that we see everywhere flowing from their use, are entirely without any sort of recompense. And now in your relation to this subject, independent to choose one side or the other, free and untrammeled to drink or let it alone, unaffected by the terrible impulse of appetite that you have seen drag so many others down to ruin, standing, as it were, at the junction of two open ways, at the threshold of active life, to take the way of drink is to hazard all without a possibility of gaining anything; with fourteen chances to one, as we have seen, against you; if you should chance to be the fifteenth, you would only save yourself, with no possible gain for the fearful hazard; you cast your soul and body into a lottery consisting of fourteen tickets written upon them *destruction*, to one of blank. I once saw an old hunter from the mountains, at a holiday bar-room carousal. He brought some saddles of venison as his only currency. A half dozen sharpers induced him to put up this property as the stake of a game of chance, with his single chance in against the six, with no recompense to him and nothing for him to win save to win back his own. That man was a fool, aye a fool, but a fool because of drink. How much bigger fool is a young man, in his sober senses, clear-headed, independent, who can drink or let it alone, to deliberately set himself up, soul and body, all he is and all he hopes to be, the subject of a game with fourteen chances against him, with just one chance against them all to win himself back no better than when he started in. And this is exactly what every young man is doing who refuses to put himself in the line of total abstainers from intoxicating drink.

But that is not all, my friends. In this game of chance, if you do not absolutely lose yourselves, it is impossible to win yourselves back as good as you went in. In these papers we have been discussing the subject of accumulating property. As we have seen, about one man in fifteen may drink

regularly all his life without being a drunkard.—
But that drinking may keep him poor all his life
and take him to the poor house at last, without
another fault in him. Or at any rate it will cost
him enough to make him comfortably rich in old
age. Now let us see what ten cents a day will cost
a man ; and any regular moderate drinker will not
get off for less than that surely. And I have
worked out the problem considerably in detail to
show the wonderful results of small sums saved and
put to use, with the interest compounded annually
for a course of years ; say

1st period of ten years : Ten cents a day for ten years is - - - - - - $	365.00
For each year $36.50. Compound interest on $36.50 at 7 per cent. from the end of each year of ten up to the end of ten years —say on that sum for 9, 8, 7, 6, 5, 4, 3, 2, and 1 years respectively, is - - -	139.28
Total first ten years - - - -	504.28
2d period of 10 years: Compound interest on above sum for 10 years - - -	487.72
Accumulation at 10 cents a day and interest as above, - - - - - -	504.28
Total for 20 years - - - -	1,496.28
3d period of 10 years: interest as aforesaid on last above sum - - - -	1,447.13
10 cents a day and interest as aforesaid -	504.28
Total for 30 years - - - -	3,447.69
4th period of 10 years : interest as aforesaid on last above sum - - - -	3,334.44
10 cents a day and interest as aforesaid -	504.28
Total for 40 years - - - -	7,286.41
5th period of 10 years : interest as aforesaid on last above sum - - -	7,047.06
10 cents a day and interest as aforesaid -	504.28
Total for 50 years - - - -	$14,837.75

So it is clear enough that besides all the hazard of entire destruction that every young man runs when he persists in the habit of drink, there is in it a *certainty* of expenses that he cannot afford, and at the most moderate rate it is likely to make him a beggar in old age unless his income is large.

In conclusion, in every aspect of this matter of drink, it is of supreme importance to every young man that he start out with a firm resolve to let it alone for life ; yea, there is scarcely a hope of him without such resolve.

IX.

TOBACCO.

Naturally there is nothing more repulsive to the human organism and the human appetite than tobacco. Usually it requires a long, persistent, sickening, disgusting trial to get the physical system inured to its deleterious effects so that the patient can endure its use in any form ; which is, I think, conclusive physiological proof that it is essentially an injurious and dangerous substance to be introduced into the human body. And it has always been a mystery to me how the use of it was first invented ; and more so, how it is that a large majority of young men and boys will persist in punishing themselves to acquire the mastery over the repulsiveness and the initiatory poisonous effects of it, while, to say the least, it is admitted by all that generally it is not of any beneficial use whatever, but an entire waste of money to indulge in it. To go no further than this, these facts ought to be sufficient to induce every young man and boy who has not acquired the habit to refrain from the severe trial of habituating the system to the deleterious effects of tobacco, so that they can be endured and the patient live along; and also to impel all tobacco users who can control their own appetites to wean themselves from it.

But there is a good deal more than that in this tobacco question. I shall not go into a scientific exposition of the pathological effect of tobacco upon the human machine; it is sufficient for my purpose to state the general result.

Tobacco, then, is a

VIRULENT POISON.

I believe this is asserted by all scientific men who have written upon the subject; it has been demonstrated by them by numerous experiments, and nobody disputes it. I think it is self-evident that a human being cannot habitually indulge in any poison with impunity. The continuous habit *must* make inroads upon the vitality, must shorten life; for the essential nature of poison is antagonism to the natural, physiological action of the physical man—nutrition, depuration, etc. In plainer terms: the renewal of the constant waste of the substance of the human machine, and the ejection of the waste matter, through the various organs for that purpose provided, constitute life. To stop this is death.   To obstruct, retard or disturb it in any respect or in any degree, is disease of some kind The natural and inevitable effect of poison of any kind is to disturb and hinder these processes, or some of them ; so that the habitual introduction of any poison into the human system, even in the most minute doses, must necessarily engender disease.   This is its nature and office.   There is no possibility of mistake about it.   It is just as clearly a philosophic principle as that water runs down hill.   Its inroads may be so gradual that the patient may be insensible to them—usually it is so— and when they culminate in serious disease, or death even, the trouble is usually attributed to other causes.   In fact it may, sometimes, be difficult for the physician to judge how far his patient, under any form of disease, and all saturated with nicotine or any other poison, owes his ailments to the poison ; but every well informed physician does know that any disease is much more virulent and more likely to be fatal upon patients infected with any kind of poison than upon those who are free from it.

We read of arsenic eaters with a great degree of horror and with commiseration for their fatuity. We know that they are killing themselves by inches, because we know that the human organism cannot indefinitely endure the contact of any substance that is inimical to life ; because we know that the antagonism between poison and human life cannot be reconciled.   Now apply the same rule to the use of tobacco, and then observe the great variety of diseases that we know are superinduced by it, and even the frequent cases where we know its victims to be gradually killed outright by its excessive use, and I would like to know what we have to boast of over the arsenic eating tribes of people.

We temperance people hold, and the fact is now pretty well established, that alcoholic drinks are poisonous, and hence it is that so many diseases are propagated by their use, and that their victims are so powerless to resist the inroads of any disease whatever; so that all drinking men's lives are shortened by the habit of drink.   And yet, while we are preaching that fearfully true theory, a large majority of temperance men are constant users of the tobacco poison that probably fills as many premature graves as do alcoholic drinks.

And therefore on a superficial view of this question of using tobacco or not, it seems unaccountable that all tobacco users will not look this matter square in the face, ask themselves what all this waste of life is for, call a halt, resolve to be freemen and not slaves; and abandon the filthy, disgusting, suicidal habit forever.

But when we go to the root of the matter ; especially those of us who have been there, we find a reason for this perseverance in manifest wrong ; the same reason that holds the inebriate to his cups —the depravity of appetite and the weakness of human nature. We exhort the men of drink to forego the indulgence of their perverted appetites. We enlarge on its uselessness, its waste, its wickedness, its destruction of life, etc.; we tell them the habit is in all respects a foolish and inexcusable one, we reach out the fraternal hand to them and tell them to come with us, that they can reject the tempter and be men again, but when a friendly hand is reached down to the temperance men of the tobacco fraternity, and their own medicine is offered them, and they are exhorted to give up the degrading, demoralizing, suicidal habit, that alters the case. Then, " oh, dear, that quid or cigar is so much of my comfort, so incorporated into my very being, if I go without it for half a day, oh, I am so all gone, and so out of sorts, and so, so, I don't know exactly how, that I must—I must. I know it is bad, wrong, hazardous, murderous, but then it is not so bad as whisky, and this appetite of mine, oh, yes. I must have it. I will have it."

That's the way temperance men, many of them, treat the subject of an intemperance which, if not quite as bad as that of drink, is very nearly akin to it, and in some of its phases identical with it. I know how this is, for I have been there. I know the power of the tobacco habit, for I was a slave to it for twenty years, and I now speak by authority. I have been free from it for ten years, and so I have a right to exhort others to come out from the degrading bondage.

Last spring a prominent business man took the Murphy pledge, and another prominent citizen, a temperance man, took an anti-tobacco pledge, to be kept as long as the former would keep his pledge. The Murphy man has held out faithful. The tobacco man struggled a considerable time—struggled, and struggled, and fought and fought with that depravity of his, until, finally, he was overpowered. He got feeling so badly ! oh, he was so sick ! so sick ! he could not, no he could not live without his quid ; so he thought. But he can ; every man can. I have been through that mill and I know. That seeming necessity for the tobacco poison is just the same that the inebriate, or the habitual user of any other poison experiences on abstaining from it. The human system can become so inured to any sort of poison, in small doses, as not only to not suffer any conscious detriment, but to really seem to need it. It is so with liquor. When a man is dying with drink, nothing seems so good for him as more of it. So with arsenic eaters. And when a reforming tobacco sot gets so sick that he thinks he must have it back, it is only the change of the physiological conditions of the system caused by the substitution of natural aliment for the accustomed poison—the effect of nature in expelling the poison without a renewal of it ; in a word, the change to a healthy condition. That is all, and a suitable time will overcome all that terrible yearning and seeming physical necessity for the deleterious drug, nature will repair the damage already done, so far as it is reparable, and at least rid the system of the accumulated festering corruption.

The tobacco habit looks like a mere foolishness only. A man sucks a cigar or pipe, and puffs out the smoke, or munches his quid and spits out the juice; that is all we see. If that were really all there is of it, it would be only a nonsensical waste of money. But in those processes there is a constant absorption of the poison of the tobacco, which creates that terrible appetite for more and more of it, driving the victim lower and lower in the thraldom of this depravity, accumulating and hoarding up more and more of the corruption and the irreparable effects of the filth and the poison, until so saturated and corrupted that he is more or less a stench in the nostrils of the uncontaminated, and a ready prey for any epidemic or other disease.

Now if the foregoing be true, I ask you, young men, and older men, too, to come with me up to a serious and candid consideration of the fearful nature of this tobacco problem as a public question, apart from its personal application to individuals.

It is a physiological fact, written down by all scientific men who write on the subject, and that we can all see for ourselves, very often, that in the propagation of the human species, as in the lower animals, like produces like. There are frequent cases where the appetite for intoxicating drinks is inherited from parents; and I have known a case where a boy inherited the taste for tobacco. I knew a child born drunk, and remained so so long as she lived—ten or twelve years. That is to say, she had the stagger and all the physical manifestations of her father when drunk. These extra cases go to show that the physiological rule above stated inevitably applies to any kind of dissipation—transmitting its effects, more or less, always, from parent to child. The habitual tobacco user is a poisoned mass of physical humanity, always diseased, more or less, whether he knows it or not; for the presence of poison in the body is always antagonistic to health. Now it is a physiological impossibility for the progeny of a corrupted, poisoned, diseased human body to be entirely free of taint from the parent; sometimes more, sometimes less apparent. In some cases, as in scrofula, consumption, etc., it is unmistakable. In the infirmities caused by alcoholic drinks, tobacco or other poisons, it is more difficult to trace them to their source, because their character is so various. But this one universal principle always holds good in procreation; health produces health; poison cannot produce health; corruption cannot produce purity; so that the progeny of tobacco users *must* be more or less imperfect and diseased, whether visible or not.

Another universal law appertaining to the human machine is that a sound mind cannot be in an unsound body; that is to say, the condition of the physical man always affects the mind more or less; any infirmity of the body always produces infirmity of mind; so that the average soundness and vigor of mind of tobacco users must be, other things being equal, inferior to that of those who are free and uncontaminated.

Furthermore: To this inherited tobacco infection must be added, all along, the current habit of the second generation of victims; so that they have the inherited infirmity and the accumulating poison of their own sin to drag them down, and degeneracy, from generation to generation, must be very rapid in those who perpetuate the habit. We cannot know how much of the physical and mental infirmities of our people are engendered by tobacco, or how much superior we would be, as a people, without it. We have no statistics as to the proportion of our people that use tobacco; but to count noses almost anywhere, I think it will be found that not less than nine-tenths of all the adult male population are in the habit; and not only so, but it is so popular that almost universally the rising generation are going into it; so that, unless a change takes place in the matter, it may be taken for granted that we are to be, practically, unanimous tobacco users—a nation of tobacco soaks. Now, apply the foregoing inexorable physiological laws to a nation of universal tobacco suckers, and the national degeneracy is fearful to think of.

Is this overdrawn? None but an Omniscient eye can discern how much of the physical, intellectual and moral defects of our people are caused by this particular vice, or how much better a people, in all that goes to make up the God-given manhood of the race, we would be if the tobacco poison had never been imbibed. But we can read in physiological law, and see in the visible effects of tobacco, the solemn, solid fact, that its damage to the race is incalculable.

We compare this habit with that of drink, and usually rate its evils inferior to those of drink; but if we consider the fact that the effects of tobacco on the physical and mental degeneracy of the individual, and of families, are held by competent physicians to be fully equal to those of drink; and if we consider the further fact that the tobacco habit reaches, substantially, the entire adult male population, whereas more than one-half of the adult male population are free from the liquor habit, it is at least a question whether tobacco is not a greater evil to our country at large than intoxicating drinks.

I do not know how much tobacco is used in this country, or how much its aggregate cost is, and I do not care to know; but I can judge of the cost to individuals. And I know that some men pay enough for cigars to make a rich man poor in a good deal less than the ordinary period of active life, or to make a poor man rich if saved. They do not know how much that one cigar costs them, or rather what that ten cents would be worth to them in a series of years if saved and put to use.

Ten cents at seven per cent. interest, anually compounded,

In 20 years is worth   -   -   -   -   39 cts.
" 30   "   "   "   -   -   -   -   76 "
" 40   "   "   "   -   -   -   - $1.56 "
" 50   "   "   "   -   -   -   -   2.94 "

Those who are wasting from ten to fifty cents a day for cigars can figure up what a day's cigar dissipation will cost them in any of those periods of time by multiplying those sums respectively by the number of tens in the day's debauch.

I will here give a convenient table to show, at a glance, what a continuous expenditure of small sums every day for cigars, tobacco, liquor or any other useless indulgence, will amount to in a series of years.

Interest 7 per cent. Compounded Annually:

	For 10 yrs.	20 yrs.	30 yrs.	40 yrs.	50 yrs.
10 cents a day...	$ 504.28	$1,496.28	$ 3,447.69	$ 7,286.41	$14,837.75
20 cents a day...	1,008.56	2,992.56	6,895.38	14,572.82	29,675.50
30 cents a day...	1,512.84	4,488.84	10,343.07	21,859.23	44,513.35
40 cents a day...	2,017.12	5,985.12	13,790.76	29,145.64	59,351.00
50 cents a day...	2,521.40	7,481.40	17,238.45	36,432.05	74,188.75

You who are paying ten, twenty, thirty, forty or fifty cents a day for cigars can see by this table what that dissipation is costing you or your family in money. And I can point out a good many elderly men of my acquaintance who have kept themselves poor by these expenses for tobacco. And I can say to my young friends in this behalf as I said in respect to drink, that unless their income be large, the tobacco habit will be sure to keep them poor all their lives. They can see it for themselves in these figures.

As with the question of drinking or letting it alone, so with that of using tobacco or letting it alone; it is a question of only one side. There is nothing in its favor. It is of no possible beneficial use to any body. It is an unmitigated evil. All its serious damages to the race that I have imperfectly illustrated are without any degree of compensation, either to the general public or to any individual.

"Oh, now," we will be told, perhaps, "you are putting it too extravagantly. There is certainly some comfort in tobacco. There is some enjoyment in sucking a cigar, a pipe or a quid. People are not such fools as to incur all the expenses and endure all the troubles and humiliation of the filth of the tobacco habit without some gratification." A correspondent of the Corning Journal says :

"There is something in a pipe that provides a solace for many woes, and smooths the path of daily discontent."

This is putting it on pretty thick to the credit of tobacco, but I freely concede that people would not endure all the confessed evils of tobacco without some *seeming* compensation—unless there were something about it that seems to be necessary, or useful or gratifying. Certainly not; there is that something in tobacco. Let us see what it is. Enjoyment or comfort is sometimes relative merely and not positive. A slight toothache is comforting immediately after a hard toothache; that is to say, a man will feel very good and enjoy it in comparison with the hard pain just palliated. But that is not to say that a slight toothache is desirable or comforting *per se*. It is preferable to the hard pain, and this is all. It is a choice of two evils. Any nostrum that has the effect of producing a very distressing state of the human body, and then of relieving part of the difficulty by its continuous use, would seem to be necessary and useful. And such is exactly the effect of tobacco. This phase of the question was tersely and forcibly illustrated by the Rev. Dr. Niles, about as follows: "Tobacco gives no positive enjoyment, but only relieves the complaint of an abused nature caused by its use." At most it can only supply a want created by itself.

A man smokes a cigar. He thinks it is a comfort to him. It is. Why? Because he has smoked before, and that previous smoking has created a morbid condition of the system that seems to require a continuation of it, and he feels better in supplying the demand of the morbid craving than by denying it. But compare him with a man who never smoked and the latter is clearly the more comfortable of the two. He thinks he cannot do without it. He cannot without great discomfort for the time being. It saves him from a distress, only, and is not a positive enjoyment. The man who never smoked has no such distress, has no need of such remedy, and his comfort is entirely superior to that of the other in sucking his cigar or pipe.

And I can vouch for all this from my own experience. There never was a time during my tobacco servitude when I did not regret having imbibed the habit; never a time when I would not have paid any reasonable amount of money to buy off the appetite if it could have been done; knowing as I did that the balance of enjoyment was in favor of abstinence, provided that the appetite, or disease, caused by its use, could be out of the way. And now, with that appetite all gone, I *know* that I was not mistaken then. I know that indulgence in tobacco is only a partial relief from the physical distresses caused by its use, and the balance of comfort is in favor of abstinence.

And I think that most of tobacco sots will agree with me in all this. They will agree that in comparison with the uncontaminated, there is no positive enjoyment in tobacco, and that they would gladly reform if they could. They can. Now we come to the question

HOW TO QUIT.

There is no mysterious process to go through—nothing complicated. The way to quit is to quit. Take it absolute, total, simple, plain. It is not an easy thing to do. It is a big battle to fight, and you must fight it out alone. There is nothing to aid you but your own free will, under God. There is no substitute or palliative that can aid you. And you cannot *taper* off. You must take the bull by the horns at once—the whole of him. I have thrown my tobacco away more than a hundred times and become pretty nearly weaned, when I would find my fingers in somebody's tobacco box —just a very little to taper off with—when the entire old demon would be instantly aroused, as with whiskey sots, and in five minutes I must have more, and then more and more until I would be back to the full use again. So I found that there could be no half way work. It must be total abstinence or total slavery. And now, with the appetite all gone, the smallest taste would at once require more, and I would have the battle to fight over again. Like the reformed drunkard, I tell my experience for the benefit of others who ought to reform. It is nothing to boast of, but is a humiliating confession to make. I make it for the encouragement of those who want to reform but

think they cannot.   As hard a thing as it is to do.
every man can do it if he will.

And yet I do not expect to see many tobacco sots
reform.   They will not.   Though they know that
their tobacco is poisoning the very fountains of
life, is of no possible benefit to them in any respect,
not even a pleasure *per se*, is in all respects derogatory to high toned manhood, costs in money
what cannot be afforded, and will inevitably shorten
life ; yet is free from some of the worst effects of
alcoholic drinks, and they have not the extreme
incentive to reform that the liquor drunkard has ;
the culmination of its damaging effects seems to
be remote, and the distresses of the weaning process are *now*.   The terrible physical demand for the
constant supply of the poison is *now*, and they will
furnish it at the cost of unknown years of what
should be their natural life.   No, they will not
stop.   There is no hope of any extensive reform in
that direction.

But I think there is a way to cure this great
national vice.   The remedy is in the rising generation.   As with the liquor habit, so in this ; it is
easier to save a hundred from learning the art of
tobacco using than to cure one after he has learned
it.   And more than this : It would probably, by a
a general agitation of this subject, be easier to
save ten boys and young men from the tobacco
habit than one from liquor, for the very obvious
reason that tobacco is not attractive to a boy or

young man until he has gone through the severe
punishment of seasoning the system to the poison ;
whereas liquor, in the palatable forms in which it
is presented to the novice, is never repulsive. In
fact I believe that one-half of the public sentiment
against tobacco that now exists against the use of
intoxicating drinks would save *all* of the rising
generation from learning the habit.

And now a word to the youth who are yet uncontaminated by this tobacco vice. You see that
there is nothing in favor of your enduring the punishment of learning how to use tobacco. There is
no good in it, but only evil ever and always.
There is no enjoyment in it as compared to your
present enjoyment in freedom from its mastery.
It will cost you in money what you cannot afford ;
it will poison your very fountains of life; it will
land you in premature graves, and degenerate your
posterity. And a boy or a young man does not
look any better sucking a cigar or a pipe on the
street or elsewhere than free from it. I know it is
fashionable to learn the art; but even now, with
nearly all the adult male population in its use,
there is no ban upon the abstainers. It is rather
the other way. The smokers, with their tobacco
fumes, are excluded from the better class of railroad cars, and from most decent parlors, and from
the society of respectable ladies in general; so
that, after all, so far as the fashion is concerned, it
is really more respectable, and high-toned, and

easier, to abstain than to indulge.   There is no reason whatever for you to go out of your way to pervert your nature by acquiring this vicious habit.
Don't you do it.

In conclusion, my appeal is to the ladies.   You
are practically unanimous against tobacco.   You
are always sufferers by it.   I need not tell you
how.   You know all about that.   You can appreciate the force of all I have said on the subject, as
men who use the article cannot.   You can see the
vast importance of a reform.   It is in your power
to effect it, not by converting your husbands, your
brothers or sons, who are addicted to the habit—
but by building up a public sentiment against it,
to be applied to the rising generation.   Save, oh
save the boys from this terrible vice, and in another generation we will be redeemed and disenthralled.

X.

GAMING.

After a great temperance revival, gaming tables
were proposed as amusement for the new converts,
to pacify them, and keep them from the dram shops.
I don't know for certain which is the worse of the
two.   If drunkenness is any worse than gambling,
it is only because there is more of it.   In individual
cases I have had occasion to know that the passion
for gambling is more infatuating, more demoralizing, more destructive than the appetite for intoxicating drinks.   But gambling is not seen.   It

skulks away out of sight. The drunkard cannot disguise his debauchery, but the habitual gambler sneaks away to a hell—yes it is rightly named, a gambling hell, for if any place upon earth is worthy of that name it is a den where gamblers congregate—the gambler sneaks away to a hell, unseen, to indulge the unholy passion at whatever cost; for when this appetite is acquired it is even more the master of its victim than is the liquor appetite. There is nothing too dear or too sacred to be sacrificed on its altar. The outside world knows nothing of the extent of this gigantic vice, nothing of the number of these dens, or the victims ruined therein.

But mere social games, parlor games, in the family, for amusement, not for money, are harmless, we are told. And so we may say that social wines, social brandies, at home, in the parlor, with our friends, moderate drinking, are all harmless so long as pent up in moderate dimensions; it is common to say so at least. But this is the seed of most of the drunkenness in the land. Banish these fashionable " innocent" parlor drinking customs, and intemperance would be greatly checked. And exactly so are the fashionable gaming tables, innocent games, family parlor games, the nurseries of the full grown gambling hells, which are one of the most effective nurseries of drink debauchery, and for aught that we can know, the original cause of more vice and crime and misery than is the intemperance of drink. Young men do not go into *them* to learn the art and imbibe the passion, any more than they go down into the lowest drunkeries to learn to drink. To show

HOW IT WORKS,

I will relate a case that occurred under my observation. A coterie of high-toned young and middle aged men was formed for cards—for amusement merely of course, and not for stakes at all; that was not to be thought of; they would not gamble, oh no. Probably the parties had learned the art of handling the cards at home. They had their stated meetings and amused themselves. The more they met the more they needed the amusement, and soon it came to be a meeting of every night. After a while it became too monotonous and dull without something to play for; just a little; anything to make the game interesting. So they put up a few sticks of candy. They would not gamble, oh no. They went on with that for a while, until that became too cheap, there was not interest enough in the game. They would not gamble, but they only put up some very small pieces of money, just to enhance the interest of the game. They then went on and on, adding to the interest of the game by increasing the size of the money stakes until the ability of the parties to raise money was the only limit. Then of course the passion reached out to wider fields. The mere local fraternity was too dull.

I had occasion to know all about one of that coterie. He was a middle aged man with an interesting family; a successful business man up to then; supposed to be wealthy—he was sufficiently so; for twelve years his ruling passion was the card table; more and more his business was neglected from year to year until he scarcely gave it any attention at all—leaving all to others. As the stakes increased in size he became more and more infatuated; sometimes he won, which only increased his infatuation; other gambling centres were visited; from year to year all available money was swallowed up in that remorseless vortex; and with a name of wealth he died a bankrupt, and left a worthy family penniless.

Thousands of similar cases are constantly going on all over the land—much of it unknown to the public—always culminating in *ruin*, RUIN, RUIN; for even the successful professional gambler's life is a failure; a failure in all that this life is worth living for—in being of no possible benefit to his fellow man, in being only an excrescence upon the body politic, in the fact that the world is the worse for his having lived in it. And not only so, he is usually a failure in *money* too, for it is notorious that the gains of the gambler are speedily wasted, and he is as poor as his unsuccessful victims. He is ruined too.

Gambling is essentially and intrinsically dishonest—criminal. There is no redeeming feature about

it.   It is worse than selling whiskey ; for this business does give something in exchange for money,
whether that something has any value or not, it is
something that the buyer thinks he wants, and
which has cost something ; whereas the gambler
seeks his comrade's money without any pretence of
value for it. The whole scheme and system are
confessedly devices and efforts of a company of
men to despoil each other of their money ; in principle as clearly so as to purloin it from a safe.
Many and various associations are formed for
mutual benefit. Even thieves and robbers affiliate
for mutual *aid*. But gamblers, and only gamblers,
associate for mutual injury, spoliation, plunder,
robbery ; for when they sit down to their game it
is for the express purpose of despoiling one another.

It is not surprising that such a pursuit as this—
founded in rapacity and wrong—is so terribly
demoralizing, corrupting its subject through and
through, extinguishing all moral perceptions, and
incapacitating him for participation in any of the
sweet and amiable sympathies and associations of
refined society ; in short, a soul of man in ruin.

I think it is an unmitigated evil. There is no
possible good to come of it. In its incipient
stages, when the play is for amusement as it is
called, it is, to say the least, a profitless amusement.
It kills time, and that is all. No instruction, improvement, or discipline of mind is left from it.
Nothing whatever of value or of satisfaction re-

sults. It is an absolute waste of time. I cannot conceive of any amusement so entirely profitless as this. There certainly is none other so hazardous. And if there is any fleeting pleasure in the senseless jargon of spades, and hearts, and clubs, and trumps, when we set that off against one lost human soul, and one ruined family from the excess of that sort of so-called amusement; make this application ye advocates of parlor card tables, and ye young men now amusing yourselves by this practice, and ask yourselves is there any pleasure in it? Link your evening's entertainment with its unavoidable consequences, to somebody, if not to yourselves, and enjoy yourselves if you can.

Probably the very common propensity to desire to get something for nothing is one of the results of the depravity of the race. There seems to be an innate disposition to shirk the sentence " in the sweat of thy face shalt thou eat bread;" and so there is a natural tendency to seize upon any thing that promises something of value without a corresponding value rendered—something for nothing. This is the fundamental idea of gambling; and it is to be seen in many attractive phases other than card playing; from the biggest lotteries down through all the innumerable inventions of gift enterprises and other frauds where something is ostensibly offered for nothing, down to the church fair where a grab bag or a cake with a ring in it is gambled off. And all this *takes*. No matter how

6

absurd a scheme of swindling is proposed, it will find takers if it offers something for nothing. Let an unknown man advertise that he will give a hundred dollars for one for all the money remitted to him in advance, and he would probably get a good many dollars. And so all the various swindling inventions, however preposterous, that are from time to time introduced through the mails and otherwise, always meet with more or less of patronage. It is all on the principle of getting something for nothing. I tell you, young man, it is all a fallacy. It cannot be done. Values are not produced by hocus pocus. If you should succeed, by any gambling process, in filching another's money, you cannot afford it. It will be too costly. First it will cost you what money cannot replace—the principle of manhood; and, secondly, it will cost you all hope of permanent prosperity, for dishonest gains are sure to be fleeting. No, you cannot afford it. The only safe foundation is honest industry, honest business, value for value. This and only this will stand the test of time and eternity.

The conclusion of the whole matter, young people, and older people too, is that your fashionable amusement parlor card tables are the training-schools that supply the customers to the numerous but unknown number of gambling hells that everywhere abound, with all the consequences that I have so imperfectly described. You cannot afford

it. I am aware that there are a great many very
excellent people who sneer at such arguments as
these—who will say that it is entirely nonsensical
to say that parlor games for amusement are the
nurseries of the full grown gambling hells, etc. I
am aware that a good many Doctors of Divinity
and Judges, and other high-toned people indulge in parlor cards, and never think of gambling;
but the question is whether that is not so much
the worse for those excellent people, and not any
the better for the parlor games? I do not say that
such parlor games, *per se*, are chargeable with the
damages resulting from gambling; but only that
they are the nurseries of the full grown gambling
hells; which is said to be nonsensical. Let us see.
A "nursery" is "that which forms and educates."
It cannot be denied, I think, that the practice of
parlor card playing always educates its subjects in
the same arts and processes that constitute the arts
and processes of the gambling hells or some of
them. The identical games are learned in fashionable parlors that are played for money stakes in
regular gambling houses, and the habit of playing
such games is there formed. And will it be denied
that more or less of the customers of gambling
houses are of those who learned these games in
parlors? And then are not the parlor games lit-
erally nurseries of gambling hells? More than
this; are not all the customers of gambling houses,
or nearly all of them, persons who have learned

the art of card playing in respectable places, where real gambling is not thought of, whether parlors or not, where Doctors of Divinity who believe in the amusement would not think it disreputable to be found? I think this must be so, for it is self-evident that very few men or boys ever go into a "full grown gambling hell" to learn how to play cards. That is not what those places are for. Their sphere in the devil's programme is higher than that. It is to accommodate those who want to gamble for money; and I venture to say that no man or boy ever went into such a place and risked money in a game of cards the first time he ever played. So it is clear enough that these innocent card tables as they are called, do actually furnish nearly or quite *all* the customers to the gambling hells. Are they not their nurseries then?

I have not said that all who play cards at home ever become gamblers; I shall not say that, for I know very well that it is not so; but I think the facts will bear me out in saying that all, or nearly all, gamblers get their primary education in parlors or other places where gambling for money is not carried on. And it is pretty safe to say that without such preliminary training they would not become gamblers.

And respectable, high-toned Christian card players and their apologists tell us that it is nonsensical to say that there is any danger in this fundamental education for the gambler's trade.

They make it respectable, and fashionable, and high-toned. They say to young men and boys: " Go on and learn all the mysteries of old sledge, seven up, whist, poker, and all other card processes; practice on them in your leisure hours; it is good for you; and anybody who does not believe in that is a fanatic." And so, with such instruction, and such habits—in very many cases amounting to a *passion*—fixed upon them, young men go out from their homes; and it is only a question of time and circumstance for many of them to find themselves in gambling houses.

There is a celebrated Doctor of Divinity in New York who advocates moderate drinking, and the liquor trade in respectable places, and in a respectable way, according to law. He thinks it is nonsensical on the part of fanatics to claim that the moderate drinking customs are the nurseries of intemperance, or in any way objectionable. Temperance parlor card players can quite easily see that mistake as to moderate drinking, but it makes a difference whose ox is gored. They cannot see anything but good in moderate card playing, although not denying that, as with drink, the moderate is the seed of the immoderate, or that the immoderate is one of the greatest evils of the day.

As before stated, if moderate drinking could always be pent up within moderation, and if cards could always be limited to moderation, in respectable parlors, then the nonsense of the fanatics on both subjects would be a good deal more apparent than it is.

In conclusion, ye men and women of the respect-able parlor card tables, you steady balanced heads who can indulge in this habit without turning your brains, without imbibing the passion that you know is all the time ruining thousands, you don't believe in gambling, you don't design to encourage it or to aid the gambler's profession in any way, but don't you see on which side of this great question your power is wielded? Don't you see that it is by your precept and example that the rising genera-tion are all the time learning the arts that are iden-tical with the gambler's arts? Don't you see that this training of the young is what eventually fills the gambling houses with their customers? Don't you see, therefore, that *you* are under a fearful re-sponsibility to God and humanity for the part that you are acting, for the power that you are wielding, upon this great question? Young man, remember that these parlor card tables are the nurseries of the full grown gambling hells—I must repeat it, for it is true. These respectable advocates of these dangerous practices are dangerous teachers. You cannot afford to follow them.

XI.

ON CHOOSING AN OCCUPATION.

In a former number I have inculcated the idea that in the order of nature's God, it is necessary for everybody, irrespective of wealth or position, to do some kind of work. The choice of a life work is a matter of no small importance; for a mistake in this may be a bar to a man's usefulness and fatal to success. It is better to be a good mechanic, or even a good hod carrier, or dirt digger than a poor lawyer dragging along through life in poverty and under a continual strain for bread and butter, who might have been comfortably independent as a mechanic or farmer. I have seen men try to preach the gospel who would have served God and their race much better by mauling rails. The way God has fixed things for us, a large majority of the race must necessarily be employed in physical labor—cultivating the soil, and in the multitudinous other vocations by which all the necessaries, conveniences, and luxuries of life are really produced. These occupations, though too often looked down upon by the unthinking, the superficial and the vain, as derogatory to what they denominate the higher grades of humanity, are really as respectable, in the eyes of all sensible and really high-toned people, as any others. When God, in His infinite wisdom, made it necessary to the life and well-being of our race that all these varieties of work should be done, He also made our physical nature to correspond with that necessity, so that every man and every woman would be the better for doing some of it. And He did not make it derogatory to any man or woman to

have a hand in it. When he made the necessity
that the ground should be tilled, that mines should
be worked, that buildings should be built, that the
thousand other trades should be carried on, that
food should be cooked, that raiment should be
cleansed, that dishes should be washed, and that
the hundred other things appertaining to the habitation should be done, He did not make it disreputable for any man, woman or child to take a
reasonable and suitable share in any of such work;
and any public sentiment that seeks to degrade
such service is false in philosophy, false to humanity, false to God.

And when enthusiastic working men and their
attorneys, in their quarrels with employers and
with other vocations, assert that they are the sole
producers of wealth, they are just as false. Without the other departments of labor, as we have
them in civilized life, the physical labor classes
would be helpless, and we would degenerate to
barbarism. A concurrence of all the forces of the
country—physical, intellectual, moral, is what produces wealth and refinement. No vocation can be
dispensed with save those that produce no good
and valuable result, as all the various grades of
crime against the State, against man, against God.

As it is so arranged in the economy of nature
that a considerable majority of the race necessarily
must be employed in what is called manual labor
in order that all the commodities of civilization

shall be produced, so I think a like majority are fitted for those employments only; that is they are so constituted that they cannot successfully prosecute any other calling. The general constitutional adaptation, and not the education or training, governs in this behalf. There is something for everybody to do, but it is not in the power of every man to be a skillful lawyer, or merchant or clergyman, or any other trade that is prosecuted chiefly by brain work and brain force. Schools cannot do it.

But any able bodied man, with common sense, can learn to dig dirt, chop wood, till the soil, or do ordinary mechanic work; and it is only stating a fact, and not making it, or wishing it to be so, when we say that a large majority of men are *only* adapted to such pursuits.

And here is where the mistakes are made in choice of occupation, that overflows the learned professions, the marts of trade, and other vocations of an intellectual character. Rich men sometimes want their sons to do something; and, as a matter of course, irrespective of their adaptability, they think it must be some high-toned calling, as it is called—something else than any kind of physical employment. Some people not rich get the same hallucination, that it is a great object for their boys to go into a learned profession, and so they strain a point to fit them for it by education, whether they have the suitable intellectual capacity or not. I think the result is that almost every-where there are too many lawyers, doctors, mer-chants, and others of light and so-called respectable employments to do the business ; and one-half of them would be much better off in some work adapted to their capacity, where they would be sure of business and sure of sufficient success for a comfortable and independent livelihood, if they had been trained to it.

The choice of a trade, then, I think, is quite easily made, as between intellectual occupations and those of physical labor. It seems to me that any boy not exhibiting peculiar adaptation to the former should not throw himself away in the fruit-less effort to compete, in a market always full, with those so superior to him that he is sure to fail, or, at best, to drag through a life of inferiority and consequent poverty, when he might, in another sphere of labor, attain to respectability and inde-pendence.

And I think there is not much danger of making a mistake in choosing this latter course; for it is not often any damage to a boy to begin life at the plow, or in a shop, or at any other hard work, and if there is anything else in him it will be pretty sure to come out in due time, and such an appren-ticeship is sure to make the better professional man, or business man of any kind.

And in choosing a life work I think it should be remembered that a simple superiority of brain power is not sufficient to ensure success in any intellectual vocation, without the propensity to industry, perseverance, push, work. Without these, genius itself cannot succeed.

Senator Sumner, with his great faculties, achieved his distinction by hard work. Here is a sample of how he began, and it is notorious that he kept it up through life. When at a law school he wrote to a classmate as follows:

"Late to bed and early to rise, and full employment while up, is what I am trying to bind myself to. The *labor ipse valuptas* I am coveting. I had rather be a toad and live upon a dungeon's vapor than one of those lumps of flesh that are christened lawyers, and who know only how to wring from quibbles and obscurities that justice which else they never could reach; who have no idea of law beyond its letter, nor of literature beyond their term reports and statutes. If I am a lawyer, I wish to be one, at least, who can dwell upon the vast heaps of law matter, as the temple of which the majesty of right has taken its abode; who will aim, beyond the mere letter, at the spirit—the law—and who will bring to his aid a liberal and cultivated mind. Is not this an honest ambition? If not, reprove me for it. A lawyer is one of the best or worst of men, according as he shapes his course. He may breed strife, and he may settle dissensions of years."

Brain power is wasted without the propensity to utilize it; while with this propensity largely developed we often see men of mediocre natural endowments rise to eminence; so that these two qualities in the make-up of a boy—brain power, and the tendency to utilize it—are what make up the real force of a man for any kind of life work. And without the latter any man is the better off in some humble calling as the servant of others, who tell him every morning what to do.

Then, as to the choice of the particular trade. Now and then we find a man of great brain powers, and so evenly balanced, that he can be reasonably successful in almost any thing. Such a man is safe to begin anywhere. As a farmer, mechanic, merchant, or professional man, he will rise to eminence if he energizes and utilizes the powers that are in him.

But most men, of larger or smaller calibre, have an aptitude, more less, for some particular calling, which should by all means be encouraged. A man with a penchant for the law would not succeed as well in the ministry. A man whose call is to the gospel will not be likely to succeed in another profession. Some are largely gifted in particular arts—sculpture, painting, music, etc.—they cannot be very good for any thing else. A prodigy in mathematics cannot make a good lawyer. A man deficient in mathematical talent cannot succeed as an engineer. One who takes naturally to mechanic work should not suffer himself to be forced into anything else. On the whole, wherever there is a marked propensity in a boy to any particular line of work, it is generally safe to cultivate such propensity.

Aside from these special gifts, and as to those destined to some kind of physical labor, I think the cultivation of the soil, at this day, offers the greatest inducements to young men. In these times of depression, when mechanics and most other hirelings find employment precarious—thousands out of work and helpless, we can appreciate the comfort of the farmer in his independent home, drawing upon his fat soil for his bread and butter, laughing at the commotions of capital and labor, secure in the enjoyment of the comforts of life, whether other schools keep or not.

And when we traverse the great expanses of rich and uncultivated lands, awaiting only the hand of labor to minister to the wants of unlimited populations, it seems to me that agriculture is to-day the permanent interest for the larger proportion of our young men to turn their attention to.

In conclusion, if every boy would adopt the vocation that God has fitted him for the best, instead of trying to strain nature by trying to do something else, I think the trades would be about rightly proportioned, and every one would be where he could enjoy life the best, for God has adapted the race, in general, to the supplying of the wants of the race to the best advantage. A man with a good mechanical talent but with none for the law, will be miserable in vainly trying to be a lawyer. He had better be a good mechanic, yea, a poor mechanic, or a dirt digger than that. And so of all other trades. Follow nature.

XII.

HELP.

When I was about twenty-one, I thought somebody ought to help me to a start in life. An old friend told me that " the way for young men to get on in the world is by their industry and good conduct to establish a credit and help themselves." And so I went to work to help myself. Young men usually think as I did, that somebody ought to help them. But I am satisfied now, upon forty years of experience and observation, that that kind of help to a young man—help that he does not command upon his own real merit, on business principles—help rendered as matter of friendship and favor—is the very worst thing that can happen to him in a business way. The best of all help for a young man is to help himself. And this is the only safe and wise condition precedent to any extraneous help—the only thing that can make such help available and profitable. A young man who has not commenced to help himself cannot be pushed into any success by other people's help. Usually any money invested in him will be wasted. This seems to be the law and we cannot help it. I have seen a good deal of this. I have seen a good many rich men's sons, having no idea that they must help themselves, helped into promising business, and amount to nothing. And I have seen the other kind of young men begin by helping themselves, and then in due time, they are pretty sure to get all the other help that they need. So, young man, it seems to me that the only sure way to begin the world is to begin to help yourself, and not begin by depending upon others. If you have not a rich father, probably that is the better for you ; if you have, his riches cannot make you ; you must help yourself, or any help you get from him will be of no avail.

I know a Corning boy, twenty-three years old, whose opportunities for earning money have been meagre, and he has saved of his earnings five hundred dollars. This is a good nest egg to start out with to be somebody, and to do some good in the world. He is helping himself. Whenever he needs any other help he will be able to get it, on business principles, if he keeps on in that way. Fathers can afford to help that kind of boys, if able, whenever the proper time comes ; but they will get along anyhow, for they start out with the best of all help—self help. And I see a great many of the other kind of boys and men, and I have seen them all along through life, who are always grumbling that they never have been helped. It never occurs to them that they never help themselves, or that any extraneous help would not be of any permanent good to them until they learn the art of helping themselves.

I don't think that any person has any just claim upon any other person for help ; not even child upon parent, however able the latter may be. I know the common opinion is that a rich man ought to shoulder his children along through life. But it is a false theory. The true philosophy of parentage, in this respect, is that a boy, grown up to man's estate, with sound health and a reasonable education, is an independent, self-existent being, and no longer a part of his father and mother. He has all the means of self-support, and the order of nature is that he shall cut loose from parental care and provide for himself; and he has no moral or other right to depend upon parents to carry him through. It is a reversal of nature. It extinguishes a man's manhood and individuality, and makes him a mere speck of his father.

All this being so, a rich man and his children being separate independent atoms in the thing that we call society, each pursuing his or her own inclination in life, each presumed to be as able to take care of himself or herself as have been the parents, I do not see what valid *claim* those children have upon the parent's bounty when they die. Their whole duty is done when the children are respectably brought up and educated; and if a father chooses to exclude a dissipated, or otherwise unworthy child, from his will, or to exclude him for any other reason satisfactory to himself, that is his own business entirely; his property is his own; nobody has any just claim upon him for any of it; he may do with it as he will; in the language of the courts, "he is the disposer of his own property, and his will stands as a reason for his actions." And then the public criticisms of a Vanderbilt and other rich men upon the making of their wills to suit themselves, are purely gratuitous and meddlesome. It is none of the public's business.

But all this is not to say that people should not, usually, leave their property, or a suitable share of it, to their children or their nearest relatives, or that parents, during life, should not prudently aid their children, when, as I have said, they are found worthy of it. I mean to say only that every man's duty is to guard his fortune, so far as he can, against being appropriated to bad uses. He has no more right to invest it in vice and debauchery indirectly, by giving it to a dissipated boy, than directly.

Furthermore: while in the main, the order of nature, and of law, and of society is that every one must depend on self help, we are not to be entirely selfish all through life. In some sense a man must depend chiefly upon himself, but every one is always dependent on others after all. Solitary and alone, cut off from association with others, a man would be miserable indeed. Association, mutual dependence, are inseparable from civilization. This, however, can all be on selfish business principles. But there are other kinds of help to one another that are worthy of our consideration if our lives are not to be shut into our own dear little selves, if we are not to be entirely selfish, if our little hearts can in any case reach out beyond our own little domicils, if we are not to steel ourselves

7

against doing any good in the world. If we are not to be all this, there are a good many things that will come in our way to do in the way of help to others that they have no particular claim upon us to do. There are many little things always occurring wherein we can help one another, where there is really no mutuality, for the time being, but costing nothing, or next to nothing, save a little trouble or labor, but of importance to the recipient. I have seen people so bound up within their own little soul boundaries that it was impossible for them to render a favor of any kind to a neighbor, to the amount of a cent, without two cents in plain sight coming back. I think the pleasure of any little neighborly courtesies is sufficient pay. I have sometimes taken a good deal of comfort in doing little matters of business for poor people who could not afford to pay professional men for the service. Only a little work for me, but of great importance, perhaps, to them. Opportunities are always occurring to do little helps to one another —and sometimes bigger ones—with no essential loss to the donor.

But sometimes such things will not be appreci ated—*i. e.*, afterwards. People will be ungrateful. It is of the depravity of human nature to be so. No matter for that. The service is not done for the pay of gratitude or for any other pay, except the satisfaction of doing a little good for somebody. This we cannot be robbed of by any conduct of the beneficiary. I once had occasion to lend a near and dear friend a considerable sum of money. I could do it about as well as not, but it was of considerable importance to her. Years elapsed, and when I wanted the matter arranged so that I would get my money back sometime, with legal interest, she thought she was injured. She thought I had wronged her. The transaction was purely as a favor on my part, and not as a matter of business; for I could have invested that money to much better advantage. She thinks I wronged her; and she is now my enemy. She intends to be a good Christian woman, but it makes a difference which way the money is to go—*to or from*. It was all right when it was going *to* her; when wanted *from* her it alters the case. Poor weak human nature cannot bear that so well. And now, shall I steel myself against all the better impulses of my nature on that account? Shall I sever all the ties of humanity and civilization, and swear that I will live only for myself? Shall I forego the pleasure of trying to make the world the better for my having living in it? and all this because of the weakness of an erring one? Not at all. Although we are not to shoulder others and carry them along, yet we are not to shut ourselves up within our own little shells and exclude all but self from our sympathies because we do not find perfection in humanity. That is not what we are for.

The foregoing general principles may, perhaps, be applied to all questions of help, and I might stop here; but there is another phase of help that is worth a paragraph specifically; and that is the lending of credit—endorsing notes, or incurring other obligations for others. It is a very safe rule, that some people adopt, to never do such a thing under any circumstances. But I think this rule comes too much within the rule of entire selfishness. If we live among civilized people, and propose to live in a civilized way, and to exercise any of the impulses of humanity and good neighborhood, sometimes the very best way to do this is to lend a name. Sometime a man *must* have bail in a considerable sum or submit to large loss by unjust judgment, or be imprisoned on false charges. Sometimes it will occur to the soundest business men that endorsement of their paper is indispensable to them. And there are various emergencies when such, or similar helps to one another, are eminently proper. Of course such obligations should not be incurred recklessly. They are purely matters of favor. Nobody has any *right* to ask them; and they never should be granted save in extraordinary emergencies, and on reasonable grounds of safety to the signer; this to be ascertained by the debtors means of meeting the obligation, eventually if not immediately, and from his habits of life and business. I don't think that any man has a right to endorse a note for another whose wife wears diamonds or any other such useless luxuries. Such a man has no right to owe any notes, or rather, a man who is in debt in his business has no right to indulge in such fripperies. Usually it is only a question of time for him to go under, and endorsers must look out. On the whole, in helping one another in this respect, we should not run any great risk. This is more objectionable, and more damaging to society and good neighborhood than to never lend the helping hand at all.

Such, in brief, I think are the general principles upon which young men should look for help from others, and upon which they should extend help to others as they go along through life. They may not be popular, but if they were practiced more the world would be the better for it.

XIII.

MARRYING.

After overcoming all the difficulties and obstructions in the way of success in life as I have tried to point them out in former papers, and getting ever so well under way in the process of thrift and reasonable accumulation, there is an institution that every young man very naturally, and very properly comes in contact with, that, in these days, is liable to counteract it all, and bring him to a miserable failure at last; and that is—a woman. *Liable* I say. It is not necessarily so. That is not an inherent quality of woman kind. It is an acquired accomplishment, a cultivated faculty, a fashionable piece of the education of young women, to indulge in habits of life that extinguish all hope of the average husband ever amounting to any certain sum. But women are not all so. And so this matter of marrying—the choice of a woman to marry—is a vital one to the thrifty young man. To the other sort it makes no difference—only to the woman.

In the first place, I think there is a fundamental principle in the ethics of courtship that should always be borne in mind by every young man and young woman. Every reputable young man and woman has, or ought to have, a conception of the character and qualities that can fill their ideal of a companion for life. In their sober senses they know what quality of a person they would be willing to marry. Now the rule that I would urge upon young people is that they never should form any very intimate associations with one of the opposite sex whom, in the first place, they would not deem suitable for them to marry. Ill-assorted flirting is very apt to culminate in ill-assorted marriages. Love is a mysterious quality of human nature. It is governed by no laws. It comes unbidden, and is uncontrollable by its victim. We can see this often in the conduct of young people —in the ill-assorted matches, in the elopements and in the general control that it holds over its subject. It is said to laugh at locksmiths. Yea, and it laughs at common sense and judgment and prudence. It overpowers them all. Too often we see reputable young women marry drunkards, or those on the road that way, or debauchees, or in other respects disreputable; and we see worthy young men ruined by marrying women unworthy of them. And all this is, I think, in consequence of improper associations—unsuitable social intercourse as it respects the selection of intimates—improper flirting. These are the fields where love is propagated and cultivated. Here is, in fact, the place where companions for life are chosen. Here, and only here, is where the misery of a lifetime can be prevented by preventing improper marriages. Let your love be cultivated in a suitable direction and all will be well.

Then as to choice. In the first place, I think that women, whatever their circumstances in life, should be of some practical use in the world ; and any young man who expects to be of any practical use in the world, should be very careful to not marry a girl who will not be that.

There is certain work that, in the order of Providence, seems to be allotted for women to do, work that all women *can* do, work that God never made a woman too good to do—the ordinary work of the house. But in these days the question seems to be whether this work is to be done by men or women, if done at all. For it is the prevailing passion with womankind to *not* do anything in that line. Young women, rich and poor, are educating themselves, and being educated by their hard-working mothers, to the idea that kitchen work is disreputable, that it is creditable to them to not engage in anything so vulgar, and that it is particularly meritorious in them to not know how to do it.

We can see multitudes of girls in any city or village—and the malady is extending to the rural districts, more or less—girls of all precuniary grades, from abject poverty to wealth, who seem to think that an indispensable element, if not the chiefest good, in the make-up of a young woman, is to exhibit tiny fingers, baby knuckles, dainty finger nails, and generally to be uncontaminated by any vulgar work. Of course they cannot think of putting their hands into dish water, or to a broom, or scrubbing brush, or any other implements of the house. If inexorable necessity compels them to any work, it must be something genteel, and not vulgar and unfashionable, like the indispensable work of the home.

I know many young women—Oh, too many of them, and I think they can be found anywhere—whose mothers are working their lives out, or whose fathers are keeping themselves impoverished by hiring other women to wait on them, but who ought to be doing the work for some neighbors who really need help. I have seen families consisting of three or four bouncing women, and two or three others, all of whom would be in the most pitiable distress on any occasion of the hired girl's leaving them for a few days; and such a commotion as the house would be in if she should leave for good, so that another must be hunted up! Yes the distress is pitiable, and the helplessness, the uselessness and the insipidness of a large proportion of American women is the more pitiable. The fathers and the husbands of that class of women are to be pitied. They should be specially avoided by young men who have any aspiration for advancement. And I notice that many prudent young men do avoid marrying altogether, because they cannot afford the expense of a wife, when it ought not to cost a man much more with a wife and a baby or two, than it usually costs him alone.

And this false education of women is the cause of all the trouble in the hired girl problem, which is everywhere the great difficulty of housekeeping. So many girls who ought to be trained to the necessary duties of the household are indulged in idleness; and when they marry their husbands, respectively, have to marry another woman or two to take care of them; that an inordinate demand for hired girls is created, and the supply is to be made up of the poorest material; for any young woman really fit to do the work and have the care of a house, very soon learns that that kind of work is too degrading for her, according to the prevailing public sentiment. Take any town of five thousand inhabitants, and probably there are not less than from 100 to 200 families depending on hired girls, where they ought to be dispensed with and the work done by their wives or the daughters, as the case may be; which increases the demand and diminishes the supply so that it is becoming more and more difficult for those who *necessarily* must have help, to obtain anything worthy of the name, for love or money.

But there are young women, even now, who are not useless, whose mothers do not think that a woman is any the better for being insipid and useless, whose fathers do not have to hire a woman to wait on them, and whose husbands will not have to marry a second woman to take care of them. I have seen such. I have raised some of them. A few of them are to be found in every community. Some of them are rich—some not rich. But they are not very plenty.

And that's the kind of girls for men of sense to marry. Let the fools marry the other kind.

In this connection, one thing more. In all this repudiation of women's work by women, the inexorable sentence : " In the sweat of thy face shalt thou eat bread," is recognized by women as applying somewhat to them. They admit the fact that they cannot all be maintained in idleness. They must do something. And so the clamor goes up *for something for women to do.*

Now, while, as Anna Dickinson demonstrated in one of her lectures, that there is nothing to hinder any woman, who is competent, from engaging in any occupation whatever, if all women who cannot succeed in any pursuit commonly reckoned as employments for men, would rise up to the real dignity of their station, and do the work that God and nature have provided for them to do, and fitted them for in every conceivable case of a common sense healthy woman, there would be no complaint for want of something for women to do; there would be no genteel lady paupers; the hired girl problem would be solved; there would be a good deal less of bankruptcy; and the world would be much the better for it.

I do not mean to say that every able-bodied woman should do her own house work continuously, or drudge constantly at any other hard work; but I do say this: that any woman, rich or poor, who sets her face against all that, looks upon it as degrading to a lady, spends her time in adorning her person and taking care of her pretty hands, never, unless under the most imperative necessity, doing anything useful to the world or to anybody in it, or if compelled by necessity to engage in something useful, then looking with scorn upon the natural and indispensable work for women; I say such a woman is not fit for any man who has a soul in him, and expects ever to be anything, to marry. And more: I say that women are just as able and it is just as incumbent on them to take a reasonable share of the work of the world, and it is just as necessary to their health to do so, as men. Of late years a new invention in hygiene has been made, called calisthenics, or the science of keeping women from dying of laziness. And I say that the best of all calisthenics are the washboard, the scrubbing brush, the broom, the dishcloth, etc. They are much better than to go to an institution and hire somebody to manipulate the limbs and muscles of a lady dying for want of the necessary exercise. And I say, further, that any young man, poor or in moderate circumstances, who is laboring and struggling to make his way in the world, has no business to marry a woman who will not, ordinarily, do the work of his house unless she brings a fortune of money to him.

After all, a good deal of such female inefficiency is the result of misapprehension. A good many women avoid work, not because of laziness, not because they do not want to do it, but because they think it is disreputable. They hear somebody with whom they associate, and in whom they confide, speak disparagingly of housework; they imbibe the same spirit, and propagate the odium of honest work. Then it amounts to just this : they reject work because it is disreputable, and it is disreputable—so far as at all—because they reject it.

This is all wrong. It is taking things wrong end foremost. I never have known a woman, in all other respects worthy, slighted in any really desirable society because of doing work for her family.

The really rich, and sensible, and high-toned, usually approve it. They have generally graduated in that school, and do not go back on their *alma mater*. The teachers in this phase of woman's education are generally those who ought to be practicing the other way—pretenders—fictitious aristocracy.

If all women who really ought to do so—I mean those who cannot *afford* to do otherwise—would at once discharge their kitchen girls, and do their own work, we would hear no more of the odium of kitchen work, and then the most industrious young ladies would be the most popular in high society or low.

In the second place, ordinarily, a poor young man cannot afford to marry a rich girl. Usually it will require a rich man to keep a rich wife supplied with the necessaries of life; i. e., what she will deem necessary to maintain her dignity and standing; for a rich girl, brought up rich, taught that she is rich, in most cases will demand a good deal more in the way of unnecessary expenses than the riches that she will bring will afford, unless she is uncommonly gifted in the way of sense. She will need a rich man to keep up her supplies. The usual process is about thus : A young woman has a comfortably rich father. He has several children. They are brought up with all the indulgences that are common with rich fashionable people. His daughter marries, but he is not quite ready to die and divide out his wealth among his

children ; and if he were, there would not be quite
enough of it to make each and every one of them
as rich as he was; they cannot begin on that where
he left off, for the reason that any sum of money
divided into half a dozen shares will not be as
much to each share as the original sum. So that
as to the common run of rich young ladies, they do
not expect to come down any in the scale of expenses and general indulgence, and poor young
men have no business with them. They cannot
afford the luxury of rich wives.

I have seen a good deal of this. And I have seen
a good deal of aping rich wives on very small
capital.   An old acquaintance of mine who started
out in life cotemporary with me, married a wife
who thought she was rich. She had a thousand
dollars or so. He was poor. She thought she
must live in the style of the rich and put on all the
airs. She did all that. He was a fair business
man, and for a time carried on a reasonably successful business; but his profits were moderate,
and insufficient to keep up his wife's *necessary*
expenses for a rich lady; and he dragged along,
under embarrassment and hard tugging to keep his
head above water for a few years, but finally he
was compelled to go under, and he never has been
able to rise since. And since then I have heard of
that exquisite lady going out washing and nurs-
ing, and anything she could get to do, and to-day
her husband perambulates the country as a book

agent, or collecting bills for a newspaper, or any other little matters that he can get to do. He might have been comfortably rich had it not been for his rich wife. This is one of numerous cases that I have seen of that character. And it matters little how much wealth that kind of a woman brings with her. There are but few cases where it is not a great damage to the husband, and ruinous unless his own income be large.

And then, in these days, it is extremely hazardous for a poor young man, who is good for anything, to marry a poor girl. The prevailing fashion now is for poor girls—even some of those who have been inured to honest useful industry—if they happen to marry a thrifty, prosperous young man, to quit business, sit down, put on airs, look down with scorn from their lofty pedestal upon honest industry, and commence a raid upon the husband's material financial substance. I have seen a good deal of this. Let one instance suffice. A very poor young lady, notoriously poor, but by good and honest industry had managed in different ways to keep up a respectable appearance, and maintain a respectable standing among her acquaintances, married a young man in receipt of a respectable salary. A house was rented, and after suitable preparations were made for housekeeping, she wanted a *housekeeper;* not a mere hired girl, but a housekeeper, who would run the whole machine, for she could not, oh no she could not think of looking into the kitchen. That would be too vulgar. And besides, she was to have so much else to do—to be a bride—to receive her bridal calls—to make her calls—it would be too much for her to do to look into the kitchen besides all that. But I learn that her husband is about as big a fool as his wife is; they are well matched; neither is cheated much; they can punish along through life in poverty together as well as in any other way perhaps. I have seen a good many of this kind of people and I never saw one that amounted to any certain sum.

Who, then, can a young man safely marry? I have said that a woman is not necessarily fatal to a man's hopes of success in life. There are women that men can afford to marry. Don't marry for riches. Don't marry for poverty. Don't marry a woman because she works, merely. Don't marry for any of the collaterals of a particular woman. But marry a woman for true womanhood, for brains, heart, soul, and common sense. Find such a woman as that, ånd then if she has wealth it will not hurt her; if she is poor her poverty will not hurt her; if she knows how to work that will not hurt her; if she does not know how to work that will not spoil her. Such a woman as that will always be a woman, and not a fool, under any circumstances. I have seen a good many of them. Such a woman can conform to any circumstances of life and be an aid and comfort to her husband.

She will. Look for that kind of a woman; make love to her; and marry her if you can, if you want to marry. Then as to

THE WEDDING.

A Vanderbilt may make a wedding to cost a half million or so if he will; it is really nobody's business but his own. But with all the multitudinous and meritorious benefactions—religious, educational, reformatory, charitable—on every hand, to invest money in, Mr. Vanderbilt and all other millionaires and other rich, and moderately rich, and well-to-do people, can make better use of their money than to inflict upon the entire household the fatigue and strain of two or three months, more or less, of a campaign for a big wedding. For it is really a hardship to all connected with it. They *endure* it as a necessary evil, and do not enjoy it, even though they succeed in having it said that the magnificence and expense of the *trousseau* ex ceeded anything before known in their particular set, or in their locality. And all engaged in such a siege, bride and groom not excepted, are ready to say, as the good woman said who sent her little child to invite a neighbor to a party, and in her instructions to the child added, parenthetically, "and I wish to the Lord it was over with;" the little one, in his innocence and truthfulness, delivered the message: "Mother wants you to come to our party to-morrow, and she wishes to the Lord it was over with." And after the great event is past,

8

they can the more truly say they thank the Lord that it *is* over with.

And so I think it is with most of the *guests* of these great matrimonial demonstrations. There is no pleasure in them. They attend because they must. It would be rude to decline without inexorable reason, and so they enjoyed it as the man enjoyed bad health. Excepting, nevertheless, and always reserving one class of people—the snobs—those who happen, somehow, to get noticed by people that they deem of a higher grade than themselves. They take a good deal of solid comfort in going to a wedding or other party above their own sphere. For example: Not very long ago a very worthy lady that I know of, with her own full share of vanity in her, with inordinate aspirations for recognition among the "first families"—in short, a snob, somehow got invited to a high-toned party. She went of course. Her success in life depended on her going to that party. She was rising in the world She had been noticed away up in the highest grade of mortals in Podunk. Oh, that was delicious. She went. The highest grade of people in Podunk amuse themselves, at their grandest parties, by playing poker—whatever that is. She found poker to be the prevailing luxury of the evening. And she could not play poker. And she was in distress. She was promoted away up high, and she didn't know how to play poker. She expected to be invited to that kind of parties all winter and she must learn to play poker. Who could teach her to play poker? She must learn. She must.

This kind of people enjoy extravagant weddings. Their amusement, and pandering to their vanity is what such parties are good for.

And then when we come to poor people, and those in moderate and straitened circumstances, these wedding splurges are positively wrong— wrong to the parties themselves, wrong to friends, and sometimes wrong to creditors; wrong in the large expenditures that cannot be afforded. I have seen a good many large and expensive weddings where that money ought to have been invested in paying debts; and other cases where it was needed to start the newly made family in the way of house-keeping or in business.

I know a man badly involved in debt, always on a strain to keep the sheriff at bay, who not long ago was deeply distressed because he could not find two hundred dollars to borrow to make a wedding for his daughter! We may say that Vanderbilt was a fool to waste half a million on a wedding, when he could have invested it in other ways for the permanent benefit of humanity, so as to afford himself and his family a life-long income of pleasure, but this man was, perhaps, a bigger fool on a smaller scale, to want to plunge himself deeper into debt and distress by wasting two hundred dollars of somebody else's money on a wedding.

And I have practiced what I am preaching, so that I know it is successful. I have been married twice, and in each case it cost me a moderate fee to the minister, and the family about half a day's extra work. And that is all. And I was just as well married, and as well thought of, as if the whole neighborhood had been in a ferment over it for a month, and money had been expended that we needed then, if ever. And I kept about my business as if nothing unusual had happened.

Young man and young woman, about to marry, if parents or other friends want to force upon you the worry and discomfort of a big wedding, because other folks do, don't you do it. Emancipate yourselves from that folly of fashion. As you are entering upon that holy state it is a good time to eschew *all* fashionable follies and vices. You have the same right to the ordinary comfort and quietude of life on the eve of marriage as at any other time. Marriage is not a crime, or in any way disreputable, that you should be punished for it by the trouble and worry and strain of a long, elaborate preparation for a fashionable splurge for the benefit of all the snobs in the neighborhood.

Another of the abominations of fashionable weddings is the present current custom of presents.— Not to say that the parents or other intimate friends of the newly married should not, on that occasion, if they desire, make any contributions whatever to them, *purely as gifts ;* but in the prevailing fashion of big weddings, every guest being expected to contribute something in the way of a so-called present, it is all simply a matter of traffic. People are invited for the sake of the presents they are to bring. They go and take the presents because they expect them to be reciprocated some time. The recipients are under obligations to contribute to all the weddings that come along. It is a sort of traffic that people in moderate circumstances cannot afford. Their presents are likely to be what they do not want, or cannot afford to have, and there is really no friendship or gift about it. To rich people it is simply a bore.

But all this is not to say that marriage should not be celebrated with a comfortable, quiet, social party of particular friends—half a dozen or so. And in this matter of invitations, remember that it is your business to choose your own company, and nobody has any *right* to an invitation. Be your wedding large or small, do not invite any for the reason that they will be offended if not invited. None but fools will take offense on that account. It is your business. I have been omitted from a good many large and small weddings in my day, and I never thought that I was insulted, slighted or injured by it, or that it was any reflection upon me, or any of my business. I may be dull of apprehension, but I never have thought that I had any claim upon any body's hospitality or their social recognition.

And then, my young friends, when the marrying

is over, I think the most sensible and comfortable and satisfactory thing to do is to quietly go about your business, just as if nothing had happened. For I never could see why a newly married pair should be, just then, subjected to the fatigue and discomfort of what is called a wedding tour. If you have occasion to travel, professionally or for instruction, and it happens to be convenient to do so just then, that is all very well; but to take a long, tiresome and expensive journey merely as a part of the programme of a wedding splurge, it is nonsense. It is starting out in married life at a disadvantage. The honeymoon should be as sweet as possible, and not embittered by unnecessary tribulations to disgust the parties with the new relation and to create a repulsion to each other. There is no need of losing your senses for a month or two before and after marriage.

XIV.

AFTER MARRIAGE—WOMEN'S WORK.

In my last number, having discussed the matter of women's work, in a general way, as a caution to thrifty young men before marriage, I propose, now, to enter upon that subject more elaborately, for the consideration of young people after marriage, as they enter upon the realities of married life. There is a good deal of agitation now-a-days, about inventing something for women to do, or setting apart something for women to do, or somehow to provide work for them to do to earn their living.

Now, I think, that with the exception of a very small fraction of woman-kind—a few sensible and enterprising women—there is a good deal more trouble in getting women to do something in the way of any useful work than in finding something for them to do. At all events there always is work enough for all the women to do. In all our cities and villages the prevailing sentiment and study, and fashion and practice, are that any woman that aspires to be anybody must not do any useful labor. The nice young lady alluded to in my last number, who could not think of looking into the kitchen because she had married a man able to support two women, is not an isolated case. So much silliness does not always crop out, but pretty nearly all the brainless women of the day seem to think that the *ne plus ultra* of feminine accomplishment is to not know how to do anything that is of any value in the world, and that there is nothing much more derogatory to a woman than to be guilty of work. And so prevalent is this theory becoming that a good many women who have better sense than that, and too many men, also, are falling in with the idea as a necessary surrender to public opinion. The other day an otherwise sensible and a really estimable lady of my acquaintance, in speaking of an enterprising young lady who is working for wages, said, "well, girls that work are not much thought of." This was said, not only to relate a fact in society, but said with an air of approval. I think, however, that this sentiment is propagated much more by fashionable *poor* people —those whose highest ambition is to ape the rich than by the really rich who can afford it.

The great want of the age, in respect to the woman question, is to get the women willing to do something. And here is a field for all the women's rights lecturers in the land.

Any women who really want to do something have not far to go. There is an abundance of work for all our native-born American young women to do, in the vocations that our mothers, and grandmothers, and all the high-toned women of a century ago engaged in—the various duties of the household that God designed for women's share in the work that He made necessary to the perpetuity and the civilization of the race, and which is now supposed must be done by an imported population.

Not that no women should do anything else but this ; let any woman do whatever she wishes to and will fit herself for ; but the idea should be cultivated and kept prominent in all phases of our civilization, that the great primary sphere of woman is woman's work in the home. Apropos to this I cannot do better than to repeat a passage from my No. XI.

"When God in His infinite wisdom made it necessary to the life and well being of our race that all these varieties of work should be done, He also made our physical nature to correspond with that necessity, so that every man and *every woman* would be the better for doing some of it. And He did not make it derogatory to any man or woman to have a hand in it. When He made the necessity that the ground should be tilled, that the mines should be worked, that buildings should be built, that the thousand other trades should be carried on, that food should be cooked, raiment should be cleansed, dishes washed, and the hundred other things appertaining to the habitation be done, He did not make it disreputable for any man, woman, or child to take a reasonable and suitable share in any of such work; and any public sentiment that seeks to degrade such service is false in philosophy, false to humanity, false to God."

A celebrated Hygienic physician, writing of the effects of the different occupations on health, puts *idleness* down as the most unhealthful of all. He says :

"Idlers generally have very poor health. Of all hygienic misfortunes, that of having no employment is the worst. A poor man is to be pitied, but an idler much more. The most inveterate cases of hypochondriasis among men, the most intractable cases of hysteria among women, and the worst forms of dyspepsia among both sexes, are to be found among those who have no regular employment. Every one who desires health should keep himself regularly engaged at something which will call forth and exercise both his mental and corporeal powers. If he must go to either extreme, it is better it should be that of doing too much."

The above needs only to be stated to be appreciated. Everybody knows it to be all true. It is verified all about us, especially in the fashionable ailments of the idle young women everywhere; for idleness in just as unhealthful upon women, as men.

Not many years ago I met with a newly married couple. The young man was a sprightly business man, in receipt of a very good salary, but in his years of bachelorhood he never had thought of saving up any of his large income. The wife had exactly the same amount of poverty, so that they started out quite evenly, only that he did the work and she put on the airs—and they were something immense. She is of the kind that cannot think of making herself of any use in creation. In a board-- ing house, listless, insipid, doing nothing to fulfill the physiological conditions of reasonable health, of course she became a fashionable invalid, proud of her delicacy. Calisthenic processes and drug medication have been unavailing; the boarding house has been abandoned as too common place; they are housekeepers, with a lusty Irish girl for the second woman. She is dying for the want of washboard, broom, dish cloth and cooking stove; he will soon be a widower.

He is the willing slave to all her follies and foibles, and of course he is always on a strain, and more or less in debt, to keep along with this pro- gramme of life; whereas with reasonable industry on her part, suited to their circumstances, and reasonable economy, she might have been a healthy woman, one-half or so of the income would have been saved, and they well on the road to indepen- dence, instead of in the slough of failure.

Women are just as able to do reasonable work, according to their strength, as men. The natural and legitimate duties of women in the order of civilized society are as necessary as those of the men ; and there is no more reason why the female part of a matrimonial partnership should be exempt from her share in the labor of life than that the other side should. And yet if a hard-working young man marries, the chances are that he must do his own work and his wife's also—*i. e.* hire a woman to do it, while with laziness and fashion the wife dwindles away by inches, for the want of something to do.

In a sermon to young people that I heard not long ago the minister truly said that young married men do not dare to venture upon making homes of their own, but must live in boarding houses, because unable to make such homes as are acceptable to their wives. He did not say that to make a home a young man must marry a pair of women—one for a wife, and another to wait on her; but that is really what is the matter.

Some years ago I was teaching a young business man how to keep his books. After I had learned all about his business, his expenses, etc., he asked me if I thought he could get through with his undertaking successfully. He and his wife were living at a boarding house. I replied that it all depended on his rate of expenses, and advised him to get a little cozy place and begin housekeeping, to save expense. Well, he afterwards did go to housekeeping, but that at least doubled his expenses, as his wife proved to be helpless, and he had another woman to provide for, with all that that implies, and nobody has ever yet found out how much money a second woman in the house does imply. His business was good, though only moderate, affording a reasonable, but not a large amount of profits. He met with no considerable losses, and had no particular bad luck. He struggled and battled along, year after year, vainly trying to overcome the inexorable leak and waste of hired girlism, and the constant expenses of fashionable lady idleness, which, with the *necessary* family expenses, constantly consumed more than his profits; his burdens and embarrassments pressing harder and harder, until, in seven or eight years he found relief in bankruptcy.

Now this man's wife was just as able to do her own house work as her husband was to do his work. And the saving of this hired girl fund would have saved him and ensured him a permanent prosperity in his business. Let us see: The full and exact cost of the common run of a hired girl—such as are usually to be had—is beyond human ken. It is past finding out. But the very lowest rate that it can be reckoned at; say wages, board, waste, and the etceteras, is not less than a dollar every day. And where the mistress is not especially vigilant and watchful, it is sure to be a good deal more.

In my friend's case, then, one dollar a day for eight years, with interest at 7 per cent. from the

end of each year to the end of eight years, amounts
to $3,744.82.   To my certain knowledge this would
have saved him.   I mention this case thus particularly as a sample of multitudes of other cases that
I have seen and that everybody can see all
along the way.   We can see them all about us under way all the time ; whether business men, to
come to a crash by-and-by, or salaried men to be
merely kept poor all the time, it makes no difference ; this useless hired girlism is ruin to thousands who otherwise might be comfortably independent.   To see how this is, let us look further
along in this figure-work :

A dollar a day for ten years, with interest as
      above, amounts to $ 5,042.80
In twenty years,   14,962.80
In thirty years,   34,476.90

These figures are an interesting, and may be a
profitable, study for young wives and their husbands.

But the foregoing class of cases is not universal.
I have seen all along through life, some cases of
the other kind.   And we may see them even now,
in any community—high-toned, respectable women
who do not think it disreputable, and are not too
lazy, to do reasonable work in aid of their husbands ; and they prosper of course.   And this
proves my theory that American women kind can
if they will, and we are not necessarily dependent
on an imported race of women to keep our houses
for us.

I may add, here, for the benefit of older people, that chronic hired girlism can be reformed. I know it is about as difficult as to reform from whisky or tobacco, but it can be done. I have seen it.

A newly married pair began housekeeping about the time that I did; both poor; the wife had been a hired girl herself. But now she had a man to work for her, and with no idea that she was to be anything to him but a toy or a doll baby, "what's the use," she said, " of my working, when my husband can earn money enough in a day to pay a girl for me a week." They dragged along for many years in poverty; she having no aspirations for anything but ease and present enjoyment of whatever of this world's comforts by hook or crook came to them, until, finally, her husband became a hopeless inefficient drunkard; then she roused up her own latent energies, found out that she was good for something besides to consume what a husband earns, went to work, economized and accumulated a respectable property on her own account.

And so there are many wives who have begun on the down hillside of this hired girlism, and are thus pulling their husbands down, who can yet reform if they will, and save the partnership from ruin.

In conclusion, I want it to be distinctly understood that I am not finding any fault with anybody; that I do not say that any woman in particular ought to do any useful work—that is none of my business; I am not anybody's monitor. I am only giving the philosophy of this disease of hired girlism—showing the facts and the law, not making them, or applying them to anybody in particular; pointing out the consequences of one course and the other, as it respects people of moderate income; on the one hand bankruptcy and life long poverty; on the other success, comfort, and independence. We might wish that our Heavenly Father had seen fit to so arrange things for us that the present fashions of the better half of humanity would not be ruinous to themselves, their husbands and their families : *that they could be healthy, vigorous, lithe and handsome in insipid idleness, instead of the contrary of all that, and their husbands able to spend their money and save it, and grow rich on investments in hired girls. But that is not the law, and we cannot make it so.

I know there are some men with incomes so large that the cost of a hired girl, or two or three of them, cannot overpower them; but with all young men with ordinary incomes it is a question of success or failure in life. It is impossible for them to support a hired girl and rise above poverty, with the chances of absolute destitution and distress always against them. It is for you to choose, young wife and young husband. Sit down together and look this matter square in the face, and work out the problem for yourselves. As you start out in life with the laudable ambition, as I must presume, to fill a position of usefulness and honor, to attain to a standing of creditable prominence in the body politic, and not to be blank in creation, or excrescences upon society, you see before you two open ways; and it is for you to determine which of them will be most conducive to what you wish to be; it is for you to decide which will be most conducive to your life-long comfort and satisfaction.

In direct connection with the subject of this chapter, is that of women's education; which is, of course, addressed to mothers and fathers of girls rather than to young men and women after marriage.

I do not propose to go into an elaborate dissertation upon the education of women. Let your girls learn anything and everything that they wish to and that you can afford, provided that the one essential, aye indispensable, accomplishment of the true woman be not omitted; *i. e.* practical knowledge of all the actual work of the home. Without this no woman, rich or poor, is fit to place herself at the head of her husband's house; in fact not fit to be a wife. For, whether necessary or not to *do* the work of her house, a woman who does not know from experience what it is to do it, is always at a disadvantage, always imposed upon by her help, and the house is usually in a state of discomfort. And a young woman who undertakes to *do* her work, without that previous education, will then find it hard to learn, and much more difficult and much harder to do, than if she had learned the art in her girlhood days.

I have seen women who, in their school days, had been educated in all the literary branches and genteel accomplishments of the schools, whose parents thought such to be all that was necessary in the make-up of a woman for life, undertake to be working housekeepers for their husbands; and although, where the will is good, such women can learn the trade after a fashion. I never have known one of them to be really good housekeepers.

I have seen a household where the mother has toiled, year after year, in the labors of the home, whereby the family grew rich. Daughters grow up in that home. The mother says : " Now, my girls shall not work as I have done. There is no need of it. We will send them to school and give them an education, with all the advantages of society and fashion that I was deprived of in my young days. That will surely carry them through."

And so they are sent to a fashionable boarding school, or college, where all the good and solid branches of book knowledge are learned, and of course not omitting the follies and foibles of fashion, whether in the curriculum or not. All that is to carry them through. There is no thought of the education of the kitchen. That is too vulgar. It is well enough for the mother. She was not educated in the higher branches; and she works her life out, or harasses it out with hired help to raise the girls in genteel uselessness. This is a sample of the current fashion of training girls, not only by the rich, but those in very moderate circumstances, and quite poor, keep themselves impoverished and on a strain to give their daughters the benefit of that kind of culture.

It is all wrong. The primary duty of a mother, in respect to the education of her girl is to drill her in the practical duties of the home. It is not a favor to her to allow her to shirk that indispensable element in the make-up of the true woman. Not to say that she shall not go to ever so many schools and learn all other accomplishments, but not let all that supersede or extinguish the primary education of woman for woman's work.

A daughter of mine was brought up by a step-mother. She was trained to all the mysteries of woman's work in the home. She thought it was pretty hard, when she saw so many of her associates who were not required to do anything of the kind. Some other people thought that was the step-mother of it. An own daughter of the same step-mother was afterwards trained in exactly the same way. They are now good for something besides being doll babies and spending the earnings of their husbands. And they and their husbands thank that mother for such an education.

I have seen a good many girls brought up in that way, and they are always the better for it. But the great preponderance is the other way, to the serious damage of thousands of families.

I think this great necessity of women's knowledge of women's home duties is generally acknowledged.   And accordingly we read of various schemes for effecting the object by the schools—in some other way than by apprenticeship in the actual work itself.   It cannot be done.   I never could have learned to hammer out a horse shoe and shoe a horse by reading all the books that the learned blacksmith could write in a lifetime.   And the only possible way for a girl to learn the art of housekeeping is by practicing it with her mother or some other good housekeeper in the home.

And this false education of girls is a serious public calamity.   It robs society of nearly all efficient hired help in women's work. It takes from this highly responsible and highly honorable department of the work of civilization, nearly all the efficiency and competent brains of womankind, and leaves that work chiefly to incompetent hands. The inefficiency of the hired girls that are to be had was tersely expressed by a lady friend of mine— in poor health, really needing help, and doing her own work, in this wise: "I am not well, and not able to wait on a hired girl."   Any good housekeeper necessarily afflicted with an ordinary hired girl will appreciate the appositeness of the remark.

XV.

AFTER MARRIAGE—STYLE.

Hired-girlism is not the worst thing that can befall a household. This is often necessary—sometimes profitable. And there are many incomes where the price of a hired girl, or any reasonable number of them is of no consequence.

But in such cases there is a greater peril than is the hired girl mania to fashionable poor people. There are very few incomes so large that an ambitious, fashionable, stylish woman, with a husband to match, cannot exhaust it all and more.

Somehow, in the make-up of the class of people, rich or poor, whose god is style, and show, and spread, there is no limit to their ambition for expense. As the opportunities for investment in that direction are unlimited, so their expenditures are limited only by their ability to command the means.

And this passion leads not only to the waste of all the honest money that a man can get, but often to much more serious consequences.

Those of my readers who read the papers of thirty years ago will remember the murder of Dr. Parkman by Prof. Webster in Boston. That horrid murder was incited by the passion for display in his wife and daughters—by their spending more money than he could earn. The facts were these: Webster was a professor of chemistry in Harvard College, with a salary that his family ought to

have been satisfied to live upon. He was a slave
to their follies, and they kept him in debt so deeply
that he was incessantly pressed and harassed for
money that was beyond his power to get. Dr.
Parkman was a creditor who had long been pressing
him for the payment of a note for five or six hundred dollars, and in his desperation the Professor
decoyed the Doctor into his room in the College,
under pretense of payment, and with the note on
the table, murdered him to get possession of it;
and he was detected and hung. In the higher
walks of life, with an unsullied reputation, and
an income sufficient for all reasonable desires, Prof.
Webster's family plunged him into a perpetual
strain of embarrassments and distresses that for
aught any human can know crazed his brain, that
sacrificed the life of the man whose money they
had wasted, and brought their own dearest friend
to an ignominious death.

Gilman, the forger, now languishing in prison,
his wife in an insane asylum, his children a hundred
times worse than orphans, committed his great
crimes, not from any innate depravity of heart,
not from inordinate acquisitiveness, but solely to
gratify the passion for display, for appearances
and show of wealth. He was respectable, highly
esteemed, and sufficiently provided with the luxuries of life when living on his honest money. But
that wicked passion for inordinate ostentation
seized him and her, and by it they are where they

are, and their children disgraced and humiliated for life.

The New York *Times* of December 13th, 1877, in giving an account of the failure of a " reputable law firm," composed of two church members in good standing, says :

" The late book-keeper of the firm, when interrogated yesterday, said that he did not think either partner carried off with him much of the embezzled funds. The trouble was, he said, that they had been living at an annual expense of $20,000 on an income of about $8,000."

But not to occupy too much space with extreme cases, which might be extended almost indefinitely, the same spirit prevails more or less everywhere ; and when it does not engender actual crime it does effect the life long discomfort and pecuniary ruin of its victims. Professor Webster's family had the unholy ambition to compete, in the way of fashionable life, with somebody a great deal richer than they. They did it on the money of Dr. Parkman and others. Gilman and his wife had the same ambition. That is all that was the matter with those two families.

To bring the matter home : there are a few rich people here in Corning ; not rich enough to hurt any body much, but rich enough to exemplify the subject in hand. There are also a good many well-to-do people here, who might become comfortably rich some day if they would ; with income sufficient, if a reasonable share of it were to be saved, to aggregate a handsome fortune in after years ;

but they cannot wait; they have the fatal ambition of the Websters and the Gilmans; they prefer the shadow of wealth now to the substance by and by; and so they kill the goose that is giving them the golden eggs; they spend all their money as fast as it is earned—usually a good while before—to ape their richer neighbors in style and spread. Young married people think they are doing a big thing to begin that way. They think they are making a large amount of social capital and popularity with the class whose social recognition they are courting. But they are mistaken. All their investment of money and of sycophancy is wasted. Real aristocracy despises the false, and when a pair of young fools start out in life by investing all they are worth, and more, in glitter and show, they are sure to receive more ridicule than approbation from those that they do it for; they are at once written down as failures. For their spreading themselves out so thin will not deceive any body; their real circumstances are known or will be; they cannot pass for rich on a little tinsel.

So, my young friends, as you start out together for your life work, instead of spreading yourselves out you had better gather up; instead of investing in public opinion, for dividends of social nods, invest in real estate, good interest-paying bonds, or a good bank account, with the real approving recognition of all really rich and sensible people; for they will soon find this out too. Instead of a large rented house, and fine carpets and furniture, and a set of tiny fingers and baby knuckles, attached to a helpless, idle, fashionable wife, and a hired girl, all with more or less of somebody else's money mixed up with it, better, far better, a little home of your own, if not more than a couple of rooms, with a rag carpet of *her* own make, and other comfortable things to match, with a healthy, handsome, rosy, working wife, and money accumulating as a foundation for real wealth.

There is a good deal said about the worship of mammon, the race after wealth, the intensity of labor for its accumulation, etc., etc. But I think that is not what's the matter. If mammon were worshiped a good deal more than it is, I think the world would be the better for it. Trace all money crimes—embezzlements, forgeries, thefts, burglaries, bank robberies and defalcations of every phase to their source—and I think it will be found almost universally, that this passion for spending money for ostentation, and not the worship of it, not hoarding or accumulation of it in any way, is at the bottom of it. One of the gigantic evils of the day is the habit of a large proportion of the people to spend more money than they earn, and I do not see that it makes much difference whether it is gotten by outright stealing or by what is called honest running into debt for what can be dispensed with, and never paid for. We hear about honest failures in business, and dishonest ones.

If the party gives up to his creditors all the property he has, it is called an honest failure; but I think that depends on what he has been doing with his money for years agone. If he has been spending more money than he has been making, and running into debt to make up the deficiency and keep afloat, so that his creditors finally have to pay for his and his wife's ostentation, I cannot see much difference between such a failure and one where the property is put away in any other manner.

This is not a question of how much it will cost, as with the matter of tobacco, or whisky, or hired girls, but it is a question of *all the money that one can get;* for with the passion for aping richer people—for living as other people do, as the saying is—the demand is limited only by the power to supply it.

This passion is fearfully demoralizing; not that all its victims commit any crimes, but its tendency is that way. A young man marries. He may have been sufficiently economical, and saved up something. His own tastes and aspirations may be in the right direction. His wife has what are called higher notions. Her ambition is to start out, not especially to suit themselves, not to suit their own convenience, and comfort, and circumstances, but for the eye of other people, under the mistaken notion that thereby they will command their applause; when the fact is that those other people, to whose fancy they are pandering, care nothing at all about them or their glitter, only as a matter of pity ; for they who have made themselves rich did not begin that way, and they know that such beginnings are wrong end foremost. Beginning where rich people end is sure to end where rich people began ; i. e., at the bottom. Well, the young husband is anxious to please his wife—she is all in all to him—and he invests his money to make a sensation. They start out under high pressure ;—their money, peradventure, proves inadequate, and they go into debt. Meantime the institution does not prove satisfying ; somebody is a little ahead ; they are fairly launched on the sea of fashion, and they must plow it through ; so the debt is piled up deeper and still deeper, until the crash is inevitable ; then the tempter comes in and to postpone the evil day crime is added to folly, and the chapter is ended. Such are the tendencies of this foolish vice, and in whatever degree that passion obtains, it is always vitally damaging, and generally fatal to the prospects of its victims, whether culminating in crime or not. There is no rational reason for falling into it.

And this foolishness of inordinate style is not limited to poor people. The really rich and moderately rich young people, who have gotten their wealth, or expect to get it, without knowing how it comes or what it has cost, are as subject to serious damage by this vice as poorer people. Even where inherited wealth does not spoil young men in other ways, it is very likely to in this. I have seen men begin poor and grow rich, raising famil-ies in the meantime—beginning with rigid economy and self-denial, but as their means increased, grad-ually and prudently increasing their expenditures, even to luxury and elegance; all of which is cer-tainly to be commended.

Then I have seen their children—all innocent of any wealth-producing power in themselves—com-mence life; commence where—where their fathers did? Oh, that is not to be thought of; perhaps not desirable, because not necessary. Where their fathers leave off? No, that is too common. As their fathers would like to have them begin? No, they are too old fogy. They do not know much of anything. The younger generation is superior to the old, and can invent so many more spreading ways than they, that they really have to cut loose and start out on their own wisdom. And they launch out.

I have seen, for example—one of many—a young family of two, not rich enough to hurt them at all if they would use common sense with it, starting out for a sensation, begin with an establishment sufficient for a family of a dozen, in grandeur ex-ceeding anything ever known in all their family connections, and aspiring to eclipse everything in the locality, at an outlay, perhaps, of all the avail-able means at their command, and involving a current expense tc run the institution, that cannot be afforded until after the father or mother of one or the other of the matrimonial partnership, from whom the expected wealth is to come, dies; or if their wealth is already in hand, involving a waste of money, altogether, that, sooner or later, is sure to exhaust any moderate fortune and land them at the bottom. Such cases are not rare. I have seen them all along through life; and I see them to-day.

Happily there always have been and always will be some men and women of brains not afflicted with that sort of mania. It is a good thing that some people have an organ of acquisitiveness; that there are some "worshipers of mammon," as they are sometimes sneeringly called by those who are eager enough for the mammon, but cannot keep it long enough to pay a single devotion to it. Without them the world would speedily degenerate to barbarism. The accumulation of money or property is not necessarily worshiping mammon. While we cannot serve God and mammon, we can serve God and respect mammon sufficiently to save some of it to serve God with, and if more of the people would do this the world would be the better for it.

Of course this matter of economy and accumulation is sometimes overdone. People who have laid the foundation of their fortunes by small savings and rigid self-denial are wont to continue the same habits when able to do otherwise. But better, far better, so, than the other extreme through life, by which no man can amount to anything. We sometimes think their benevolent contributions too meagre for their circumstances; but how much do the spendthrifts who accumulate nothing, with like opportunities, contribute? The fact is that all the benevolent enterprises of the day are carried on chiefly by the thrifty " worshipers of mammon."

For example: take the matter of church finances. Brother A. has always been a man of moderate income, but by severe economy and self-denial he has managed to accumulate something all along through life, while living in a sufficiently respectable style, and always paying reasonably toward the support of his church, and other meritorious benefactions; and he is comfortably well off in the way of property. Brother B. has had about the same income as A., but his cigars and the kid gloves, et. cetera, and his wife's diamond rings, and pretty shawls, and hired girls, and other pleasant things that A. and his wife could not think of indulging in, have exhausted all his income all along, so that he could not contribute much of anything to the church or any other benefactions, and now he is entirely poor. A. is expected to pay largely to the church, and B. comparatiyely nothing, because the Lord has prospered A.; when the fact is that the Lord has prospered B. just as much as A. The difference is that B. has used up his prosperity as he went along, for his own gratification, and A. has saved some of his. A. must pay because he can do it without self-de-

nial, whereas years of self-denial are what has produced his present ability ; so that his contributions
are as much the fruits of self-denial as B.'s would
be if he should deny himself of *present* indulgence.
And I have seen many a poor church brother who
can afford more extravagances than their prosperous brethren would think of indulging in, and
when the church expenses are to be made up they
are too poor to pay much of anything. Do they
get their cigars or their fineries, for themselves and
families, any cheaper because they are poor ?

And then there is an intermediate grade of current style and fashion, not ruinous, but to a considerable extent mischievous.   I was told by a
very worthy Christian lady, the other day, that she
had not been at the church for two years, because
she could not afford clothing suitable to appear
in at the House of God! Good Christian people
make a specialty of exhibiting their fine and expensive clothing at church. People *must* dress richly
to go to church. And so people who cannot dress
richly cannot go to church. Poor people must not go
to church. All this is about as imperative, upon the
feminine community, as if it were the law. It *is*
the law—the law of fashion—and there is no more
inexorable law than this. A woman must not go
to church in a plain, cheap dress that she can buy
for a dollar or two, not because it is not respectable
in appearance, but because it is not costly.

Now, I think it is a bad law for good Christian

people to make that deprives people of the means of grace for their poverty. Unknown numbers of church sittings are always vacant because those who ought to be in them cannot dress up to the church-going standard.

A respectable, well-to-do farmer, in this vicinity, heard the Rev. Mr. Chandler preach two funeral sermons outside of Corning village. He is not a professor of religion. He was strongly impressed by the discourses. He said to a member of the Corning M. E. Church: " If that man could preach at Gibson, or Knoxville, or in a school-house anywhere convenient to me, I would like very much to be a regular attendant, with my family. But in your Corning Church the style and grade of dress are so far above what we can think of indulging in, that we would be very uncomfortable to meet with you there. We cannot think of such a thing." The force of this reasoning was appreciated and all that the good brother could do was to offer a seat in his pew, with stabling for his team, at any or all times, and cordially invite him to come in.

The only possible remedy is in a change of the law. The ostentation of dress is not a necessary part of the service of the sanctuary ; nay, its abolition would promote the spiritual interests of all churches ; for it would be conducive to sincere Christian devotion to leave the god of fashion at home, if it were possible that such a thing should be. I do not say that Christian people should not wear upon the person all the value that they can afford, elsewhere than where it is essential for all Christians, rich and poor, to congregate. Here, certainly, all should meet on one common ground, with no possible cause of repulsion to any. But "it is the pride of the poor that keeps them away." Certainly it is, and they have no excuse that will avail them at the bar of God. It is the pride of the rich, too, that makes the church regulation grade of dress. And so long as human nature is as it is ; so long as the sisterhood will persist in so many ridiculous modes of dress, to their own discomfort, and the distress of all sensible people, all because other folks do, and so long as the well-to-do sisters dare not go to church without exhibiting their wealth of dress, it is not to be expected that the poor will venture on the road to heaven with less than the orthodox grade of church dry goods.

XVI.

ON RUNNING INTO DEBT.

It is quite common for public teachers to inveigh at wholesale against running into debt. "Never, under any circumstances," they advise everybody, "run into debt." If I were asked by a young man just starting out in life whether to take that kind of advice or not, I should say *that depends*. It depends on several things. It depends upon what the debt is to be for. A long time ago I heard an old experienced farmer say that he had rather owe

a hundred dollars for a good pair of oxen than ten
dollars at a store. The idea was that he would
have the oxen to show for the hundred dollar debt,
and nothing to show for the store debt; it would
be used up before paid for. And that philosophy
will generally hold good. And when I see a man
with a fixed income—be it more or less—who cannot wait till his month's wages is earned before he
must use it, and in debt at the stores wherever
they will happen to trust him at the highest prices,
instead of taking his money after he gets it and
buying his goods at the lowest prices, or sell his
time, as they call it, at a large discount, because he is
too hard pressed by creditors to wait till the pay-
master comes along, I think, as the old farmer
said, he had better owe a hundred dollars for a
pair of oxen, or something else that he would have
to show for it. If a man, working for wages, is
determined to spend it all, there is no need of
spending it before it is earned and keeping himself
in the distress of debt. He can economize sufficiently to get a month's wages ahead and be thus
far above board.

And then the expediency of running into debt
for a pair of oxen, or any thing else that it is proper, sometimes, to go in debt for, depends on certain other things. If a young farmer should run
in debt for a pair of oxen, so as to produce more
on his farm, and then on the strength of having
oxen and producing more, he should incur extra

10

expenses in his living more than his extra income, that debt would be a damage to him, although the oxen might be on hand to show for it.

The young man mentioned in my No. XIV, who incurred a debt for business purposes, made a mistake, in view of the fact that his expenses were to be more than his profits. He had no business to run into that debt. He should have kept himself a hired servant. He would have been the better for it. But in the other phase of that business—the economic phase—if that man and his wife had taken my advice, and lived cheaply, that debt would have been the making of them. The business was better than wages, and he might have been above board and in an increasing business to-day. As it was, I think the debt was bad for him.

And so, my young friends, in all cases of going into debt for business purposes, it depends very largely on the habits of yourself and your wife after the business is in blast. If you intend to put on style and make a splurge upon the strength of your business that you owe for, I say by all means do not go into any such debt. It will be pretty sure to extinguish you. Beware of that kind of indebtedness. You have no business to be in debt with your wife wearing diamonds or other extravagances. But if you see a good opening for a business that you are competent to do, and you have the energy, industry and integrity to run it successfully, and you and your wife are determined to begin down upon the hard pan of fortune to build yourselves up, then I say by all means go into debt for such a business and such a life as that, if you can do so on fair terms. It is scarcely possible that you should fail. I have seen many fortunes made by running into debt, and seen many insignificant people get down flatter than they started, by it, all by adopting or rejecting the rules aforesaid. It all depends on that.

Then there is another sort of debt that I think is to be recommended. In one of my articles on "doing something," I advised young men out of work to go West, or go somewhere, and locate themselves in the cultivation of the soil, to build for themselves independent business and independent homes. This involves the idea of buying land on credit. I think it is always safe for a young man to buy land on credit for that purpose, provided only that he buys good and productive land and at a fair price. Whether he is thrifty or unthrifty he will be none the worse for having land and owing for it. It is like the old farmer and his oxen and a hundred dollar debt for them : the land will be worth the money. The most of the western part of this State was settled in that way —poor men buying the land on credit—and most of the old generation of rich farmers made their wealth by buying land on credit, with ample time to pay for it from the produce of the soil. And I think most new settlements are made in this way.

But in this business human nature is about the same as in any other; some will be improvident and fail. Success depends on the same principles as in any other business—on habits of industry and economy. Those who indulge in the luxury of continual large indebtedness at the stores and elsewhere, for current consumptive expenses, will fail and give up their land to more prudent and sensible people; but, as I have said, the land debt will make them none the worse, because the land will be there to show for it. The other kind of debts are what does the mischief. In all my experience as a land office clerk, I never knew a thrifty land debtor, woiking on his land for a business and a home, who was not benefitted by such debt. And I never knew an industrious man, working as aforesaid, whether thrifty or not, to be injured by such debt.

Nevertheless we hear a good deal about the oppressions of land creditors, and the hardships of land debtors. But I have noticed that that hue and cry always comes from the imprudent, improvident, spendthrift class of land debtors—the inefficients, who never pay much of anything on their land, and never would accumulate anything anywhere, in any work or any business. They are the agitators—the anti-renters, who boldly strike out to dispute the title of their creditors, merely because they have been indulged to live upon the land a good while without paying for it, as their more provident neighbors have done, just as this same class of people in other vocations take possession of railroads and burn buildings to compel the giving out to them of what they have not earned.

On the whole, while debt is not desirable *per se*, the facilities that it sometimes offers to poor young men of the right make-up, for a start in life, are valuable and should be accepted.

XVII.

DECISION OF CHARACTER.

The phrenologists tell us that there is an organ of the brain that they call firmness; whose office is to hold the individual to his purposes, and prevent a wavering, zig-zag, undecisive, vacillating course of life. This faculty of the mind, like all others, greatly varies in strength in different individuals. Some people are naturally so firm and stubborn that it is well-nigh impossible, in any case, to change their preconceived opinions or their practices; others are so deficient in this quality as always to be drifting about, never having any mind of their own, always liable to be persuaded, even against their own better judgment—weak, unstable, and therefore inefficient.

All the desirable qualities of the mind can be improved by habitual use—cultivation. As the muscles of the blacksmith's right arm become enlarged and invigorated by the continuous wielding of his heavy hammer, so the various organs of the mind become invigorated by habitual use.

The faculty of firmness—decision of character—more especially, perhaps, than any other quality of the mind, is within the control of the mind itself. While an individual may be naturally fickle and indecisive, if he has an ordinary degree of common sense, he can, at will, and at once, overcome that defect in his character, as it represents all essential matters in business, and especially as to refraining from any habits that his own better judgment tells him are improper or inexpedient. Every sane man is the master of his own actions in these respects—he can control himself if he will. With a deficiency in the organ of tune it is very difficult to become a good musician. Without a fair development of the organ of constructiveness, it requires a good deal of cultivation to become a good mechanic. And so of most other organs of the mind. But with defective firmness a man *can* be sufficiently firm. If he has been indulging in any bad habit, he can change it all if he will. Without a certain amount of natural endowment a man cannot learn a tune, or learn to build a machine, or learn to be a good mathematician, though of strong mind in other respects; but any man of common understanding can refrain from bad associations, or bad habits, can refrain from wasting his money, or doing anything that his judgment tells him that he had better not do; and yet thousands go to ruin, in spite of themselves, really against their own will, to please somebody, merely because they drift along listlessly, without asserting their own individuality; having no distinct identity, being only atoms of a general mass—a part of somebody else.

And this matter of self-control—independent decision of character—is an important factor in the make-up of a young man with reference to his success in life, and it is especially apropos just here in this series of papers—applicable in respect to all the instruction and advice that I have given to my young readers; for all the information that can be given, and all the convictions that can be produced, are wasted upon any man without the decision of character to utilize them. For instance, a young man in receipt of a large salary, will say—if not out loud, he will say it in his actions—"Yes, I know that Mr. Heermans is right in his lectures on economy; I know that I ought to save a good deal more of my income now in my days of prosperity than I am saving; I know that many others with a good deal less income have saved a good deal more, and have really made themselves quite independent; but somehow, I don't know how it is, but really I —I cannot; my habits are so fixed—this and that and the other thing come along that call for my money, and really I cannot refrain. And then, I know he is right about these social customs—the cigars, a little wine or beer, the social games and small gamblings, the fineries and embellishments, etc., etc.; but really, like the charm of the serpent they seem to draw me on and on, and if it carries me to destruction I cannot help it."

You can. It is only to put on the manhood of a man, and learn to say NO. If you are not an imbecile you can control yourself. You can control your own money. To say you cannot is to renounce your own manhood, to write yourself down a blank in creation, and submit to bondage. All you have to do is to begin the process of saying NO. When the impulse comes upon you to expend any sum of money for anything that can be dispensed with and you be none the worse for it—anything that your own better judgment tells you that you have no need of, in any of the thousand ways in which such useless demands will come upon you, learn to say NO. If you have a wife victimized by style and fashion so that she wants you to invest all your income therein, and even, perhaps, spend your money before it is earned, learn to say NO. If you have a good chance to relieve yourself from some onerous labor by faithlessness to an employer, when you think he cannot know it, learn to say NO. Whenever you see a first-rate opportunity to make a large or small speculation by any kind of sharp practice, by dishonesty in your business, when you think you know that no human being can ever find it out, learn to say NO. When you meet with brilliant young friends, in gilded places, which would be wicked but for the gild, and it would be pleasant, and social, and friendly, and fashionable to indulge in a cigar or a drink, learn to say NO. When you find yourself in social intercourse, in your mother's parlor, it may be, or elsewhere, attended with all the brilliance, and sparkle and enjoyment of fashionable society, and the elements of the gambler's trade, or of the drunkard's education, are introduced—the hospitalities of high life, peradventure, are prostituted to the cultivation of the arts of these trades of hell, oh then of all other times in your life, learn to say NO. Finally, in respect to all the innumerable follies and foibles, that seem to demand your attention and that your better judgment tells you that you ought not to indulge in, learn to say NO.

As I have said, this matter of self-control—decision of character—is entirely subject to your own volition. The first negative to a habit of life requires more or less of nerve and self-denial ; but any sane man *can do it* if he will ; and the habitual use of that will power soon makes it easy. In fact the habit, with the enjoyment of its beneficial results, soon makes itself enjoyable.

In short, this quality of decision of character is an indispensable element in the make-up of real manhood, indispensable to any real success in life. The destitution and distress, the vice and immorality, the intemperance and crime, that the world is afflicted with, are due largely, very largely to the want of it. Cultivate it, young man, and start out as a full grown man, and not always be a pigmy.

XVIII.

HOW TO INVEST.

Those of my young readers who have not determined to practice upon the advice that I have already given in these papers, so as to have something to invest as a saving for the future and to help them to earn something more all along, need not read this number. It will not be of any use to them. Any man who has no money to invest, and is determined to not have any, has no need to spend any time to learn how to invest it. But the matter of investment is of the highest importance to those who have something to save; for I have often seen the savings of the severe industry and rigid economy of years, yea, sometimes of a lifetime, swept away at a single swoop by bad investment. First, then,

HOW NOT TO INVEST.

Not in banks. In general there is this about banks as depositories of money for customers : the management is independent of the depositors, and really they have no reliable security for their money. So long as the bank is prosperous and the management is honest, the depositors may be regarded as safe ; but of this, ordinary depositors cannot know ; their money must run the risk of the unskillfulness, the misfortunes and the dishonesty of the bank. I need not cite particular cases to prove all this. All are familiar with sufficient facts in point to show the impropriety of bank deposits as permanent investment of money. In fact our ordinary banks of deposit are not intended for such investment, but only for the temporary custody, for the safe keeping of the loose money of business men.

And I do not see that savings banks, designed for the more permanent investment of money, and on interest, are any less liable to the objections named than other banks, as the great number of recent failures of large and popular saving banks will show. Within the last few years immense numbers of savings bank depositors have been compelled to pay largely out of their hard earnings, for the misfortunes, the mistakes and the dishonesty of men not under their control.

And more than this; if saving banks could be made entirely safe to their depositors, they only undertake to do for them what they can do for themselves much more to their own advantage. The legitimate business of a savings bank is to borrow money at a low rate of interest, and lend it again at a higher rate. The theory of the transaction is that the bank takes good mortgage security for the money, which is an indirect security to the depositor. And so it amounts to this: say the bank pays six per cent. to the depositor and receives seven per cent. from its debtor; the depositor pays the bank one per cent. for investing his money for him, besides running all the risks before alluded to, when he can just as well do it all himself without any risk, or expense, as I shall try to explain further on.

Not invest in friendship. I have known a good many hard-working, thrifty people ruined by lending their money to relatives, or by dealing with them in other ways. The adage that " there is no friendship in trade," is always just, and the only safe one to be observed in dealings between relatives or special friends. Its philosophy is very simple. For instance, if I deal with a brother, and he expects me to be more liberal, or lenient, or careless with him than I would with a stranger because he is my brother, the ready answer is that I am just as closely related to him as he is to me, so that I have the same claim upon him for liberality and a good bargain in any respect as he has upon me, and this matter of friendship exactly neutralizes itself, and we should deal at arm's length, precisely as we would with strangers. So, my friends, if you have money to invest on interest, lend it to a friend if it will be any accommodation to him, but be sure to require the same security that you would require of any stranger. I long ago found out that friendship is no security for good solid money.

Not invest in charity. I do not mean by this that you should not make suitable contributions to all meritorious charities—on which subject see further on—but when you invest your money to make it earn you something, and to get it back some time, never try to do that on charitable principles. Never lend a man money merely because he needs it badly, because he may suffer loss if he does not get it, or because of any other exigencies of his, unless his security is all right. His needs, or his troubles, or his exigencies will not pay back your money when your own needs or troubles or exigencies may require it. Business of any kind cannot be safely mixed with charity. I have often heard men clamor for employment upon the ground that they needed it, when they were notoriously unfit and unprofitable hands to be employed; that is, they were poor workmen and shiftless, slouchy workers. And I have often heard people plead for loans of money merely because they needed it badly, when their security was insufficient for a prudent man to accept. It cannot be done. The employer who hires unprofitable hands because they need employment is sure to go under; and the money-lender who lends his money merely because the borrower needs it, will soon find his money all gone, with nothing to show for it but wasted paper. No, my friends, let your business always be done on business principles, and let your charity stand by itself.

Not invest in mere personal securities. I shall not say that this should never be done; but as a general rule I have observed that it is an unsafe practice for those who are seeking permanent investment. For small sums temporarily, while accumulating sufficient for a permanent investment, it is of course allowable. By proper precaution it can be made reasonably safe; but for investment for years there is no need of taking any such risk, and it should not be thought of. I have seen many well-to-do men ruined by lending their money to so-called rich men on their personal obligations without security.

Not invest in life insurance. Notwithstanding the general popularity of life insurance as a supposed necessary investment for everybody, I will venture to have my say about it. I think it is unbusiness like, wasteful, and objectionable in many respects; and,

First, it often defeats the very object for which a poor man toils and economizes, *i. e.*, to accumulate a fund for *himself* for old age or time of disability, as well as for his family. No member of a family —not even the wife—has any right to ask a husband to impoyerish himself during life for her benefit after death. He who earns the money surely ought not to put it out of his own reach during his own life. He ought to have at least an equal share in it with his family during his life in case of need. But it is not uncommon for men in moderate circumstances to take large life insurance policies, requiring all their surplus income to keep them up; in fact keeping them poor and on a strain all their lives to make their wives or somebody else rich when they die. It is unjust. I do not appreciate that kind of accumulation, and especially as there is no need of it; it is so easy for any man to invest his money, not out of his own reach, and yet for the benefit of his family too.

Secondly, life insurance is an extremely hazardous investment. In this respect it is liable to all the objections above noted as to banks, and more. When we invest in a life insurance company it is for life. We cannot draw the money out at pleasure as from a bank. We not only risk the solvency of the company for the time being, but for life. The return of the money, or any of it, depends on the skill, success, and honesty of somebody, we know not who, so long as we shall live. I think the recent wholesale collapse of life insurance companies is a sufficient demonstration of this point; and it is only a very common result of trusting poor human nature with large sums of money without security. Some of the surviving companies are boasting of their own success and their solvency, but how can a creditor be safe for twenty years to come with any of them? If a young man takes a policy in the best of them to-day, who can know how many sharpers and thieves will get control of the funds before he dies? In any other shape no prudent man would think of investing on so long credit without the best of security. They talk about legislative protection to policy holders. Time out of mind legislative wisdom has tinkered at this problem of securing bank creditors and insurance creditors against loss, and the more they tinker the more we see that there is no security. It cannot be done until human nature gets a good deal improved.

Thirdly, irrespective of the foregoing objections, life insurance is too costly. If all the companies could always remain solvent, and all policy holders should get all they contract for, it would cost about twice as much as it comes to. Life insurance companies are careful to publish their extreme cases, where somebody has received a large amount of money for a very small investment in life insurance. For instance: Mr. so-and-so paid a hundred dollars for a five thousand dollar policy, and in thirty days or so he was dead, and his family were saved from want by that life insurance. We very often see such items floating in the papers—paid for of course by life insurance agents. That all looks very well; but that is the lottery part of it. When they print one such case they do not print the other hundred cases where the policy holders do not have the luck to die so soon, and pay enough more than they are to get back to make up such large sums as are advertised as aforesaid, together with expenses and profits of the business. Take a prosperous, honest life insurance company, and it must make out of its policy holders, altogether, 1st, all that it pays out for death claims; 2nd, all its expenses; 3d, its profits for the shareholders, whatever they may be. And from my observation of the rate of expenses of the best companies, in the way of commissions, salaries, and otherwise, I think it is not too much to say that the cost to the policy holders, on an average, is not less than two dollars for one received back upon death claims; so that by investing money in life insurance, we must pay one dollar for taking care of another dollar for us; which we can do a great deal better for ourselves and keep both of the dollars.

Some companies are quite ingenious in making up nice schemes and figure work to show that policy holders are to get their fingers on the large surplus funds, or something else, and get all their money back during life, and more too, and leave a pretty good fortune for their heirs. But all this is of a piece with the thieves and sharpers who are always offering us something for nothing. It is a fraud.

Put your money into some safe investment, on interest, and in the average of cases it will amount to twice as much for the beneficiaries as they would get from life insurance, if not somehow cheated out of the whole. It will not quite do to say that life insurance is a fraud, but very many people have found it so.

Not invest in railroad stocks, or any other joint stock concerns that you cannot know much about, and that are beyond your control; or in any other institutions that offer wonderful inducements to investors. These are always hazardous, if not entire frauds. Now the question recurs:

HOW TO INVEST.

A young man in business on his own account, be it what it may, should, of course, invest his money in his own business. As to others.

11

1. There can be no better investment of a suitable amount of a thrifty young man's savings than in a homestead, whenever the time comes for housekeeping. But this requires some discretion. Many years ago an old friend of mine in Geneva told me his experience in buying a house. He was a clerk in an office at a good salary, and had been living in a passable house, at little or no rent. The speculating times of 1836 came on, and in a little fever of fictitious prosperity he must have a better house ; and so he bought a high-priced house and paid for it, but in a course of years that house cost him a fortune. That is to say the interest on the investment, with the concomitant extra expenses, all along, all of which would have been saved if he had been content in the old home, would have made his family comfortably rich ; and they would have been just as comfortable and as highly respected all the time. Such experiences are worth something ; and yet they are only a matter of a little figure work that any body can do, after all. Let us see what an excess of $2,000 in the price of a homestead will cost the owner in a course of years, in the mere interest at seven per cent. compounded once a year.

In one year,	.	.	.	$	140.00
In ten years,	.	.	.		1,934.31
In twenty years,	.	.	.		4,739.39
In thirty years,	.	.	.		13,224.56

So to persons of moderate income who wish to

accumulate something through life, it is important that their homesteads shall not be too high priced.

When I see a young couple starting out with twice or three times as costly a house as they need, and perhaps owe for some of it, I thing of my Geneva friend, and think that such a house may be the wasting of a little fortune.

2. Judicious investments in land are usually good and profitable ; but of course this all turns on the question of what investments are judicious. I think that vacant lands in a growing town, or good farming lands in an improving locality, at fair prices, are always safe to buy ; while lands in a dead town, or poor lands in a poor neighborhood cannot often be profitable to a buyer. Improved farms in a high-priced neighborhood are not likely to be profitable as a mere investment. It is usually difficult to make the income and the advance n price pay the interest and expenses, unless some fortuitous circumstances add to their value. The great advantage of farming land to a man is for him to live on it, and work and improve it himself, to make his living on it while it grows into wealth.

Land speculation, like all other speculative business, is always a good deal of a lottery. Sometimes fortunes are made in it—sometimes the re verse. But for a mere investment of money, to earn something for a course of years, the average young man would do a safer and better business to invest on interest than in land, and so

3. Good real estate money securities are to be recommended as the best of all investments of money for a course of years to earn money for its owner. There cannot be any better or simpler way of investing money on interest than this. There is never any need of trusting money in savings or other banks—or on mere personal securities ; for it is always easy to invest any sum, from $50 upwards, on good real estate security, and at good interest—not depending on anybody's skill in business, or their success or honesty—security firm and steadfast, that cannot take to itself wings and fly away.

4. Government bonds are always to be recommended as good and safe investment, and always convertible in the market—always desirable to those who have not a horror of being bloated bond-holders ; but not now as profitable as good real estate securities.

XIX.

BENEFACTIONS AND CHARITIES.

Hoarding money, or accumulating property, for its own sake, is not "the chief end of man." Worshiping Mammon should be especially guarded against. " Ye cannot serve God and Mammon." But the accumulation of property is the foundation of civilization. There is a good deal of senseless clamor about wealth ; its greed, its oppressions, and its wickedness in general, as if it were reprehensible, *per se*, for a man to be the owner of any property ; but I would like to know what these croakers would be but for the property accumulated by somebody.

Benefactions and charities and poor taxes come mostly from the provident, accumulating classes. They *must;* for the other sort never have much of any thing to invest in that way.

But what I started out to say is: all through life every man, when prospering, *ought,* systematically, to invest something in beneficial enterprises for other people. If you are of the spendthrift kind— using up all you make as you go along—you can just as well as not halt a little in your extravagances, now and then, to aid a meritorious charity. If you are of the provident sort—trying to lay up treasures for the future—of course you cannot afford to omit some investment, all along, in that kind of " banks."

I think we have no right to live entirely to self. All through these little discourses I have tried to inculcate the idea that a material part of our business in the world is to be of some practical utility to our fellow men. And while there are many other ways to do this, reasonable contributions to meritorious benefactions cannot be omitted without the loss of much satisfaction, not to say a dereliction of real duty.

But then this matter of donations requires great care and discrimination. It is not everything that comes along, pleading for aid, that should be aided, by any means. He that donates indiscriminately to every so-called charity that presents itself with a plausible story, will be quite likely to do as much harm as good by his liberality.

I think the work of the voluntary, systematic church charities, organized in the name of aid societies, or any other names, and other organizations, for the purpose of hunting up people to provide for, is mostly of that character. There is always plenty of pauperism to be found if we look for it; always an unlimited number of people ready to be provided for by others. And when it is understood that an aid society is ready every winter to relieve all the destitution in a town, that fact will create an unlimited quantity of destitution. Many who might save money enough during summer time to carry them through the winter, relying on the aid society for a comfortable winter, are pretty sure to spend all their earnings in summer, and claim their winter's support at the hands of the public. The story of a woman who called at a society's quarters to inquire how much they allowed to their beneficiaries to buy dress trimmings with, and that of another who wanted a baby carriage, are not entire fictions.

One of the great social problems of the day is how to provide for all the pauperism, and make it very comfortable and respectable without inciting the propagation and cultivation of pauperism as a business. It cannot be done. Start a free soup house, in any town or city, and you will at once have twice as many soup eaters as can be supplied. Offer to distribute a thousand loaves of bread a day to the needy and you will be sure to have two thousand calls as soon as known—no difference whether there is any real destitution or not. Build a luxurious Poor House, provide it with all the comfort and enjoyment, and respectability, and you will always have it full if it be understood that all destitute people are to have a chance.

Probably more than three-quarters of all pauperism is self-imposed. As I have tried to show, in former papers, extraordinary calamities excepted, every man and wife can, if they will, accumulate enough in health to carry them through ordinary sickness, and accumulate enough through life to support them, comfortably at least, in helpless old age, if they come to that. And as to able-bodied pauperism there is never any good cause for any considerable amount of it, and none only temporarily. There is always something somewhere for everybody to do to earn a living. Even in this exceptional time of stagnation in business and labor, it has just now been ascertained by detectives that the great armies of tramps are not men who cannot get work, but those who do not want to get it. The best way to deal with that kind of pauperism is to let it starve to death if it will.

" The world owes me a living," is the plea of the

spendthrift, as he goes along through life, using up all his earnings, and depending upon the public to fill out his living at the last, or when disabled at any time.   And boldly and brazenly he asserts this *claim* when he becomes a public charge.   And on this theory our public charities are instituted and conducted.   The plea is false.   The world does not owe anyone anything only what he makes for himself or gets in some other honest way.   All that is done for pauperism and mendicancy, by law, or by voluntary associations, or otherwise, is pure benevolent gratuity.   To come down to original principles, the recipient has no shadow of *right* to it.   To go back to first principles : the true theory of human life, as well by Divine law as by human philosophy, is that every individual, independent, self-existent man is to provide for his own wants through life ; and to this end he is entitled to all the fruits of his own industry.   Nobody else can have any just claim upon any of them.   Two men go out upon pieces of earth, to subdue and cultivate them, and to make for themselves a living.   Both are equally fruitful according to the labor and care bestowed. One is laborious and prudent ; his fruits are abundant and he economizes them ; hoards them, if you please, for future use.   The other does not quite see the need of all that hard work and hoarding. He has a plenty for the summer time, and he consumes all his productions or lets them run to waste. The winter comes, and he has no corn, no bread, no anything. Then, like the foolish virgins, calling upon the wiser ones for some of their oil, he demands of his thrifty neighbor: " Give me your corn, lest I starve and die—you owe me a living." In this simple illustration the fallacy of the plea is clearly seen. The just penalty of his indolence and waste, imposed by the laws of our being, is starvation. There is no just claim upon anybody for relief.

Do the complications of civilized society change that law so as to give one man any right to live upon the fruits of any other man's labor? In entering into that state each man surrenders some of his natural rights for the general good, as a consideration for his own protection in his life and his property ; but no man acquires a right to omit to provide for himself and his own house, and depend on neighbors for what he might have secured and hoarded up for himself. So that the just penalty of the natural law of human life—the law of self-preservation—for improvidence, remains the same as in the rudest state of life—distress and starvation.

And then, if every self-made pauper should be left to starve, he would have no just cause for complaint. It is his own deliberate choice. " Whatsoever a man soweth that shall he also reap." And if there were no interference with that law I think there would be much less suffering from poverty than there is. Then people would not waste their surpluses, in prosperous days, on unnecessary luxuries until after making ample provision for themselves and families for future contingencies. As it is, the ample provisions for the care and comfort of every species of destitution is the cause of most of it.

Well, what then? Shall pauperism be cured by starving it? Not at all. All persons destitute of the absolute necessaries of life, and unable, from physical disability, to earn them, must be provided for. The conscience and the benevolence of this age cannot see people starve, be the cause of their destitution what it may; even though, as an example, it might, in the long run, be beneficial to the. race. But I think the multitudinous charities of various phases, hunting up objects of care, and thus encouraging and cultivating the profession of mendicancy, should be discountenanced. I think there should be one uniform system of State Poor Houses, not luxurious or attractive, but providing for the bare necessaries of life for all destitute individuals; for I do not see why it should not always be understood that the spendthrift improvident class are to suffer some of the just and natural penalties of their misconduct. Then, all individual beggary, and all able-bodied beggary should be summarily crushed out. Contributions to those are worse than wasted.

With pauperism cared for entirely by the State, under laws sufficient to take in all its phases, our whole duty is done when we pay our taxes.

Of course all this does not preclude us from the

pleasure of neighborly aid to friends, or respond-
ing to the humane impulses of consanguinity.

Now, having disposed of the question of common pauperism, to my own satisfaction at least,
there are various other subjects of voluntary contribution that demand everybody's attention all
along through life, more or less of which belong in
the same category where I have placed promiscu-
ous contributions for common pauperism. Of
course every individual must be guided by his own
judgment as to the choice of objects for his bounty;
but I will venture a few suggestions.

The support of the gospel ministry is a duty
that devolves on everybody. If you are a member
of a church organization, a reasonable share of its
expenses is an honest indebtedness upon you.
What that reasonable share is, is a question for
every one to decide for himself; for there is no
compulsion. It is usually expected that church
members are to contribute in proportion to the
money that they are worth. I think this business should be done on business principles, exactly
like any other business, and not upon charitable
principles. For illustration, take a church of two
hundred members, costing, for all expenses, three
thousand dollars a year. Say fifty of them are
really poor, and not able to pay any thing. So far
as they are concerned the church is a charity. They
are conceded all the privileges of the sanctuary
without price. The other hundred and fifty we

suppose to be able to pay, each, an equal share of the $3,000—say twenty dollars. But some are richer than others. Now I would like to know on what principle of business, or of equity, or of morals, it is that fifty of them should be expected to pay fifty dollars each, and the other hundred only five dollars. For everything else that they indulge in—food, clothing, cigars, fineries, jewelry, and all other embellishments to go to the sanctuary with, they all pay for alike; and why one should pay more than another toward the church expenses —all being able to pay their equal share—I do not know. Then as to the ability: any man who pays ten cents a day for cigars or any other unnecessary indulgence, or fifty dollars a year for style for himself or family, is able to pay twenty dollars for the support of his church, whether he has any accumulated capital or not. And if a man has denied himself, so as to save something, all through life, I do not see that this is any reason why he should pay a higher price for his flour, or meat, or coal, or clothing, or church sitting, than he who expends all his income as he goes along.

But church covenant obligations require the members to pay according to their ability, I may be told. Let us see about that. I do not suppose that means that every member shall pay all that he is able to pay for the local church services. A church of two hundred members, costing $3,000 to run it, may have a membership able to pay a hundred thousand dollars. It does not mean that they shall pay that sum. It does not mean that a millionaire member, who can pay the whole $3,000 as well as not, shall pay it all. It does not mean that he shall pay $2,850 of it, and the other hundred and fifty members, who are well able to pay their equal share, pay only one dollar each, if an assessment upon the value of the property of each would bring it so. That would substantially extinguish all obligations of the 150 members. It would be to require one man to pay the obligations of a hundred and fifty who are abundantly able to pay for themselves.

A local church organization is a sort of business partnership, for the equal benefit of all its members, and not a charity. A preacher is hired, fuel and lights, and other incidentals are provided, strictly on business principles, for the equal benefit of all, and not as a charity to all, or to any portion of the members who do not need such charity. So that I think the covenant obligation means that every member who is able to pay his or her equal share shall do so, and those not able to pay such equal share shall pay what they are able to. It is not benevolence, but business.

But then there is another class of church and other enterprises that are purely charitable, that are worthy of every man's attention; and they come under a different rule. To send the Gospel to other lands, to give the Bible to the poor, to

inaugurate church work anywhere away from home'
etc., are purely charitable. They are for the benefit of
other people and not for ourselves. That is *giving*
and not *paying*. And such gifts should be graduated chiefly by the wealth of the donors.

If you are not a church member, I think the obligation upon you to support the gospel ministry
is not much the less for that reason. The Church
of Christ does not exist merely for the benefit of
its present members. It is for *you*, reader, whether
now a member of it or not. It is for your family,
if you have one, and if not it will be for your
family when the time comes that you have. If you
are not an entire unbeliever, you expect, some time,
to embrace it and profit by it. At any rate you
know you cannot afford to dispense with the
churches in your locality. I think there is no man
of common sense, be his religious belief what it
may, who would think of making his permanent
home, and investing his money, in a town of no
church—no gospel preached. Not long ago, on a
railroad train, I heard a discussion between a
Christian and an infidel, on the subject of the
Christian religion. After a good deal of sharp talk
the *infidel* closed substantially as follows: "But
the world cannot do without the churches. Without the restraining influence of the Christian faith
upon the depravity of human nature, vice and immorality would run riot, and the world would go
to the bad," which I think is generally admitted,

even by infidels, to be true, and is tantamount to saying that Christianity makes people better; infidelity makes them worse—in this life at least, by infidel admission—and then if there is any hereafter at all, is it very unreasonable to conclude that these results are to continue over, in-as-much as we see everywhere in nature, the truth of the scriptural declaration that " whatsoever a man soweth that shall he also reap." And then what is the infidel doctrine good for? What are all the labors, and arguments and publications of infidels, from Thomas Paine down, for? When it is admitted that the world cannot afford to do without the Christian religion, that admission extinguishes all the arguments that ever have been or ever can be adduced for infidelity. When it is admitted that Christianity makes people better—and infidelity makes them worse—it is clear enough that we cannot afford to dispense with the Christian religion —cannot afford to indulge in infidelity. If Christianity makes people in general better, it will make *you* better, my infidel reader. If infidelity makes people in general worse, it will make *you* worse. If society in general cannot afford infidelity in place of Christianity, *you*, as an individual cannot afford it. I think this is conclusive, and you that persist in infidelity are persisting in what you confessedly know to be the worse for the race—what you know to be wrong. And this is the end of argument on the question. How futile and how profitless is the hunt for a substitute for Christianity when it is so frankly admitted that the world cannot do without Christianity. The explorations on this subject prove only that the natural man is dissatisfied with himself and wants to find an easier road to Heaven than through Christ. It cannot be done. "There is none other name under Heaven given among men, whereby we must be saved."

And the conclusion of the whole matter is that everybody—spiritual Christians, nominal Christians, and infidels ought to take a liberal share in the support of the Christian ministry, not as gift or charity, but as honest indebtedness to civilization.

In this connection I will venture a criticism that may be disapproved of by many of my readers. It is claimed by some ministers of the gospel that in devoting their lives to the ministry they are making great pecuniary sacrifices. They think so, because they see some men in other vocations earning more money than they do. I think they are mistaken. An ordinary New York lawyer, or merchant, struggling along with hard work to make a bare economical living, might look upon Henry Ward Beecher, or T. DeWitt Talmage, or Chapin, or Crosby, or many other high-salaried clergymen, and say that they are making great sacrifices to society by being lawyers, or merchants, just as the common run of preachers—or more commonly the lower run of them—look upon here and there a successful man in other business and think that they are making sacrifices by preaching the gospel. I was told by a young Methodist preacher some years ago, that he could make a good deal more money in some other business, when he was making more money than any man of his age and ability within my knowledge, unless where large capital was invested. Undoubtedly there are cases where men of ability do sacrifice pecuniary interests by preaching the gospel—work for less money pay than their talents would command in some other business; but as a rule I think preachers are as well paid, according to their abilities, as any other profession or pursuit. If there ever was a time in this country when the ministry was not adequately paid, that time is past. But there are a good many preachers whose salaries are very, very small. Yes, and so there are other people who earn not more than seventy-five cents a day for the year round; but they get all they are worth in the market. And my opinion is that the lower-priced preachers are getting all they are worth, and all they would be worth in any other work.

There are a good many men, in all vocations, who think they are making great sacrifices by condescending to live. They are always badly used. They are not appreciated. They are worth more than they are rated at. So they think. It is the inefficient class of men—those who not only can-

12

not earn much money but do not save any that they do earn; for, as I have shown in former papers, it is not those who earn the least who go through life the poorest.

And probably it is that class of men among clergymen who think they are making sacrifices.

I do not see any good reason why clergymen generally have not now about the same opportunity and the same obligation upon them to accumulate a reasonable competency as other people.

This is not written in a spirit of fault-finding with ministers—any of them. I would that they all might be better paid than they are; for there is no more essential trade or profession than theirs; and nobody, beyond my own family, can have a firmer hold upon my sympathies than a faithful pastor. But what I do say is that the pecuniary dealings between preachers and people have become established on business principles; and when the salary is paid the *obligation* is ended. It is a good thing to know when our debts are paid.

While, as I have tried to show, all necessary and reasonable expenses of the churches should be cheerfully borne, not only as a duty, but as a profitable investment, it is not to be disguised that there is a good deal of church *begging* that is not of that character, and more or less of which is not to be commended. As a single example—and the reader will meet many other phases of them as he goes along—when a silver-tongued canvasser comes along, boring the churches of his denomination for money to build a church, or any number of them, in some far-away field in the Master's vineyard, I cannot help thinking that in the matter of meeting houses, as with everything else, everybody ought to live within their means. People who are not able to build a sufficient house to worship in do not need any. In any community, ever so poor, if there are not enough people interested in the preaching of the gospel to erect as good a house to preach in as they occupy themselves, they can be sufficiently provided for in school houses or private houses. Fine churches are not essential to the spiritual success of church organizations, but rather the contrary. The older people can remember how churches were planted, and how they flourished, in this part of the country without any fine buildings, and without any buildings, and without the continual din of church debts. I was once traveling on horseback in the wilds of West Virginia, and halting one night at a small log cabin of one room on the ground floor, for a night's hospitality, I found the inmates preparing for a quarterly meeting of the circuit, of perhaps ten or fifteen charges, to be held at that house. Travel the thinly settled portions of that State to-day, and you will find, here and there, a log meeting-house, built, usually, by the joint *labors* of the whole community where located, with but the merest trifle of money cost; and this can be done wherever a church edifice is needed. And the Lord will meet the people in such a house just the same as in any other.

And yet there is no objection to fine and costly churches if the people of the locality are able and willing to build them. What I do object to is the building of churches that they are not able and willing to pay for, and boring the community for an indefinite number of years with church debts, and the attempts to build churches at a distance, that the people of the localities do not need, or ought to build for themselves. In this matter all people can live within their means without detriment to the cause.

After all that can be said in respect to donations to the multitudinous charitable enterprises that are always coming to us for aid, every one must be a law unto himself. One will approve one thing; another, another thing. This one general rule is always safe: Any enterprise that is calculated to make the world better should always receive encouragement and support.

XX.

LAW AND LAWYERS.

Every man is liable, some time in his life, to be compelled to go to law to protect himself and his property from spoliation by evil doers; and so a little discourse on law and lawyers may not be inappropriate in this series.

In the first place it is safe enough to advise young men to start out in life with a determination never to go to law for mere sentiment, for mere feeling, for mere right, justice. Perhaps you cannot afford it. And I think it is true that most small matters of litigation cannot be afforded by the winning party. They cost him more than they come to. These questions should be settled in your own mind on business principles, and not on the principle of fight. Never go to law for the sake of beating somebody, if it is likely to cost you more than it comes to. Don't bite your own nose off. In every case of proposed litigation there are two questions for you to consider: 1st, is your case just? and 2nd, will it pay? In deciding the latter you must consider the probable chances of success, and the expense in money and time and fret that it will cost you if you win; and if, on a fair comparison of these with the amount involved, there is a fair preponderance in your favor, then go to law; if not, haul in your temper and make the best compromise you can, or let it all go. If people would act upon these principles a good deal of petty litigation and a good deal of bad neighborhood would be saved.

In the matter of law and lawyers in general I think there is more or less of radical error extant, which I propose here to discuss. In so doing I shall not say that the common sentiment of the masses is that lawyers are entirely useless, that the profession is a fraud upon society, and that law itself and lawsuits only devices for a useless class of people to get their living out of the producing classes, but the current popular fashion of driving at law, lawsuits, and lawyers does imply, and I think the fact is, that there is a wide-spread sentiment in all communities that law itself is unstable, unreliable, fluctuating, that lawsuits are evils *per se*, and that lawyers are non-producers, living upon the bounty of the producing classes, and everybody ought to have as little to do with them as possible, and the fewer of them in the world the better, and if none at all the world would be the better for it; as if it were by their own *ipse dixit* that their work and their profits come.

It is for the instruction and benefit of that class of croakers of law and lawyers, and to caution young men against their extravagant theories, that this discourse is made, and not for a vindication of the legal profession, as if they needed any defense for being lawyers.

It is to be confessed that lawyers, and judges, and sheriffs, and all other court officers do not really produce any values, but are supported from the productions of other people. Instead of cultivating the soil, or fashioning any of the products of nature into intrinsic values—creating property out of nothing, their trade goes only to the distribution of the wealth created by others, and taking a share to themselves. An expensive litigation over a property, to determine who is the owner of it, does not enhance its value, but practically diminishes some other property to the amount of fees paid to the lawyers and others. An estate is to be settled. The lawyer's services do not increase the acres, or the amount of invested securities, or increase their productiveness, or make them better in any respect; but he is sure to take a share to himself. And so of all other work of the lawyer.

But we must go deeper than this. To understand thoroughly what lawyers are good for, we must not stop at the surface of things. We must go down to the foundations of civilization.

We used to hear a good deal about the Divine right of Kings: by which I suppose was meant that Kings were, by Divine appointment, invested with the power to rule the masses perpetually, in contra-distinction to the claim that the masses have any right to govern themselves, or any right to a voice in the selection of their rulers. I do not propose to discuss that question here; in this country we decided that a hundred years ago. But I will say this: The Divine right of Kings to rule would be a very fine theory of government and the best and cheapest practical government that could be devised, if we only had a Divine *race* of Kings—a race of men devoid of the infirmities and the depravity of common mortals. With such a race for rulers, government would always be pure, just and perfect. Kings and all other rulers, however, being afflicted with the same infirmities and depravity of other people—the same that makes government necessary for the protection of the weak against the rapacity of the stronger—a government vested in the hands of a particular class is pretty sure to be prostituted to the very purposes that its legitimate province is to prevent—rapacity and wrong. That is to say : the necessity of government arises from the tendency of people to plunder one another of the fruits of their labor ; and government is a mighty engine, capable of that same kind of plunder, when a particular governmental class is recognized ; for the reason that government necessarily has unlimited power to reach into the pockets of the masses. And a governing class are pretty sure to appropriate the government to themselves as a property vested in them for their own benefit, instead of for the benefit of the governed, as by the true Divine theory. That there is a remedy for such governmental plunder, in republics, is exemplified by the impeachment of New York Judges, and Tweed in prison.

And so, to go down still deeper into fundamental principles, were it not for human depravity, there would be no need of law or lawyers. But with this law : " In the sweat of thy face shalt thou eat bread," and the ten commandments, and other laws of God, came the necessity for human laws for the application and enforcement of those laws in human society. The statesman who said it was not necessary to re-enact the laws of God, was wofully mistaken. The re-enactment of the laws of God is substantially what human laws are for.

" Thou shalt not kill."

" Thou shalt not steal," etc., are re-enacted by all civilized countries. They *must* be.

Human laws, then, being indispensable to the protection of individuals against the rapacity of others, in their persons and in their possessions, those laws are the very foundation and groundwork of the right of property—of property itself; for without them there would be no possibility of property.

Then to go a step further, there must be umpires, arbiters, courts to administer and enforce the laws There must be lawyers, for Courts must be made of lawyers ; and there must be practicing lawyers also, for without them there could be no administration of justice in any civilized or intelligible way. So that, on the whole, law and lawyers really constitute the basis of the social fabric. They are not secondary ; not a useful convenience merely; they are a fundamental factor of civilization. On them the body politic largely rests. Every cultivated acre, every habitation, every factory, every working mine, every public improvement, together with all their varied productions, and all invested capital, in every phase and manner of investment, all, all owe their value to law and lawyers.

There is a great deal of croaking about the un
certainties of the law. There is nothing positive
in it; all is doubtful and uncertain, for the benefit
of the lawyers, we are told. It is said of the late
Judge Grover that he gave this account of himself:
When he first went into the Court of Appeals of
the State of New York, he expected to find that
court made up of very profound lawyers—men who
knew every thing about the law, and could readily
grasp all the points of every case and square them
up to the science of law every time without any
mistakes. But he soon found that the only difference between that Court and inferior courts was
that the Court of Appeals had the last guess upon
the law, as he said.

Suppose that all to be so; what of it? Let us
see. That applies to litigated properties only.
Nine hundred and ninety-nine men out of a thousand, hold their properties without question, *because the law is certain as to their property*. Mr.
Croaker, why is it that some stronger man than
you does not drive you from your house, or your
farm, or take your cattle, or your crops, or your
merchandise, or whatever else you are possessed
of? Because the law is certain. Why does not
some rapacious neighbor go into Court to dispos-
sess you of these properties? Because the law is
certain; for the law applies to all property, and
stands as a bulwark to shield it against all evil
doers, and not merely applying to disputed cases.

We used to hear a good deal about a government of consent. There is no such thing as a government of consent. It it a solecism. Government is coercion. Law is coercion. The consent of the evil disposed is assured by the coercive power of the law. You hold your property undisputed because this coercive power is sure to award it to you—because the certainty of the law is in it and all about it.

But as a matter of course there is always uncertainty in litigated cases in court. If there were no uncertainty there would be no litigation; for nobody would go to law with a certainty of losing his case. From the imperfections of humanity it is impossible that all the processes of trade, in all their ramifications, can be carried on without cases of disagreements as to fact and imperfections in the application of law, which necessarily lead to litigations. These disagreements and uncertainties are what make the litigation, and not the law that makes the uncertainties.

And then, admitting the uncertainties of litigation, in all courts from lowest to highest—uncertainties in the application of law to facts, and in the fine and difficult discriminations often involved in important cases, there is science in the law after all; it is not a jumble; not a guess work, if Judge Grover did say so. In my explorations of law, in my own cases, for I am not a lawyer, I have found that in every case of any magnitude that comes before a Court, where any disputed question of law is involved, there is an underlying principle of law that reaches it, and should govern it, and will govern it in the hands of a competent well-inform-ed lawyer and an upright and competent judge.

And in passing, I may as well say to the young members of the profession, seek out that governing principle in every case that comes to you, and you will be able to save many a client from unsuccess-ful litigation, and achieve more than an average of success in your profession. Prepare your cases well by exploring the law to the bottom, so as to be able to show to the Court all the merit that they admit of. The more you do this the easier it will be to do it. Such preparation of one case will, perhaps, prepare you for many others in future. When you commence practice, you are just ready to commence to learn the law. Work, therefore, is I think the principal secret of success. Great lawyers are always great workers.

From what I have already said on this subject, the profession of the law is not a mere invention for the benefit of the lawyers, as many intelligent but superficial people seem to imagine. It is not a necessary *evil*. It is purely beneficial *per se ;* as much so as the trade of agriculture, or any other purely productive vocation. It may be said to be a contribution to the productions of all other classes. The support of the legal fraternity is not in any sense a drain upon the national wealth. The lawyers are just as well entitled to a share in all litigated properties as is the working man in the goods that he aids in manufacturing. And litigations are just as necessary to the good order of society, yea to society and civilization themselves, as is the cultivation of the soil or the operations of the mechanical processes.

As to going to law, probably there is too much of it. A good deal of it might be dispensed with if people would not stand so much on their " grit," and more of it if all lawyers were well qualified for their work, so as to avoid the bringing of desperate and really hopeless and unnecessary actions, or encouraging desperate and hopeless defenses. Not that a lawyer must know positively the result of a suit before he begins—that, as we have seen, is impossible; but great numbers of suits are battled through, which, on one side or the other, a competent lawyer, by exploring to the bottom, would know to be hopeless from the beginning. And then, furthermore, lawyers are made up of the same sort of humanity as other people. A few men get into the profession who have no right to be there. Without the moral principle in good faith to pursue the labors and the arts of the true lawyer, they disgrace the profession by all the sharp practices of shyster necromancy. These excresences upon an honorable profession are always ready to foster litigation, whether needful or not, provided only that they can get their hands into somebody's pocket—no matter whose.

I think it is a commonly received opinion that the practice of law is *necessarily* more or less untruthful, and dishonest. Of the two sides of every litigation, one side is wrong, and the lawyer on that side always exerts his skill and ingenuity to make it out to be right; and all that is surely wrong; he cannot be an honest man to do that. Such is the theory of many superficial people. But that is begging the question. In litigation, the question of the right or wrong is what is to be tried, and each party is entitled to a full presentation of all that there is in the case in his favor, and in the best possible light. This is the lawyer's business to do. This is fair and honest. It is his bounded duty. With less than that, courts would be a farce. There would be no administration of justice. Beyond this a lawyer is not bound to go, and the true lawyer will not. And this does not require anything false or disreputable. But the lower grade of so-called lawyers that I have described above, will stoop to anything—fraud, falsehood, any sort of chicanery or swindling to carry a case, or to get one; and they care not who is cheated—whether client or others, so that they make a fee. But I have good reason to know that there are *true* lawyers. In my numerous litigations, in several States, I have found them; and have not had the misfortune to employ any of the other kind.

We hear a good deal of clamor about lawyers' fees. Sometimes it so happens that a lawyer gets large pay for little work, and that, perhaps, of an ordinary kind.   It is the price ; the law gives it to him.   It is an incident of his business, a profitable job, perhaps, just as the merchant makes a hit in an honest trade, whereby he makes a hundred dollars in an hour ; or as any other business man makes a few hundred with very little exertion. With the exception of the class of lawyers above described, whose highest conceptions of the province of the lawyer is that it is to get fees, and whose aim always is to make fees whether necessary or not, I think it cannot be claimed that lawyers make too much money.

A Court in session is one of the grandest spectacles in civilized society.   Look in upon it.— Sovereignty of the people embodied.   The power of a state determining rights of property—liberty —life.   Look upon its work.   The case may be a trifling one.   The parties may be foolish to take it there.   It may cost the county more than the sum involved.   But there is a wrong on one side or the other that it is the province of government to redress.   There is a right of property involved that the parties have the same right to carry there, and society is just as deeply interested that the wrong shall be righted, as if a million were at stake. The trial of that little suit is a part of the price of good order and civilization, just as is that of every one, large or small, that parties choose to litigate. Society cannot afford to ignore the rights, however small of any individual, however humble.   If it is ·

costly to care for them, it is more so to omit it. Intruders may come upon our borders, as they do sometimes, and plunder our people of a few hundred cattle. For the time being it may be cheaper to furnish cattle to replace the stolen, than to send an army to stop it. But to begin that process is to invite a repetition and multiplication of the plunder to an indefinite extent; and the only safety is in immediate redress at any cost. And so with legal litigations. It is the boast of the law that there is no wrong without a remedy, and the State cannot afford to ignore the slightest wrong. As I have said, the party may better afford to waive his rights than to prosecute them, but the State must enforce them if required, or her dignity and power cease, and the government is a failure.

Judicial prerogative, and the lawyer's office—the grandest province of humanity in respect to human rights. A vast interest, peradventure, to be adjudicated in a Court. A lawyer on either side, holding up his client's case, in the best of its aspects. One seems to have the better of it, and he wields all his advantages of law upon his antagonist, and holds him in the well-woven net-work of his case; the judge decides the controversy; the end is reached; vast property is handed over, this way or that, by the fiat of a man; the chapter is ended. Yes, it is grand. It is a fearful power in human hands, as it respects the immediate parties, but it must be so. The decision may be wrong, for this is only to say that judges are men. It may be wrong in principle, wrong in law, but right nevertheless, in the larger political sense, for there must be an end of property strife somewhere. The last end of a judicial controversy must be taken for the right. It is the law of the case; it is the legal right.

In conclusion, the true lawyer is a fundamental factor of civilization, the conservator of all property rights, and of the peace and good order of society. Let him appreciate the dignity, power and responsibility ot his office, and seek to maintain its integrity and honor. The false lawyer is the contrary of all that: the fomentor of strifes and litigations, a mere schemer for business—fees—self; an excresence upon society; deserving of all the opprobrium that is sometimes heaped upon the profession in general, and more; of no possible beneficial use in the world; inviting the scorn and detestation of all honest men.

XXI.

TONGUE.

Some people go through the world at a disadvantage for the want of a sufficient fluency of speech; but I think there are more who are troubled with too much volubility of tongue. Not that any degree of fluency, and ease, and oratory in the expression of ideas can ever be unacceptable; for such is one of the grandest and most attractive faculties of man. But the trouble is the talk without the ideas, or too small a proportion of ideas to the quantity of talk.

If a person has anything to say, it is a good thing to know how to say it, but it is a better thing to know how to stop when he gets through, and still better to know how to say it without any surplus of talk. And this will hold good in any kind of public speaking, in business, or in ordinary conversation. Of course all that is a big thing to know, and very few can know it to any degree of perfection. But I think there are some general principles that may be hinted at here that may be useful to young people; for the world is suffering of too much talk.

I have seen many a lawyer tire a jury and damage his case by a too elaborate threading out of unimportant and fine-spun theories and arguments; as if his success depended upon the length of his speech. I do not say that a short speech will always do, or that the shortest is always the best; for a certain amount of talk is usually necessary, longer or shorter, according to the nature of the case. A five hours' speech may be shorter for one case than one hour's would be for another. What I do urge is that by seizing upon the prominent features of a case, and setting them out with studied conciseness and perspicuity, a lawyer will usually do better with a jury or a court than by a redundancy of words. All young lawyers may profit by studying the art of condensation and terseness. I have heard of discourses so put together and applied to the subject that "every word was a sledge hammer." And that is the kind of talk that all young public speakers should aim for. I think it is done only by grasping the gist of the subject and presenting it with plainness of diction and condensation.

In printed talk, too, I think there is great waste of words. In the productions of many popular writers we see a good deal of fine writing about nothing. When they undertake to discuss any subject they have more to say all around the edges of it than upon the vital matter in hand, all of which is some times quite readable if the reader has nothing else to do; but to a busy man I think it is a good deal of a bore to endure so much embellishment for a little substance; to search through so much ornamental chaff for the kernel of the subject. I often tire of wading through the mazes of elegant diction, to find the merits of a subject that ought to be embodied in a quarter of the space that is taken up.

In writing on any topic, for busy men to read, the very best way is to pitch right into the merits without any circumlocution, go through it without surplusage or trimmings, and stop when through. This, too, is a good deal of a trade to learn; but it is the true art of the really fine writer, that every young aspirant should aim for.

And then there is the abuse of talk in the way of gossip—mischievous, news-bearing, from one to another, from the mere unimportant tattle to actual slander, which should be studiously avoided. It is always damaging to somebody and never useful to any one. I do not say that we should say nothing about our neighbors, for this would be not only impossible but undesirable. It would pretty nearly shut us out of all sociability. But I think there is a general rule that may easily be observed, and that would be the better for everybody; and that is, simply, to not report or repeat anything disparaging of another, true or false, with these exceptions :

1st. Where it is for the ends of public justice that it should be told.

2nd. Where a matter is under judicial process; and

3d. Where any person is being injured in reputation or otherwise, by talk or otherwise, by another. In this last case I think it is the special duty of any person to inform the injured party. That is to say: Suppose A and B to be in ostensible friendly relations, socially or otherwise; but B is doing something by talk or otherwise injurious to A in his good name, or his business; A is treating B as his friend; I think it quite clear that A has a right to know of B's conduct, and it is the imperative duty of any other person knowing it to inform A of it, so that he may not longer be deceived and cheated. To keep it from A is to do him an injustice; to tell it is not doing B any wrong or injury only so far as it may be an injury to be cut off from cheating.

I think these garrulous people often injure themselves by their propensity to talk. They are always so hungry for talk that the supply of gossip of others does not suffice, and so they peddle everything they know about themselves. They cannot have any matter or scheme of business without telling all about it to everybody they come in contact with, and thereby often get supplanted or injured. If they happen to have a lawsuit, they continually talk, talk about it to everybody they see, revealing all the secrets of it, and sometimes get beaten by their own imprudent talk. Reader, it is always safe to make your talk about yourself as small as possible.

But the most extensive grievance of all, in the way of talk, is in business; or rather, around the edges of business. The most of men never know when any little piece of business talk is done. For instance: one of that kind calls on a business man on business; and in stating his case he cannot do without telling the whole history of himself and his family and all of his neighbors. Or if that is stating it too strongly, perhaps he will pitch straight into the subject, and tell all he knows about it, with the most elaborate particularity, through all its labyrinths, three or four times, over, together with everything that every other person that has had to do with it has ever said or done about it. And then, if he ever does get choked off from that, he cannot think of retiring without an elaborate talk on matters and things in general that somehow seem to be suggested to him by that business. These two phases of that nuisance, in various degrees of intensity, embody the principal substance of this kind of superfluous talk.

A little case in point. Not many days prior to the present writing, I was trying to write one of these little chapters. A man called on me for a matter of business that ought to be done in about fifteen minutes. Before I could shake him off without rudeness I wasted about two hours. Then another call of the like character used up the entire half day

Sometimes an acquaintance, having nothing to do—waiting for a train or something—will call on a business man who wants to be at his work, and entertains him with a couple of hours or so of talk. An editorial friend has just now had such an entertainment, and they are quite too common with all business men. These examples are given as merely illustrative of what all business men are more or less afflicted with all the time.

Reader, learn to avoid all such unnecessary talk; when you call on a business man on business, make your discourse directly 'to the business in hand,

and when you get through with that don't forget that he does not want to be entertained with any thing else in business hours. He wants to do his work.

XXII.

HOSPITALITY.

I think young people commencing to keep house can and ought to improve upon the current ideas of entertaining visitors. My observation leads me to doubt whether there is much of the old-fashioned, comfortable, enjoyable hospitality left. It is overdone and underdone. The fashion is to overdo it so much, when undertaken at all, that it extinguishes nearly everything in that line. People cannot afford it. They cannot do it. It is too severe a burden for the average housekeeper to undertake unless under a great pressure. It is a big job to take a visitor or two for a day or two. It ought not to be so; there is no need of it.

Go into almost any house where the mistress of it is a good housekeeper, a few days before visitors are expected, and you will find a hurly-burly of preparation; the house, perhaps, overhauled from cellar to garret; the culinary department in a distressing tumult; as if the visitors were so superior to their entertainers that nothing but such a strain as that could render their visit endurable; and in general the aspect of affairs so uncomfortable that all in their hearts wish the visit was over with, instead of looking forward to it as a pleasure, as should be the case; for the entertainers are just as well entitled to enjoyment in the visit as are the visitors. And when the auspicious day arrives, and the company are on hand, the household are so tired out and so surfeited with the agitations of the subject, that the whole thing is a bore; the visit that might be a pleasure is really a burden and a grievance. All this by over-kindness—overdoing the matter of hospitality. By these extraordinary efforts to make the visit pleasant and enjoyable the mark is so overreached that the enjoyment of real free, familiar, social intercourse is extinguished.

Of course that process of preparation for guests cannot be endured very often; for it may as well be confessed, for everybody, that they do not like to do it. And it is well understood by all that nobody likes to do it. And nobody can think of visiting the nearest friends at a distance without first ascertaining if it will be agreeable to them; in plainer words, if they can endure it. The tendency is to do just as little of it as possible; and on public, religious, or other occasions, where visitors ought to be cared for by free hospitality, such entertainment is very difficult to get. Not long ago, a meeting of a religious body of forty members was held, in a village of five thousand inhabitants. Notice was given out a week before the day of meeting for volunteers for boarders for two days. During the week the pastor received reports from two persons—one that none could be taken; the other offering to take two; that was all. And then it was by importunity that entertainment was secured for that little gathering without going to the hotels.

Another case: On invitation of the prominent temperance people of a large village, a Temperance Convention was called at said village. Accommodations were asked for fifty or sixty for a night and part of two days. This, of all benevolent gatherings, ought to be taken care of without charge, for it is well known that the mass of temperance workers have to work for nothing and pay their own expenses. From a sharp lady canvasser I have a fund of valuable information on this subject. But not to divulge details, the subject was very generally repulsive to those whose ability and sympathies with the work would naturally suggest that the doors would be opened. All sorts of excuses were interposed—of course some were good and valid, but probably not more than one in ten of those who had no real hindrance could be induced to accept a single guest; and many who did so did it with the greatest reluctance.

I do not speak of these facts and these tendencies to complain of the *results* of the prevailing fashion, but to complain of the fashion itself. Hospitality is pretty much played out. It ought to be —*i. e.*, the kind that I have tried to describe. It is too repulsive to the average housekeeper, and too costly—in labor and in money. People cannot afford it. When a brother writes to a brother that about a month hence he proposes a visit by himself and family for two or three weeks, *"if agreeable,"* that means a month's labor and expense in money and a commotion for the two or three weeks' visit that often sends back the answer that it will not be agreeable, or it will be for special reasons inconvenient; when the fact is that the visit would be extremely agreeable and not at all inconvenient but for the fashion aforesaid. And in many cases where the "agreeable" reply is given, it ought to be the other way, because the labor and expense cannot really be afforded. In most of such cases the fault is in the host and hostess themselves, for the visitors would prefer to not inflict such a strain upon the family, but knowing that the friends would be horrified with such visit without such great preparation, the notice is given as before stated. And when entertainment is asked for any benevolent meeting, the call is supposed to involve a feast of fat things, and other incidental labors that not many can very well endure.

It is all wrong. There is no need of overdoing this matter of entertainment. And by not overdoing it we can do the more of it; and then there would be no trouble in entertaining a few friends on any suitable occasion. And then it would be quite easy, in any good sized town, to care for any large gathering whenever necessary and proper.

Hospitality can and should be enjoyable on both sides, and not a source of distress to the entertainers which often creates great uneasiness, not to say discomfort to the guests.

Reader, if your brother and his family, or other relatives, are to make you a visit, remember that you are exactly as much related to them as they are to you, and there is no reason why you and your family should take upon yourselves a burden for their entertainment that you cannot really afford, and that will spoil all of your side of the visit, even if they should desire you to do so, which in nine cases out of ten they would not. They have no right to any such thing. It is not just and mutual social intercourse. If you are to take a stranger for a day or two, he is no better than you and your family—or if he is, he has no business there—and there is no reason for straining to make a great feast for him, and he has no right to expect any extra preparations that will disturb the equanimity of the family or make them in any way uncomfortable. If I am invited by an acquaintance to dinner, casually, for my accommodation, that should not involve an overhauling of the dining room, any inconvenient change of food or extra work. If the dinner happens to be very plain or common-place, I have no right to complain of it, and I do not see why the lady of the house should be at all embarrassed. And there is no reason why my friend should incur an expense of a dollar or so to reconstruct a dinner to save me a half dollar at a hotel. If I am invited to a free entertainment for a few days, and I am given such fare as the family usually have themselves, the probability is that it is as good as I have at home, and surely that ought to be satisfactory to me. If not it is my privilege to buy something better and pay for it. This matter is usually treated as if everybody else are better than ourselves, and our way of living is not fit for any body else.

But all this is not to say that visitors do not necessarily make some extra work and expense, or that reasonable preparation should not be made so as to make them comfortable. Less than that would be an inexcusable insult. All that I complain of is the superfluous, unnecessary strain, that is usually the biggest end of the preparation, and that in nine cases out of ten the guests would much prefer should not be done.

But "such slip-shod hospitality is not showing a proper respect to guests," some will say. Very well, let us see. The respect should be reciprocal. One side is entitled to about the same respect as the other. The respect due to the guest is that he have a comfortable and respectable entertainment, and that due to the entertainers is that they be not subjected to inordinate burdens on account of their hospitality. Each has rights that the other ought to respect. The pleasures of social intercourse should be mutual—can be mutual—enjoyable by both sides, and not merely enjoyed by one side and endured by the other.

After all, I hear some people say that "most of this matter of free entertainment is a bore any how. On these public occasions, such as Religious Conferences, Presbyteries, Associations, Temperance Conventions, etc., let the delegates provide for themselves at hotels."

Well, if these gatherings are to be treated as matters of mere money making business for the members, like Bankers' or Manufacturers' Conventions, and the like, then that is very well. But if we treat such institutions as benevolent organizations, for the general benefit of the world, that alters the case quite materially. It resolves itself into a question of the expediency of such meetings and of paying their expenses some how. The world needs these benevolent bodies, and they are not primarily for the benefit of their members, and their meetings must be supported somehow by their patrons. And I think the best way and the cheapest way to do it is by voluntary entertainment.

And more than this: I think the object of all such benevolent organizations is always considerably promoted by social intercourse of the officials with the people at their homes, at such meetings. It cultivates interest in the work that cannot be done in any other way. Think of a Conference of three hundred ministers of the Gospel spread through the masses of people of a town or city, in social converse at their homes, instead of coldly plodding along, at hotels, as if this world were for nothing but mere selfish money getting. What a vast fund of valuable information, with its impetus for progress, must remain in such a community. And so of all other high-toned benevolent bodies.

And this is not all. If we can get rid of the useless family strain of hospitality before alluded to, I think the care of such public bodies can be made enjoyable all round. I think I am not extremely social in my disposition, but it is usually pleasant to me to entertain a few guests on such occasions, and some of my most interesting acquaintances have been formed in this way.

XXIII.

CONCLUSION.

In these twenty-two little discourses I have tried to impart to young people, from the experience and observation of a laborious life, such instruction as seemed to me, if accepted, would make the world the better. In discussing the property interests of the masses, I have endeavored to inculcate the principles of practical Christian piety as a necessary factor in the make-up of a man for success in life. But I cannot bid adieu to my readers, in this connection, without an exhortation to accept the Christian religion from the better motive of the higher life, and not merely for dollars and cents.

Drink it in spiritually, experimentally, in all its length and breadth, and not stop with the cold and passive theory, and the money profit of it. Embrace it for its spiritual consolations here, and for its assurances for the future life, and not merely accept its secular advantages and reject the higher. To this end you must accept Christ as your Savior, put your trust in Him, confess Him before men, do your life work in His name, and in subordination to the requirements of His Gospel. And now, commending you to His grace, mercy and peace, and in the hope that the object of these papers may not be entirely unattained, I close this series.

PART SECOND

ALCOHOLIC MEDICATION.

1.—INTRODUCTORY.

In all the range of activities, and principles, and habits, that all people, young and old, have to face, and consider, and act upon, one way or the other, all through life, there is nothing more vitally important to every man, woman and child, than the subject of temperance.

On the mere question of indulging in the use of alcoholic beverages, I have already given my views, to which I have nothing to add in these pages; but intimately connected with that, there is a phase of the temperance question that has not yet been generally discussed, but is now coming to the front as an important factor in the temperance work; to wit: alcoholic medication.

To all deep thinkers in the temperance cause it is now well understood that the use of alcohol as medicine is an important agency in the propagation of the drink habit—that a large portion of the intemperance in the land originates in the use of the article as medicine. And whether alcohol is good for sick people or not, there can be no doubt that the sale of it in the name of medicine is doing immensely more harm than good.

A child trained by the family physician to the idea that alcoholic stimulants are necessary in sickness, does not have very far to go to conclude that they are good for well people too.

And when we look over the field of battle between temperance and intemperance, I don't know for certain which is the more formidable enemy of the temperance cause, the hotels and saloons, or the doctors and drug shops. We have many temperance doctors, but I think they are no improvement upon the other kind in respect to alcoholic prescriptions. There are very few cases of disease that the regular allopathic practitioner can think of attending without more or less of such prescriptions; and in a variety of cases alcoholic stimulants are the chief reliance.

" Get a little brandy, good brandy ; go to the drug store for it, they keep a good article, especially for medicine : put so and so in it, and take two or three spoonfuls three times a day ; it will build you up ; you need stimulating."

Or, "get a keg of the best beer, and take three or four glasses a day. It is nourishing as well as stimulating, and that is just what you need."

And so in a hundred ways the great elixir of life, as they would have us think it is, is drawn upon by the profession, day by day ; and the people are educated to the idea that it is good for everybody when they do not feel well. And the people make their own prescriptions in most of common cases of not feeling well

The drug stores keep a good supply of "pure

14

liquors—for medical purposes only." To get a bottle filled there is not tippling. When the bottle is out the patient again feels not very well. And so probably more than half of the drinking customs of society are propagated and cultivated by the use of the article as a medicine.

But after all, the question is whether alcohol is ever good for sick people. To this chiefly I propose to address myself in these papers.

I do not cast any reflections upon temperance doctors. They are conscientious and true to their convictions in this matter. But they are mistaken at one end or the other of this question. I think an alcohol-prescribing doctor cannot consistently be a temperance man. If alcoholic stimulation is good to build up exhausted nature in a sick man, it is good to build up an exhausted well man. If there is any vitalizing power in it, it is good for everybody ; and the temperance ideas of the present day are all wrong. But I think I know what I am saying, when I say that alcoholic stimulation is never useful to sick or well. It never increases, but always exhausts the vital forces—always tends to kill and never to cure. And I think no physician can give an intelligible or physiological reason for prescribing it.

I am aware that all this will be deemed fanatical by the generality of readers, but I shall try to produce good scientific and practical proof of it before I get through.

II.

ITS TENDENCY—ELEMENTARY PRINCIPLES.

THE DRUG SHOPS.

The meanest of all our institutions that the law has provided, and that temperance men and Christians are voting every year to perpetuate, for the propagation and cultivation of intemperance and debauchery, are the drug store grog-shops. The other sort do not pretend to any benefit or value in their goods, but generally admit that they grasp the money of their victims for what is worse than useless, and that their business tends only to debauchery and crime. The drug store grog-shop is founded on a relic of barbarism—the popular delusion, perpetuated by the doctors, that alcoholic stimulants are good for sick people. They think that the sick cannot get well without them, just as all the world once thought that people could not endure any severe labor, or any hardship, or exposure, without them. Professedly for the purpose of supplying afflicted humanity with this cure-all, the druggist obtains his license, and he is thus relieved of the odium that attaches to the common vulgar liquor dealer.

Large and general as is the demand for these goods by orders of the doctors, this is but a trifling part of the trade. Theirs are charmed liquors. They are for medical purposes only. They are absolutely pure. They are good. They are to do

sick people good.   The doctor had prescribed them
for his patient.   The patient got well in spite of
the prescription.   The medicine is pleasant to take,
and it has the credit of a cure.   Afterwards the
same patient takes to feeling not very well.
What's the use of paying a dollar for a prescription.   He can go for the cure-all just as well
without it.   About a quart of the best, with some
orange peel or quassia in it will do the job.   He is
a reputable citizen; he is sick; the druggist is
anxious to relieve him; his liquors are of the very
best: for medicine only; he makes three or four
times on them; and the customer is cured for a
very little while—so long as the medicine lasts—
and then the same over again, and again, until he
becomes an open undisguised drinker anywhere.   In
this way I think thousands of people are all the
time on the road to drunkenness.

Another way: A convalescent having exhausted
his doctor's stimulant prescription, he feels a
" goneness," without something to brace him up;
or any other person who feels such goneness, goes
to the drug store for the bracing up then and
there.   The dispenser of medicines, ministering to
the needs of suffering humanity, and not to the depravity of human nature as with the common
liquor seller, and seeing a good twenty-five cent
piece for what costs him three or four cents, is
quite easily persuaded that a little drink of the
purest and best is good for the customer; and so

a nice little back room sees a very good run of that kind of custom. And then the proprietor soon becomes convinced that his pure liquors are good for every body ; and any one, money in hand, can get a drink, for the health, at any time.

I do not say that all drug stores are that kind of grog shops, but I think they are not very uncommon.

THE DOCTORS.

Now a word to the doctors. Whenever and wherever the practice of anti-alcoholic medication is advocated by any respectable authority, the alcoholic practitioners usually take it in a belligerent way. They may as well keep cool. It is not for us to educate them. But in view of the notorious and enormous propagation of the drink habit by alcoholic medication, it stands them in hand to study out this matter for themselves, and see if those members of the profession who deny the efficacy of alcohol as a remedial agent, may not be correct, and the majority wrong, as the entire profession has many a time been wrong in vital matters of practice ; for this doctrine of anti-alcohol in medication is not an invention of mine, and it is not very new. And this study is especially worthy of their attention in view of the fact that there is not to be found in their books any specific therapeutic theory, as to how alcoholic poison operates to cure disease. If it does cure, there must be a particular elementary action upon the vital forces, somehow, by which the cure is effected. Let these knowing sprigs of Esculapius study out this problem and publish the result to the world, so that the profession may not longer grope in the dark, and continue to poison people with alcohol merely because their books tell them to, without knowing whether they need poisoning or not.

And then, further, failing to discover any good reason for the alcoholic practice, when they say to a rigorous temperance patient that he must take alcohol or die, and he does not take it and does not die, as is not at all uncommon, it stands them in hand to stop and think whether the other side is not in the right after all, and whether those desperate cases that survive alcoholic medication do not get through in spite of it, instead of by virtue of it.

It is high time for the medical profession, as conservators of the public health, to reconsider this matter, go down to elementary principles, and do a little thinking for themselves, instead of following the practice of darker days merely because some distinguished writers keep it along in the books.

And in these papers I shall try to present such common sense theories, and sustain them by such preponderating authorities of medical science, that the majority of doctors may profit by a careful study of them.

THE THEORY.

I think this question of alcoholic medication is a

simple one, and easily understood by anybody who has a very slight knowledge of physiology.

Without here undertaking to describe the physiological processes of a living human body, it is sufficient to say that life and health is the constant renewing of the continual waste of tissue, or elementary substance of the body, by the process of assimilation—nutrition—the appropriation of the usable particles of the food, to supply the waste aforesaid; together with depuration or excretion of the effete or wasted matter through the various emunctories or outlets of the body. These processes in perfection constitute perfect health—the maximum of vitality. Any interruption to them in any respect, in any part of the body, is disease of some kind—a loss of vitality. Their entire suspension is the extinction of all vitality—death.

Now, I think alcohol is administered to the sick, chiefly, if not entirely, in cases of exhaustion—low vitality. For instance: in fever, where the vitality has been nearly all wasted by the disease—the patient nearly dead—alcohol is given to recuperate the system from the waste of vitality that has been going on without the physiological renewal, accelerated as it has been by the poison of the disease. And in multitudes of cases, of the same character as to this particular phase, and of varying intensity, I think this drug is uniformly relied on by the most of allopathic practitioners.

I believe it is admitted by the profession that alcohol is a powerfully irritant, caustic poison. Now put that and that together, and tell me how alcohol is to restore the wasted vitality. Vitality is produced by nutrition only. Instead of nutrient material you introduce poison into the body of the almost dying patient. It cannot be assimilated, cannot be converted into tissue to supply the indispensable want of life ; but on the contrary, when any poison, especially alcohol, is introduced into the human body, all the vital forces are at once brought into action to expel the intruder. And when this is effected, as it will be if sufficient organic power remains in the patient's system for self-defense, the alcohol will be expelled, leaving no beneficial result behind ; the patient remains as before, minus the vitality expended by the violent action of nature's scanty forces in expelling the enemy of all life.

There is only one way to build up the wasted tissues ; only one way to renew the strength ; and that is by alimentation. Poison cannot do it. Its apparent effects are illusory. It is the rousing up of all the remaining life forces, but is not an addition to them. It is the exhaustion of them in doing a work that the doctor should not make necessary. Who has not seen patients alcoholized—not to say drunken—to keep them up, as they call it ; all the vital forces kept on a strain of activity, until extinguished, oftener, perhaps, by such strain than by the original disease, and life going out without a moment's warning.

Temperance men and women, such is the effect of alcoholic medication, in any form, upon the debilitated human body. You can see for yourselves that it never can be useful, but is always injurious —dangerous. And when your doctor tells you to use it, don't do it. When he tells you that you will die, or your friend will die, if it is not administered, tell him that it can only help to kill. And with this peremptory instruction the doctors will soon be in a way of learning the true philosophy in this behalf.

III.

SCIENTIFIC PROOFS.

I remember very well when it was just as fanatical to say that alcohol was not good for people in health to take—that people could safely endure severe labor, or any kind of physical exposure, without alcoholic drinks, as it is now to say that sick people can get well without them, or even that they are much more likely to get well without than with them.

But that old fight is over. Nobody, now, save here and there a fossil tippler, pretends that alcohol is good to put into a human stomach except as medicine. I think a large majority of drinking men admit that it is bad for them. And now the true temperance platform is anti-alcoholic medication. The only way to stop the propagation of intemperance is to stop the use of alcohol as medicine.

But when it is intimated that sick people can do without alcohol, the doctors rave, and the people —temperance people as well as others—stand aghast. And yet to those who have critically studied into the subject, outside of professional prejudice, and beyond professional power, it is really mournful and distressing to see the multitudes of people who are all the time being slaughtered by alcoholic medication.

I have already given the true theory of the effects of alcohol upon the living human body, by which it appears that this poison must necessarily always be injurious and dangerous to the sick; but this matter does not rest on any theory or argument of mine. And I now introduce some of the highest medical and scientific authorities in support of my position.

"Alcohol cannot supply anything which is essential to the due nutrition of the tissues.— *W. B. Carpenter, M. D.*

" Alcohol is a poison to our organization. It is never digested and converted into nourishment.—*Dr. Murray.*

" Beer, wine, spirits, etc., furnish no element capable of entering into the composition of blood, muscular fibre, or any part which is the seat of the vital principle.—*Liebig.*

" A small quantity of pure alcohol injected into the veins of an animal causes immediate death. The poison having been absorbed, carried to the heart, and propelled to the brain, the nervous centres become paralyzed, and the heart ceases to beat.—*Prof. Monroe, M. D.*

"The use of alcoholic drinks diminishes man's capacity to endure both mental and physical labor, increases his predisposition to disease and shortens the average duration of life.—*N. S. Davis, M. D.*

PARKER.

Prof. Willard Parker, of the New York College of Physicians and Surgeons, says:

"Distilled liquor, I will use that term for the greater clearness, is never, under any circumstances, a food. It adds nothing to the substance of the body. It is never digested. It adds nothing to the forces of the body. On the contrary, it weakens force. It acts as an irritant; and so diminishes force by compelling the body to put forth efforts in order to get rid ot the intruder. The effect is the same as that produced on the eye by the presence of a grain of sand. The eye is excited to a state of great activity to cast the intruder out; but its real force as an eye is not increased; it is weakened by the unnatural exertion.

"Nor is distilled liquor a fuel. It is not burned; if it were we should find the ashes, and of the ashes no trace is found.

*　　*　　*　　*　　*　　*　　*　　*

"It is true that a dose of alcohol will sometimes produce a sudden external glow, but it does not add to the real warmth of the body. This fictitious glow is thus produced: Alcohol introduced into the body as a foreign substance acts, as I have previously explained, as an irritant in the manner in which a grain of sand acts upon the eye. The nerves of the stomach, and of the heart, and of all the vital organs are thrown into a state of excitement; the alcohol is passed directly undigested into the body; the blood hurries to get rid of the intruder; the rapidity of the circulation is increased, and the warm blood of the heart is thus hurried too speedily to the surface where it cools off. But no additional fuel has been furnished to the body to supply the heat thus exhausted; the temperature of the body has on the contrary been unnaturally lowered, and the vital organs have been overworked in the process. This has been proven both at home and abroad by frequent experiments.

" Alcohol adds neither food, force nor fuel to the human frame ; what does it do ?

" It has been ascertained by a distinguished *savant* at St. Petersburg, that alcohol taken into the stomach passes into the blood, in one minute and a half, undigested. It acts there disastrously upon the blood corpuscles. These are the little cars freighted with oxygen and constituting the beginnings of life. The alcohol impairs their vitality, robs them of their oxygen, and destroys their usefulness. The impaired vitality produces the disease known as fatty degeneration. Its operation upon the system is precisely that of increasing age. It hastens the inevitable approach of death. In health the blood has 8¼ parts of fat in a thousand; in a drunkard the blood has 117 parts in a thousand. The result of this radical change in the constitution of the blood is felt in every part of the body. Bad blood can no more make good brains, good nerves and good muscle, than bad flour can make good bread.

*   *   *   *   *   *   *   *

" Poisoning the blood, alcohol poisons the whole system, and affects with disease every vital organ— the lungs, the liver, the kidneys, the stomach. These are the physiological effects of alcohol as discovered by careful scientific investigation by the most eminent pathologists. They are confirmed by widely extended observation of the practical effects of drinking as witnessed in daily life."

HUNT.

In September, 1876, the International Medical Congress, consisting of over 600 delegates, met in Philadelphia ; and it was the most important medical body ever convened in this country. In its proceedings a paper was read by Ezra M. Hunt, M. D., on "Alcohol in its therapeutic relations as a food and a medicine," which was adopted as the sentiments of the Congress. From that paper I quote as follows :

"What consumption is among diseases, that is alcohol among medicines. How to limit the causes of the one is not more a professional question with us than how to abate the necessity for the effects of the other. It can not be concealed that the habit of the employment of alcoholics as a beverage is supported by the persuasion that they have an important value as a food, or are reparative and recuperative, and so medicinal. Thus, as half food and half medicine, they are accredited into popular use."

*   *   *   *   *   *   *   *

" Any article to rank as a food must be convertible into tissue or force, in such a way as to contribute to healthy vitality, and aid the body in the performance of its normal functions."

"It has been conclusively proved, says Lionel Beale (*Med. Times*, 1872), that alcohol is not a food, and does not directly nourish the tissues.

" There is nothing in alcohol with which any part of the body can be nourished." (Cameron, Manual of Hygiene, p. 282).

" It is not demonstrable at present that alcohol undergoes conversion into tissue " (Hammond, *Tribune*, Lecture, May, 1874),

" Alcohol contains no nitrogen ; it has none of the qualities of the structure-building foods ; it is incapable of being transformed into any of them ; it is, therefore, not a food in the sense of its being a constructive agent in the building up of the body " (Richardson on Alcohol, p. 21).

"There has been such unanimity of consent among those of divergent views in other regards, that alcohol is not a tissue-building food, that it is by quite common consent excluded from this class."

" Not detecting in this substance any tissue-making ingredients, nor in its breaking up any combinations, such as we are able to trace in the cell-foods, nor any evidence either in the experience of physiologists, or the trials of alimentarians, it is not wonderful that in it we should find neither the expectancy or the realization of constructive power."

Then, after quoting numerous authorities showing that *alcohol does not sustain animal heat,* the learned lecturer says :

" 'This fact, then, that alcohol is shown by the direct test of experiment, confirmed by experience, not to be a sustainer of animal heat, goes far towards necessitating its expulsion from the force-imparting class of foods."

Next the learned doctor says :

" *In further search for it, however, as an originator or conserver of force, the next point is to find whether it increases the excretion of carbonic acid (carbon dioxide)* which, as usual, would take place chiefly through the lungs. This is a leading proof of the food-value of the hydro-carbons of oils or of such liquids as are changed so as to impart vital force."

And after citing the authorities on that point, he sums up the result as follows :

" It in no wise bears this second great test of a heat-producing food. Nor does it in any way in the system show such affinity for oxygen as to form water.

" So far from this it is a great water consumer in every tissue to which it finds its way. It dries the stomach, the liver, and the lungs. It even steals moisture from the very corpuscles of the blood, and so far interferes with the supply of water and with its value as the universal medium of exchange amid the tissues, that for this very reason it oftener than any other article in common use initiates degeneration of important organs (R., pp. 41, 42). With water and alcohol the endosmosis is toward the alcohol, and alcohol requires four times the pressure to pass through the same membrane that water does (see Dalton's Physiology).

" When we consider how much all the functions of life depend on what the chemists and physiologists call osmosis, or the transfer of liquids with their soluble ingredients through various membranes, and that water is the all-important vehicle of this transfer, we must regard anything that interferes with this as involving serious risk both to function and to organ. A derangement of this all-pervading life-function is involved more in the continued administration of alcohol than in any one of the articles of the Materia Medica. It is fraught with imminent peril to the whole vitalized and vitalizing structure. So alcohol does not so combine with oxygen as to provide moisture and thus show one of the results of its appropriation by the system as an energy, but it makes grand larceny of the very thing it should contribute."

Then he comes to the question : *Is not fat recognized as the evidence of a nutritive process, and does not it result from the use of alcohol?* And after elaborate discussion of this question concludes as follows :

" The most constant effect of alcohol seems to be to cause that fatty degeneration of organs which is a sad substitute for healthy alimentation.

" If alcohol should ever be shown to cause increase of fat, with the facts of animal chemistry as thus far elucidated, it would be far more likely to be found to be a pathological result of some obstruction to necessary change, than a healthy and vital contribution of force."

*   *   *   *   *   *   *   *

" There may be a forced retention of the debris of the system which simulates the normal storing of vital force, but which is nevertheless so abnormal as to be damaging."

And that is exactly what takes place in the bloated drunkard. It is the arrest of the necessary depuration, or excretion of the effete matter of the tissues. And this is why a drunkard's body is always so corrupt, so liable to disease, and so difficult to cure.

The same principle is set out by the lecturer under " metamorphosis of tissue." He says :

" *But the form in which the idea is now most prominently advanced that alcohol is, somehow, a food, is that it delays the metamorphosis of tissue, and, so, in a secondary, but, nevertheless, effective way results in nutrition.*

" By the metamorphosis of tissue is meant that change which is constantly going on in the system

which involves a constant disintegration of material;
a breaking up and voiding of that which is no longer
aliment, making room for that new supply which is
to sustain the life. Vital power itself is found to be a
process of reparation and decay.

" A usual division is to call the process by which food
is converted into tissue *progressive metamorphosis*,
and that by which tissue is converted into force *regressive metamorphosis*. For this latter the term
destructive assimilation (Dalton, p. 325) is also used.

" Both these processes are physiological, and the regressive metamorphosis or destructive assimilation is
as healthful as the progressive process. It sounds
conservative of health to say of a substance, that it
delays the breaking down of tissue, but the histologist or physiologist does not allow a substance which
occasions such delay, to possess, because of that, either
dietetic or remedial value. To increase weight by
prolonged constipation is not a physiological process.

" Speaking of this regressive metamorphosis or destructive assimilation, Dalton says : ' The importance
of this process to the maintenance of life is readily
shown by the injurious effects which follow upon its
disturbance. If the discharge of the excrementitious
substances be in any way impeded or suspended, these
substances accumulate either in the blood or tissues,
or both. In consequence of this retention and accumulation they become poisonous, and rapidly produce
a derangement of the vital functions. Their influence
is principally exerted upon the nervous system,
through which they produce most frequent irritability,
disturbance of the special senses, delirium, insensibility, coma, and finally, death.'

" The description seems almost intended for alcohol.
To claim alcohol as a food because it delays the metamorphosis of tissue, is to claim that it in some way
suspends the normal conduct of the laws of assimilation and nutrition, of waste and repair."

*   *   *   *   *   *   *   *

" Having failed to identify alcohol as a nitrogenous
or non-nitrogenous food, not having found it amenable to any of the evidences by which the food-force of
aliments is generally measured, it will not do for us to
talk of benefit by delay of regressive metamorphosis
unless such process is accompanied with something

evidential of the fact—something scientifically descriptive of its mode of accomplishment in the case at hand, and unless it is shown to be practically desirable for alimentation.

" There can be no doubt that alcohol does cause *defects* in the processes of elimination which are natural to the healthy body and which even in disease are often conservative of health. In the pent-in evils which pathology so often shows occurrent in the case of spirit-drinkers, in the vascular, fatty, and fibroid degenerations which take place, in the accumulations of rheumatic and scrofulous tendencies, there is evidence that alcohol acts as a disturbing element and is very prone to initiate serious disturbances amid the normal conduct both of organ and function.

" To assert that this interference is conservative in the midst of such a fearful accumulation of evidence as to result in quite the other direction, and that this kind of delay in tissue-change accumulates vital force, is as unscientific as it is paradoxical."

*   *   *   *   *   *   *   *

" With abundant provision of indisputable foods, select that liquid which has failed to command the general assent of experts that it is a food at all, and because it is claimed to diminish some of the excretions, call that a delay of metamorphosis of tissue conservative of health ! ! !

" The ostrich may bury his head in the sand, but science will not close its eyes before such impalpable dust."

*   *   *   *   *   *   *   *

" It seems hardly possible that men of eminent attainments in the profession should so far forget one of the most fundamental and universally recognized laws of organic life as to promulgate the fallacy here stated. The fundamental law to which we allude is, that all vital phenomena are accompanied by, and dependent on, molecular or atomic changes; and whatever retards these retards the phenomena of life; whatever suspends these suspends life. Hence, to say that an agent which retards tissue metamorphosis is in any sense a food, is simply to pervert and misapply terms."

*   *   *   *   *   *   *   *

"The study of the laws of nature in the animal econ-
15

omy, and the results of chemical analysis, give us no warrant by which we can certify alcohol as a food."

* * * * * * * *

"In searching for alcohol as a food by all the tests afforded to scientific investigation, it eludes the grasp."

* * * * * * * *

"It may be the fabled food of gods, but alcohol is not an actual food for man which can be tried and proved such by any known laws of any known science, or by any test of any known art."

* * * * * * *

"It is apparent that it is too often Bacchus that would appear in the robe of Ceres, or with the wand of Esculapius, and so call that food or medicine which is taken merely as a luxury or to satisfy an appetite. We shall have done essential service when in our own peculiar sphere we shall have removed all the false supports for alcoholic beverages , attempted to justify its use as a daily or occasional self-selected food or self-advised medicine."

The careful reader will have observed that in the foregoing passages from the learned lecturer, he has demonstrated not only that alcohol is not a food in the sense of being converted into tissue, as a nutrient material ; but also that it never, directly or indirectly, imparts force or strength to the human system.

And this is pretty nearly conclusive of the question of alcoholic medication ; for it is administered by the doctors, chiefly, if not always, to add strength to the patient.

I now introduce, from the same lecture, some passages on the question, "Is alcohol a medicine ?"

"As we come to inquire into the value of alcohol as a medicine, after having found it unsustained as food, it is well to remember that the terms food and medicine, are often more nearly allied than the mention of the words is apt to indicate. A medicine is that which

helps to heal or repair, for that is both the etymology
of the word and the practical design of the article used.
The process of restoration or repair is often but an application of the process of natural nutrition. Amid
the progressive change of food into tissue, and the regressive disintegration which all life means, we must
not deceive ourselves by terms. Much of the discussion, therefore, as to the value of alcohol as a material
for medicine, is in reality to be determined by what it
can do toward repairing the waste of tissue which occurs in disease. What it can accomplish in this regard is largely the determination of the question of its
food-value. This we have seen to be so small and in-
determinate that *it will not do to push it forward* as a
valuable medicine in those regards in which a medicine chiefly concerns nutrition and the production of
animal heat. 'The more we investigate,' says
Lankester, ' the relations of food to the human system, the greater must be the conviction that food is
not only capable of maintaining healthy life, but by
proper modification can be made the means of curing
disease ;' and again, 'In the management of food we
have the great means for the cure and removal of
disease.'

"When we find that alcohol has no nitrogen with
which to nourish ; that it does not respond to the laws
by which animal heat is usually evolved; that it at
best undergoes such imperfect change in the system
that much of it is found unchanged in secretions, excretions, and tissues; that the products of its primary
or secondary change can not be identified ; that it is
not settled whether it diminishes the carbonic acid, or
urea, or other excreta, or that such diminution would
be reparative, we may well hesitate to assign it a
place in the category of medicinal nutrients. While
it has eluded the ingenuities of science, the persuasions of art, and the astute diligence of interest to ex-
temporize it into a food, it has failed not less signally
to vindicate itself as a medicine in the one particular
in which it is most frequently urged as of value.

"Another consideration that should make us exceed-
ingly modest as to clinical assertion of its value as
a medicine is, that the very next important thing to
nutrition of tissue which it has been claimed to accomplish, viz., the sustaining of animal heat, is now

the very thing which it is claimed to reduce. We
have examined with some interest the different records of the value of alcohol furnished by authors on
Materia Medica and Practice of thirty years ago and
those more recently in print. New editions of the
same author show often an entire shifting of the line
of defense, or else repeat the old dicta in ignoring ignorance of the most defined views of modern analysis
and experiential use. Many others have come to deny
its value except within very narrow limits.

In speaking of the testimony of the profession, he
says:

"It will not do to assume unanimity of testimony,
and so carry a position, when page after page can be
quoted from medical authors in nowise identified with
any special reform, in opposition to such views (see
summary by Parkes, pp. 280–285).

"An examination of the leading books on Materia
Medica and Therapeutics within the last twenty years,
and of the limits which both science and practice have
demonstrated, will serve to show how narrow is the
field in which we are to look for the therapeutical
effects of alcohol.

"Excluded by common consent from the list of ordinary aliments, eliminated from most of modern die-
taries where foods are studied with precise relation to
force and effective endurance, and from all systems of
athletic training, pronounced so unreliable as a sustainer of animal heat as to be used on a directly opposite hypothesis, identifying itself with toxics to a
degree that almost organizes use into abuse, its field is
so far narrowed as that the only classification it will
admit is that of GENERAL STIMULANT."

That is to say, its only effect upon the patient is
to excite the scanty vital powers to abnormal action to expel the intruder and further exhaust
those powers, and not to aid them in any way to
cure the patient. And then it is significantly
added:

" Many a horse which might have reached its journey's end, at a snail's pace, it is true, but still safely, has utterly broken down on the road in consequence of a too frequent application of the spur."

And this is exactly what alcohol does to a sick man : it helps to kill him. Richardson says :

" The heart beats faster because the contractile force of extreme vessels is weakened, and so there is less resistance than natural." "It gives evidence not of increased, but wasted power."

*　　*　　*　　*　　*　　*　　*　　*

" *Besides the effect of alcohol as a stimulant to the circulatory system, some claim for it a value as a nerve stimulant.*"

" ' It is of all other causes most prolific in exciting derangements of the brain, the spinal cord, and the nerves' (Hammond). ' The effect had on the nervous centres starts them directly in the path of nervous exhaustion' (Richardson). As its direct action is ' to lessen nervous force (Edward Smith), and as it is an irritant of nervous tissue, it is difficult to dissociate its vaunted nerve-stimulation from nerve-irritation.' "

" *The next prominent defense of alcohol as a medicine 'is to aid in the assimilation of food.' *"

" The phrase has been so often used, and the general popular and professional impression, like that of its heat power, has been so prevalent that men cling to to this view with the tenacity of an antiquated error. Pathology appears to tell us that alcohol coagulates albumen, and that it acts upon digestive fluids in a disturbing rather than a beneficial way."

I have drawn thus copiously upon this great lecture of Dr. Hunt, because the auspices under which it was delivered invests it with an authority that no regular physician can consistently reject. That Congress was composed of over six hundred representative physicians of England and America. They adopted that lecture as their sentiments, and so it may be said to be the embodiment of the authoritative medical opinion of this country and England on the subject in hand.   And what is it? The plain import of it is that there are no established facts to sustain the use of alcohol, in any case whatever, as a medicine.   And more, it is not mere opinion, but it demonstrates that the *science* of this question, so far as facts have been so established as to constitute science, is that alcohol is always injurious and never useful as medicine or otherwise.

And Dr. Hunt does not speak as a temperance man, but as a physician—for the healing art merely; —radically so, for he says:

"If I knew that brandy would save my patient, and that a thousand, copying from his restoration, would make self-resort to the same remedy and die, I would in solemn sorrow, yet in holy fealty to my patient, give him the brandy, and hold myself not responsible for the self-inflicted result to others."

And he is so cautious, and so loyal to his profession, that he studiously leaves the question open for further scientific investigation, without giving his individual opinion, further than it is embodied in the scientific facts that he has presented, notwithstanding that those facts, bearing as they do on every phase of the question of alcohol as a medicine, render it impossible that alcohol can be a medicine in any case; for science never contradicts itself.

So that, on the whole, we have the representative medical opinion of England and this country that alcoholic medication is always bad; and such opinion is founded purely on medical science.   Any thing to the contrary is yet to be discovered, to say the least.

RICHARDSON.

And that is not all. In the Cantor Lectures, delivered by B. W. Richardson, M. D., F. R. S., before the Edinburgh Society of Arts, in 1875, we have a full and fair exposition of the present state of medical science in respect to the effects of alcohol upon the human body. And he, too, speaks as a physician and not as a temperance man. In his introductory note to the printed lectures, he says :

" I have spoken out freely the lessons I have learned from nature, no pledge binds me, and no society banded to propagate particular views and tenets claims my allegiance. I stand forth simply as an interpreter of natural fact and law."

And the American edition of these lectures is endorsed to the public in a highly eulogistic preface by Dr. Willard Parker, of the New York College of Physicians and Surgeons. These lectures are more in scientific detail than that of Dr. Hunt, from which I have copied so largely, but in their conclusions they are identical with it ; so that I shall content myself with a very few quotations. He says:

"In the end, all these alcoholic fluids are depressants, and although at first, by their calling vigorously into play the natural forces, they seem to excite and are therefore called stimulants, they themselves supply no force at any time, but cause expenditure of force, by which means they get away out of the body and therewith lead to exhaustion and paralysis of motion. In other words, the animal force which should be expended on the nutrition and sensation of the body, is in part expended on the alcohol, an entirely foreign expenditure.''

His third lecture is devoted to a full and minute scientific examination of the physical action of alcohol on the human body, showing conclusively that it always, in large or small doses, in sickness or health, deranges the healthful action of every vital organ; so that its use is always more or less damaging, *per se.*   And then in the fourth, he takes up the question whether there be ever any compensation for such damage; stating the question as follows:

"We have studied in the previous lecture the purely physical action of alcohol on the animal body, that which stands apart from the action of the food, and we have learned from the study that over the nervous system and over the vascular supply this spirit exerts a specific influence. We now inquire whether the influence ends there, or whether there may be, in addition, either a sustaining, and constructing, or a heat-giving power—that is to say, a force-giving quality in it. If there be, then the simple physical effects are perchance tolerable, or at all events are not sufficient to militate against the advantages which lie on the food side of the question.''

*   *   *   *   *   *   *   *

"Let us then ask the question : Can alcohol be in any sense accepted as performing any other part in the body save that physical part which we have considered?''

After a full discussion of the replenishing of the tissues, he answers that part of the question thus:

"In conclusion, therefore, on this one point of alcohol, its use as a builder of the substantial parts of the animal organism, I fear I must give up all hope of affirmative proof. It does not certainly help to build

up the active nitrogenous structures. It probably does
not produce fatty matter, except by an indirect and
injurious interference with the natural processes."

And proceeds to the further question :

"If alcohol be not a substance out of which the animal tissues are formed, may it not be a source of energy of actual motion; may it not supply the power of
doing work ?"

.Now, let the reader bear in mind the scientific
fact that the only possible way of supplying force
or strength to the human body, is to administer
some substance which, by its digestion and assimilation, renews the wasted and wasting tissues, or
by its combustion or decomposition furnishes heat
to the body. Then it is to be stated that the
learned lecturer goes on to demonstrate, to scientific certainty, from actual experiments of his own,
that instead of supplying heat, alcohol always reduces the temperature of the body, and says :

" Here, however, I leave the theoretical point to re-
vert to the practical, and the practical is this : that
alcohol cannot by any ingenuity of excuse for it, be
classified amongst the foods of man. It neither supplies matter for construction nor heat. On the contrary, it injures construction and it reduces temperature."

And after relating a further experiment by which
it is proven that alcohol does actually diminish
muscular power, he thus states the general result :

" In man and in animals, during the period between
the first and third stages of alcoholic disturbance,
there is often muscular excitement, which passes for
increased muscular power. The muscles are then
truly more rapidly stimulated into motion by the
nervous tumult, but the muscular power is actually
enfeebled."

"Once more : I would earnestly impress that the systematic administration of alcohol for the purpose of giving and sustaining strength is an entire delusion."

*　　*　　*　　*　　*　　*　　*　　*

"Again, the belief that alcohol may be used with advantage to fatten the body is, when it is acted upon, fraught with danger. For if we could successfully fatten the body we should but destroy it the more swiftly and surely ; and as the fattening which follows the use of alcohol is not confined to the external development of fat but extends to a degeneration through the minute structures of the vital organs, including the heart itself, the danger is painfully apparent."

On the whole, then, the result of the demonstrations of this distinguished scientist and physician is that all the known facts as to the effects of alcohol on the human body go to show that it is never useful as a medicine or otherwise, but always injurious.

EDMUNDS.

And that is not all. We have also the testimony of James Edmunds, M. D., member of the Royal College of Physicians of London, to the same effect, as to the medical use of alcohol, in a series of lectures delivered in New York in 1874—he also speaking only as a physician and not as a temperance reformer—and also endorsed by Prof. Willard Parker.

I need not tire the reader by quoting from Dr. Edmunds the same scientific facts that I have already given ; but in my next number I shall avail myself of his instruction on another phase of the subject.

In concluding this part of the subject I refer the

professional reader to the works from which I have quoted herein, to wit:

"Alcohol as a Food and Medicine." 12 mo, 137 papes. By Ezra M. Hunt, M. D. Pager, 25 cents; cloth, 60 cents.

"On Alcohol." 12 mo, 190 pages. Paper covers, 50 cents; cloth, $1. By Benjamin W. Richardson, M. A., M. D., F. R. S., of London.

"The Medical Use of Alcohol." 12 mo, 96 pages. Paper, 25 cents; cloth, 60 cents. By James Edmunds, M. D., of London.

Sent by mail, post paid, on receipt of price. Address, J. N. STEARNS, Publishing Agent, 58 Reade St., New York.

IV.

PRACTICAL FACTS AND MEDICAL ARGUMENTS.

HUNT.

Dr. Hunt, to whom I introduced the reader in my last number, says :

"Science, at least, has failed to indicate how alcohol in any one way aids assimilation. Just so has exact practice failed, and testimony rests too much on a general impression and clinical belief. This, though worthy of respectful consideration, recent investigation shows to be suspicious for want of accuracy of evidence. We need clinically tabulated and classified results from which sources of error are eliminated on which to base any extended use of alcoholics for medicines. Such expressions as that it "bridges over weakness,' 'assists assimilation,' 'acts as a quick nutrient,' etc., can by no means pass as axiomatic in the face of the fact that they do not stand the test of dietary studies, and are not accepted by many of the most advanced professional thinkers and clinicians of our day."

* * * * * * * *

"In all Chronic Diseases, the place of alcohol, as a remedy, is, by quite general professional consent, still more restricted.

"The poor inebriate no longer needs to be assured that a hair of the dog that bit him can avail to cure the bite. Few would now say with Anstie that alcohol is 'good to prevent epilepsy;' that it is the best treatment for the convulsions of teething; the sovereign remedy in neuralgia, the cure-all for dyspepsia, and the eradicator of tubercle in phthisis.

"Facts of pathology, as to brain, and nerves, and stomach, and lungs. have of late come in upon us too rapidly for this. Fatty and fibroid degenerations in every organ of secretion, warn us as to the serious import of the embarrassments which it is the normal tendency of alcohol to initiate and confirm."

* * * * * * * *

"The dividing line in medicine, even between use and abuse, is so zigzag and invisible that common mortals, in groping for it, generally stumble beyond it, and the delicate perception of medical art too often fails in the recognition."

* * * * * * * *

"Any medical man who has been in practice for the last quarter of a century, cannot but recognize the wonderful change which has taken place. We have come to understand more thoroughly the laws of alimentation, and to see how much more can be accomplished by nutrients in cases in which stimulants were once the chief reliance."

* * * * * * * *

"'The fashionable plan,' says an advocate for their employment, 'of giving great quantities of strong spirits, is happily dying out, and is being replaced by a more careful practice.'

"In the whole management of lung diseases, with the exception of the few who can always be relied upon to befriend alcohol, other remedies have largely superseded all spirituous liquors. Its employment in stomach disease, once so popular, gets no encouragement, from a careful examination of its local and constitutional effects."

" In candor it must be admitted that many eminent physicians deny the efficacy of alcohol in the treatment of any kind of disease, and some assert that it is worse than useless."

*   *   *   *   *   *   *   *

"Abundance of opinion can be found both in adulation and condemnation, but it is very noticeable that those who feel themselves bound to speak in accord with the physiology of function, and the pathology of organic changes, and those whose experience is such as has derived clinical observation of that looseness which must occur where alcohol is administered amid manifold nutrients and medicines, are expressing their views with far more doubt as to the efficiency of alcoholics."

*   *   *   *   *   *   *   *

" We can see how the normal expenditure of force increases progressive metamorphosis. We can meet the demand not by giving doubtful liquids, but by such foods as by quick digestion or rapid assimilation supply the want. In disease we are fast finding out that the demand created by accelerated waste is of the same nature, and that such foods become the real medicines. If change of tissue goes on so rapidly as to exceed the limits of conservative waste, we may also begin to study how to make the given amount of food go further, or to make up for weakened heart-action. But this is to be done by sedation, by the recumbent posture, by reduction of temperature through unquestionable methods, rather than by the use of a medicine claimed to retard change in an inexplicable way, and known in its physiological action to entail functional defects and organic lesions such as never attach to water, quinine, phosphorous food, or to various direct sedatives.

*   *   *   *   *   *

" Whatever may have been the preconceived views of physicians, we believe any one who will candidly sit down and study the leading authorities on materia medica, and therapeutics, and the practice of medicine, and by their side study the details of chemical physiological investigation, and the methods of general medicinal use, will be satisfied that the therapy of alcoholics needs to be carefully reviewed from a strictly dietetic and medicinal stand-point.

" While on the one hand it is alleged that the prejudices of reformers in the interests of abstinence may lead them to extremes, we have in various ways evidence that traditional and popular beliefs, and the forces of habit and authorized practice handed down by mere weight of general authority, need careful reviewing by the light of those more exact methods of test and of observation, which are now the aim and tendency both of our science and art.

"If we are to shut out the testimony of the devotees of total abstinence on an assumption of bias, we must also shut out all those who themselves use alcoholic drinks in any form, and leave the unprejudiced investigation of the question to those physicians who are not identified with temperance movements on the one hand, and on the other are not under the unsuspected influence of that prejudice which the self-joyment of a daily glass of wine is equally apt to induce."

*   *   *   *   *   *   *   *

"Our preconceived notions must not lead us to attribute to alcoholics properties which neither science nor art can prove.   Unable to ascertain food-value or medical-value according to the usual rules of evidence, we must not imagine evidence. If the article used were inert, the case would be different and the assertion of food or medicinal-values of little practical import. But the opposite is too severely and intensely true as to the material in hand.

"The capacity of the alcoholics for impairment of functions and the initiation and promotion of organic lesions in vital parts is unsurpassed by any record in the whole range of medicine. The facts as to this are so indisputable, and so far granted by the profession, as to be no longer debatable. Changes in stomach and liver, in kidneys and lungs, in the blood-vessels to the minutest capillary, and in the blood to the smallest red and white blood disc disturbances of secretion, fibroid and fatty degenerations in almost every organ, impairment of muscular power, impressions so profound on both nervous systems as to be often toxic—these and such as these are the oft manifested results. And these are not confined to those called intemperate.

"We are aware that '*when used in excess*' is the cylinder escapement for all this, but with facts drawn not from intemperance, but so-called moderate use, with the facts as to the physiological effect on man and animals of doses not toxic; with its tendency to evil, and only evil, and that continually, the burden of proof of its medicinal value lies entirely with those who advocate it. When practical medicine tells us that three-quarters of all diseases in adults who drink at all, are caused thereby, and when pathology shows 'its greatly predominating action to be that of a neurotic,' even where its general effects are not so obvious, we may well watch it with a careful eye. The practitioner needs to respond with incontestable evidence of a value which rigid science pronounces untenable, and which variable experience has not established.

"When the wailing cry of evil to society reaches us, high moral obligations require us to make out a clear necessity of use, or else ignore the article. If there is doubt, society in this case is entitled to the benefit of the doubt.

"The medical, the pathological, the social, the moral questions are so imminent and urgent, so critical and crucial, that it is right to put each physician in the witness-box, and let him tell how he knows that alcohol is ever a food or ever a remedy. It is right to confront him with the results of manifold experiments, with the facts of skilled observers, with its failure to respond to the tests which estimate real food, and its inability to define its precise sphere as a medicine."

*   *   *   *   *   *   *   *

"It is asking too much of us to be empirical as doctors lest some medico-beverage advocate should stigmatize us as a profession of reformers. We are called upon to vindicate its use as a medicine by the most exhaustive evidence of its curative agency."

GILMAN.

Dr. N. Gilman, of South Deerfield, Massachusetts, says:

" Take a patient reduced low by fever, for instance. Look at the state of the system and the condition of the various functions. Apply sound physiological and pathological principles, and ascertain the wants of the system ; then look at the properties of alcohol, and see if it is capable of supplying them. When reduced low by fever, the vital powers are nearly exhausted by the previous excitement and deficient nutrition. Is stimulation indicated? Does the patient need to have another excitement produced in the system, which will make a still greater draft on his latent nervous energies? Does he not rather require perfect rest and suitable nourishment? Undoubtedly; for nothing else can impart *real permanent* strength, and restore the wasted powers of life. This is so plain that it can be understood by any reflecting person, without any knowledge of physiology. When the mass of the people, who have no medical education, shall get their eyes open, and look into this subject for themselves, some of our learned craft will be ashamed of their own stupidity.

" We will next look at alcohol, and learn its nature; then determine whether it imparts any strength to the human body. Alcohol, in all its forms, is a mere *stimulant;* or rather, with more propriety, it might be called an *irritant poison*, possessing no tonic or strengthening properties whatever. The digestive organs have no power to change it, or extract from it any nourishing principle. Without undergoing any change, except what is produced by dilution, it is taken up by the absorbents, carried into the blood, and goes the rounds of the circulation. Thus every organ and tissue of the body has an irritating poison brought into actual contact with it. This must be expelled without delay, or their vitality is endangered. An additional task is thus imposed upon the vital organs. The apparent increase of strength is nothing more than the latent nervous energies, aroused for the sole purpose of driving out this enemy from the body. When this task is over there is still greater exhaustion. Nothing has been gained by the operation, but a positive loss has been sustained."

Then, after quoting Dr. Carpenter, wherein he shows that alcohol disturbs the vital functions by interfering with nutrition, by coagulating the soluble albumen by preventing the decarbonization of the blood, etc., Dr. Gilman continues:

" The injury arising from this source is proportionate

to the quantity used. In health no appreciable effect might be produced by the small quantities administered in sickness; yet we may safely infer that when the system is so much prostrated that the lungs can, with great difficulty, so far purify the blood, as to enable it to stimulate the heart and brain to action, a very minute quantity of alcohol, by imposing an additional task, may cause a fatal result. The physician who prescribes alcohol under such circumstances, thwarts his own purpose. It has long since been known that it never imparts any new strength, but only makes a draft on what one already possesses. As in health, so in sickness, it is never capable of affording any other strength than is imparted by the lash to the jaded horse.

"This being the case, it would seem to be self-evident that it can, in no case of prostration from fevers, or any other debilitating causes, facilitate recovery. On the contrary, it must hasten death, when the nervous energies are too much exhausted to allow of the recovery without stimulation, and actually *cause* a fatal termination, when the vital powers are barely sufficient to keep up the action of the heart till they can be invigorated by rest and nutrition. It is only in cases where the patient has more strength than he actually *needs*, that it would be safe to stimulate with alcohol. The physician who prescribes port wine, or any other alcoholic stimulant in such cases, does not understand the difference between stimulation and nutrition, consequently he fails to prescribe scientifically or successfully. A patient thus reduced may be compared to a lamp with the oil so nearly exhausted as to present but a slight flickering blaze. The gentlest motion or breath of air will extinguish it. It will burn for hours if not disturbed; yet, if you pick up the wick, a momentary flame is produced, and then entirely disappears. If you had carefully filled the lamp with oil, the flame would have been *permanently revived.*

"So much for theory; now for practice. A person is sick of fever, a crisis takes place at the proper time, the patient is convalescent, and the doctor recommends a little wine to strengthen him. Under its use the patient feels better, an appetite is excited prematurely, and indulged too freely. He grows worse, and

16

is soon apprised by his physician that ' he has been imprudent in eating, and caused a relapse of the fever.' Another has typhoid fever, is very feeble, and wine is resorted to, for the purpose of keeping up the strength. The vital powers are rallied, and strong hopes are entertained of his recovery. But the next day, perhaps, an inflammation is developed in the brain, lungs, or abdominal viscera, and the symptoms become alarming. The doctor is summoned, and assures the friends that ' another fever has set in, and he fears it will go hard with the patient.'

"It may be laid down as a rule, that if alcoholic liquors relieve, or seem to cure one disease, they cause some other, as bad or worse. The pleasurable feelings resulting from the stimulation lull all suspicion of the mischief going on, which is usually referred to the patient having ' taken cold or eaten something to hurt him,' or, as not unfrequently happens, that modern scapegoat, *Calomel*, is obliged to bear away all the sin and reproach of this deleterious article. The necessity of stimulants, in such cases, is not so great as is generally supposed. The patient is not always dying when the pulse becomes very feeble and intermittent. This is no very uncommon occurrence when the excitement of fever is gone. If there are latent nervous energies, nature will call them into action; if there are none, stimulants will have no effect."

In the above, Dr. Gilman has given us, very compactly : science, experience, and argument—altogether entirely conclusive of this question.

TRALL.

The late Dr. R. T. Trall was a regularly educated Allopathic physician, and he practiced the alcoholic system of medication for many years. But being a man who did his own thinking, he became convinced by his own practice that much of the medical practice of the schools was radically wrong, and became a convert to the hygienic treatment of sick people, and the latter years of his life were devoted to the advocacy and practice of that system. And now I will let him speak for himself as to alcoholic medication in fevers :

"I have tested this question of stimulation both ways. For many years after graduating as an M. D. I prescribed alcoholic stimulants in 'low fevers and cases of debility.' I lost about the usual proportion of patients; that is to say, of mild cases, one in fifteen or twenty, and of severe cases, one in four or five. In due time I became skeptical as to the benefit of stimulants, used them less, and had better success. Finally I came to the same conclusion that Sir John Forbes, M. D., F. R. S., arrived at by a somewhat different process of reasoning, viz., that 'more patients recover in spite of the medicine than with its assistance.' It is now more than fifteen years since I prescribed a particle of stimulus of any kind, and although I have treated hundreds of cases of all the febrile diseases incident to New York and its vicinity, including measles, scarlatina, erysipelas, small-pox, remittent, typhus, typhoid, congestive and ship fevers, pneumonia, influenza, diphtheria, childbed fever, dysentery, etc., etc., I have not lost one. And this statement I have repeatedly published in this city, where the facts, if otherwise than as I represent, can be easily ascertained."

The above statement is perfectly reliable, for Dr. Trall was a man well known in New York. And many other physicians have testified to the same effect.

EDMUNDS.

The distinguished Dr. Edmunds, of London, referred to in my last number, says :

"I believe, in cases of sickness, the last thing you want is to disguise the symptoms—to merely fool the patient; that if alcohol were a stimulant, that is not the sort of thing you would want to give to a man when exhausted from fever. If your horse is exhausted, do you want to give him food, or would you give him rest and food ? So, if your patient is exhausted by any serious disease, surely it would be the more rational thing to let him rest quietly, to save his strength, and in every possible way to take care to give him such food as will be easily absorbed through the digestive apparatus and keep the ebbing life in the man. Well, those are the considerations, ladies and gentlemen, which I would submit to you as an answer to the question so pertinently put by our chairman here to-night, Dr. Parker. And when we come to take up specific diseases, I will consider that disease which we know is produced by alcohol—delirium tremens. It is a disease not unknown on this side of the Atlantic; certainly, it is not unknown to us in England. What is the theory ? The notion is to cure the man by a hair of the dog that bit him. I do not know whether that commends itself to you as a reasonable proposition or as a reasonable theory of curing a man.''

*　　*　　*　　*　　*　　*　　*　　*

"The theory is with very many eminent physicians, to whose opinion I should defer with the greatest possible respect, although I should strenuously argue against it from my own theory and experience—the theory is that you should let them down gradually; that you should go on and give them spirit. We have had many eminent men on our side of the Atlantic who have given these patients enormous doses of spirits. Suppose one of us had an affectionate friend who for many weeks had been putting poison in our coffee, and at last we found ourselves getting ill, and the ordinary symptoms of arsenical poisoning coming on. Would you think it the proper thing to go on giving it to him, or would you stop the arsenic at once ? I submit, you would have it stopped all at once. So, I maintain, when you have a man in a state of delirium tremens, you should stop giving him that substance which poisons his nervous system, and has contributed to bring about that state out of which the exhausted condition of the mind comes. I submit that is an ordinary common-sense position. I would tell you this also: that we have found, in looking into the statistics of delirium tremens treated in the old way, that the mortality was very great; and while I have gone through all those phases of treatment when younger, and I thought, immensely cleverer, I have come to the conclusion that the use of spirits in the case of delirium tremens does nothing but worsen the patient, and probably hasten his death.

"I now, without the slightest hesitation, in every case, should immediately stop the spirit; and I find that very few cases of delirium tremens that I have are fatal, provided I can have a responsible nurse or a resolute wife who will stop the miserable patient from getting out or sending a servant for a bottle of brandy, which he might have under his pillow and drink on the sly."

*　　*　　*　　*　　*　　*　　*　　*

"The physiological laws by which vitality is conserved and maintained, are precisely the same in the essence, whether one is sick or whether one is well."

*　　*　　*　　*　　*　　*　　*　　*

"I wish to submit very strongly that, when a lady is suffering excessive strain—we will say she has to provide for the wants of an infant, and she is told by her mother perhaps, or lady friend, that she must take a little stout two or three times a day, must take a glass of wine or a little spirit—I wish to submit to you very clearly and positively that the same law must come in when you want simply to maintain health in the most robust and vigorous person."

That is to say, if alcohol is good to restore the strength of a weak person, it is also good to maintain the strength of a vigorous person.

In closing this chapter, therefore, I think we may safely conclude that the science of this question, as given in my last number, will always be held good in practice.

V.

THE OTHER SIDE CONSIDERED—THE PRINCIPAL ERROR.

The fundamental error upon which the alcoholic practice of medicine has hitherto rested is that alcohol is a heat-producing food, and therefore a

force or strength-giving material.   After long con-
troversies on that question, the researches and experiments of Dr. Anstie seemed to establish the
fact that alcohol is not all eliminated from the human body in its natural state, but that a portion of
it is somehow consumed or decomposed in the
body, from which it was inferred that it is respira-
tory food, oxygenated or burned, and gives up
heat and force to the system, which appears quite
reasonable.   But after that, and quite recently, the
distinguished Dr. Richardson, for the "British
Association for the Advancement of Science," instituted and executed a careful and elaborate series of experiments by which it was proven to actual certainty that alcohol *diminishes the heat of
the human body, and also diminishes the muscular
power*, as stated in my third number of this series.

All this seems to be unknown to the generality
of practitioners.   At any rate it is unheeded, and
they are practicing upon the old theory of alcohol
as a heat and force-producing agent.

STIMULATION AND EXERCISE.

A distinguished writer of the other side speaks
of the "beneficial agency of a stimulus (alcohol)
which is so very analogous to the stimulus of a
sharp mountain walk."

Now, I think that no doctor would prescribe a
sharp mountain walk, or any other severely fatigu-
ing exertion, for a patient exhausted with fever,
or in any other case, for the purpose of imparting

strength. Intense physical exertion exhausts the vital powers, and it is well said that the stimulus of alcohol is analogous to a sharp mountain walk; for alcohol exhausts the vital powers too. Both excite an abnormal action of the vital organs; in the one case to get rid of the alcohol, in the other to sustain such extraordinary outward exertion: both consuming an extra amount of tissue—in other words, vitality. Not to say that physical exercise is not healthful; it is. A certain amount of it is indispensable, ordinarily, to keep the body from dying of torpor—laziness. The physical system is so constituted that the necessity that is upon us of physical labor to supply the wants of the body, carries with it the corelative necessity of a certain amount of physical exertion to maintain the body in health. And to a healthy, vigorous person, I think a considerably severe and continuous labor year after year, even to every day fatigue, so long as none of the physical powers are really overstrained and overtaxed, and with reasonable periodical rest, is not unhealthful—it only requires a greater amount of alimentation to replenish the excessive waste of tissue and keep up the vitality. But such excessive exertion is never necessary to health; and much less is very *tiresome stimulating* exercise, such as excites unnatural action of the vital powers—as a brisk mountain walk—promotive of strength or recuperation in a debilitated patient. The benefit of exercise—for sick or well—is not from that kind of exercise. In case of very low vitality, where the life is in danger of going out, absolute quiet is indispensable. Any exertion to stimulate the system as aforesaid is extremely hazardous. And the doctors will persist in giving alcohol to do exactly the thing that they will not permit to be done by exertion.

We know that reasonable exercise is essential to recovery in many chronic diseases, just as it is to maintain health in a healthy person; but I think the physiological rule is that the exercise must not be such as to tire or stimulate. That is not what it is for. Its purpose is to keep the vital organs from stagnation and clog, so as to keep up their natural action, but not beyond that. And this, alcohol does not do. Its effect is all abnormal, stimulating, exhausting.

Dr. Hunt, from whom I have heretofore quoted, sums up this matter as follows:

"Now, recollect, food is that which puts strength into a man, and stimulant is that which gets strength out of a man; so that when you want to use stimulants, recollect that you are using that which will exhaust the last particles of strength with a facility with which your body otherwise would not part with them."

Dr. Trall puts it in this way:

"The system spends its force to get rid of the alcohol, but never derives any force from the alcohol."

PARKER DOES NOT KNOW HOW TO DO WITHOUT ALCOHOL.

Dr. Willard Parker, after writing all that I

quoted from him in my third number of this series, from which I copy as follows :

" Distilled liquor is never, under any circumstances, a food ; adds nothing to the substance of the body ; is never digested ; adds nothing to the forces of the body ; it weakens force ; acts as an irritant, and so diminishes force by compelling the body to put forth efforts to get rid of the intruder ; is not a fuel and is not burned ; does not add to the real warmth of the body, but unnaturally lowers it ; overworks the vital organs ; passes into the blood undigested and acts disastrously upon the blood corpuscles, and impairs their vitality and destroys their usefulness ; hastens the approach of death ; poisons the blood, poisons the whole system and affects every vital organ with disease."

After all that he says :

"There is a use for distilled liquor in the human body. It is essential medicine in some forms of disease."

And he gives his reasons—the best reasons that the case admits of, for there is none abler to do it than he. What are they ? He says :

" I am called to visit a person who has suffered some sudden shock by which the heart has been affected and the whole circulation depressed ; his surface is cold and his system collapsed. I put the alcohol into his stomach, and in one minute and a half it rouses the exhausted system, spurs it to an unwonted activity and thus enables it to spring the chasm into which it would otherwise have fallen."

This is ingenious. It looks plausible. But it will not stand the test of science and common-sense. Let us see. The Dr. says his patient's system is exhausted. That is, the vital forces are diminished so that there is danger that they will go out entirely. He is in the same condition as if the vitality were impaired in any other way.

What is wanted is to prevent it from running lower, or as little lower as possible, and to recuperate it. Now what I want to know is, how alcohol in the stomach can do this, by "rousing the exhausted system and spurring it to an unwonted activity," when as the Dr. says "it diminishes force by compelling the body to put forth efforts in order to get rid of the intruder, overworks the vital organs, and impairs vitality;" which is simply exhausting, wasting the life, and increasing the chances of a fatal termination.

But how about the chasm that Dr. Parker uses alcohol to enable the patient to spring over instead of falling into it? Is there any such thing in the case of a sick man, as if a man were in a position that he must leap over a literal chasm or fall into it and lose his life, and when a stimulant to excite all the vital forces to unnatural action for the moment, even at the expense of unnatural depression afterwards, would undoubtedly be useful. Is this the case with the sick? I guess not. When the patient takes alcohol does it lift him over a chasm? I guess not. What does it do? Let Dr. Parker answer. He says:

"Alcohol introduced into the body acts as an irritant in the manner in which a grain of sand acts upon the eye. The nerves of the stomach, and of the heart, and of all the vital organs are thrown into a state of excitement; the rapidity of the circulation is increased," etc. What for? to lift over a chasm? No. "To get rid of the intruder" as the Dr. says; *i. e.* the alcohol, and that is all.

No, Dr. Parker's chasm is a mere figure of speech. There is nothing analogous to it in case of the sick. There is no chasm to spring over, for which an unnatural exertion of the remaining vital forces is necessary? All that is wanted is to keep them in motion; and to this end all that are left must be economized, and not wasted on the unnecessary work of expelling an intruder that is guilty of all the bad things that Dr. Parker charges alcohol with.

It requires no medical or physiological knowledge to understand that the abnormal action of the vital powers of a debilitated patient, exhausted from whatever cause, cannot increase those powers, or save them from further exhaustion. Again Dr. Parker says:

"I do not know how I could treat ship fever without distilled liquor. When my poor patient lies in an utterly exhausted condition, his system without vitality sufficient to enable him to digest and assimilate his food, I give him a spoonful of alcohol with milk, and under the stimulus of the alcohol the stomach will digest, and the system will assimilate the milk."

This is really wonderful, in connection with the learned doctor's theories as to the effects of alcohol. Let us see. The patient's "system is without vitality sufficient to digest and assimilate his food." Alcohol does not impart any vitality or increase it in any way, but impairs and diminishes it—so the

Dr. says.   We all know that alcohol does not digest food.   Its nature is to preserve it in its natural
state.   The stimulus of the alcohol merely excites
all the vital organs to unnatural action to expel
the alcohol—so the Dr. says.   Now, the patient,
without sufficient vitality to digest and assimilate
milk, a spoonful of alcohol, without increasing the
vitality, will enable him to digest the milk, and do
the extra work of expelling the alcohol to boot!
This is one of the mysteries of alcoholic medication.   To the common mind it would seem that if
a patient is unable to digest food for want of sufficient vitality, nothing less than an increase of
vitality can enable him to do so ; for the vitality
must do the work.

But alcohol is an aid to digestion in general, the
Dr. thinks, but is not sure of it.   He says :

"If taken with food, it *may* be an aid to digestion ;
if taken before food it prevents digestion."

He is sure it prevents digestion when put into
an empty stomach, by coagulating and destroying
the pepsin, and with that the power of digestion,
because the operation has been seen, in the case of
a man who had an opening in the stomach so that
the operations within could be seen. But he
guesses at the other side.   He *thinks* it may be an
aid to digestion when taken with food.   This is
another curiosity of alcoholic medication.   Taken
before food it destroys the digestive power ; taken
with food it *may* aid digestion.   How it can have

such opposite effects merely in consequence of the *time* of taking it, how it can aid digestion, when there is no digestive power in it—its nature being to preserve food intact—or how " a poison dangerous and deadly," as the Dr. says it is, which all the forces of the body are at once excited to violent action to expel as an enemy, and to drive out from the stomach and into the circulation on its way out of the body in one minute and a half, as the Dr. says they do, how these things can be is entirely unaccountable.

On the whole, Dr. Parker's reasons for alcoholic medication are only excuses for a barbarous practice that he seems to think must be kept up because he found it in the books, and has kept it up all his life, and because, as he says, he knows no other way ; excuses that are clearly antagonistic to all the science of alcohol, and its effects upon the human organism, as given by himself and well established by the scientific world.

EDMUNDS, RICHARDSON AND HUNT.

Our scientific friends by whom we have been so largely instructed in the science of this matter, and against the use of alcohol as a medicine—Drs. Edmunds, Richardson and Hunt—are not yet entirely satisfied that alcohol *may* not be useful in some cases. They do not say it is, but they expressly leave the question open, so far as their science has not foreclosed it. For instance, Dr. Edmunds says :

"I cannot but believe that alcohol also, potent drug as it is, *may* be useful in many cases of disease; but the cases in which I use it in may own practice, I confess, become less and less frequent every day. And I should feel that I lost very little were I deprived of it—indeed, I almost think that if mercury and many other remedies that are used so freely now were used less freely the practice of medicine would be more successful than it has hitherto been."

Dr. Richardson says:

"*I am not going to say* that occasions do not arise when an enfeebled or fainting heart is temporarily relieved by the relaxation of the vessels which alcohol, on its diffusion through the blood, induces."

Dr. Hunt says:

"Yet in some sudden attacks of faintness, as resulting from failure of heart-action, or some profound nervous impression conveyed to the heart, alcohol *may* cause a reaction, and if no other article is at hand, *may* be never so good as a medicine in such an emergency."

And this is all that is left of alcohol as a medicine, according to these eminent scientists and physicians. What does it amount to? Only that they are entirely unprejudiced, and give to alcohol the benefit of the doubt—leaving the question open where it is not absolutely closed against alcohol. I might rest here, but let us examine these reservations. Dr. Edmunds thinks it "*may* be useful in many cases," but his own experience is teaching him that the science of the matter, that he has given us, is correct, and so he is using alcohol less and less every day. Certainly he cannot hold out to use it at all very long at that rate.

Drs. Richardson and Hunt may well leave it problematical whether alcohol can be beneficial in fainting. Fainting is a deficiency of blood to the brain, inducing unconsciousness—unequal circulation; that is all. Alcohol accelerates the heart's action and the circulation, but it is difficult to see how it can equalize the circulation, inasmuch as its tendency is to pervade all parts of the system alike. And it is also difficult to see how "the relaxation of the vessels which alcohol induces" can equalize the circulation.

ALCOHOL A FORCE—BARTHOLOW.

A distinguished medical practitioner of my acquaintance pins his faith in alcohol upon the following from Bartholow's Materia Medica:

"At present the weight of authority and the deductions of experiment are in favor of that view which maintains that, within certain limits (one ounce to one and a half ounce of absolute alcohol to a healthy man), alcohol is oxidized and destroyed in the organism, and yields up force which is applied as nervous, muscular, and gland force."

And I think this is now the principal reliance of the alcoholic medical practitioners. But they are behind the times. This theory, long in dispute, and always contradicted by the obvious manifestations of alcohol, has been entirely exploded by the experiments of Dr. Richardson, as stated in my third number, wherein he has demonstrated to absolute certainty that alcohol never, under any circumstances, yields up force in the human body.

And Dr. Willard Parker, of the New York College of Physicians, has adopted that view. He says:

"Distilled liquor is never, under any circumstances, a food. It adds nothing to the substance of the body. It is never digested. *It adds nothing to the forces of the body.* On the contrary, *it weakens force.* It acts as an irritant; and so diminishes force by compelling the body to put forth efforts in order to get rid of the intruder."

*   *   *   *   *   *   *   *   *

"Poisoning the blood, alcohol poisons the whole system, and affects with disease every vital organ—the lungs, the liver, the kidneys, the stomach."

It may be added that it is quite a reckless assertion to say that an irritant poison—as alcohol is admitted by the profession to be—can be a useful food, that it can be assimilated, converted into living tissue, constituting life and vital force. It cannot be. It is a contradiction. Poison is inimical to life. Food is exactly the opposite. It is what life is made of. There never was a more absurd theory than that poison can have any vital force-giving quality in it.

SPECIAL CASES.

But almost every one has a special case where alcohol has been good. My friend, appearances are delusive in this matter. And your preconceived opinion in favor of alcoholic medicine constitutes more than half of your faith in its virtue. You administer the alcohol; if the patient gets well you attribute the cure to the alcohol, of course, without inquiry whether the recovery was not in spite of the alcohol instead of by virtue of it. Or if the patient dies, you do not ask yourself whether the alcohol killed or he died in spite of a remedial power in the alcohol. The fact is that we are so indoctrinated in the theory that alcohol is good for sick people, that the scientific facts in relation to its effects on the living organism are entirely lost sight of. Although, as Dr. Willard Parker says, "*it hastens the approach of death*," yet we keep on using it, and when it kills, we shut our eyes to the facts of its deadly nature, especially in its effects upon a small remaining fraction of vitality, as I have explained it in these papers, and solace ourselves with the reflection that "all has been done that science could suggest."

But, more specifically : a friend tells me that a lady was run down with puerperal fever, the system in a state of collapse, the surface getting cold. A little brandy was administered internally, the surface was briskly rubbed with alcohol, and she came up. Now the science of this matter, as given by Dr. Willard Parker, is that this patient would have gotten up the easier without the alcohol; for he says that when taken internally it does not impart any heat, but exhausts it, especially from the surface, and we know that when applied to the surface its rapid evaporation abstracts the heat of the body; and in its effects upon the system in general, its only result is to further exhaust—use up—the scant vitality, as heretofore shown from Dr. Parker's and others' writings, and thus further endanger the life. "But the patient at once improved and finally recovered, and so we

17

know that the alcohol was good;" I will be
answered, No, you don't know that. Nature does
the curing, and how can you know that she can
more easily restore the patient after the excitement
and abnormal action of all the vital powers to
expel the alcohol and to overcome the blood poisoning that the alcohol produces, thus largely
wasting the slender stock of vitality, than to
simply restore the patient without that extra
work?

And then, I have a case exactly in point by
which I know. Thirty-six years ago I had a boy
all run down with fever, in a state of collapse, the
surface getting cold. No alcohol or other stimulant was used, but I applied artificial heat by hot
blankets and rubbing. He speedily revived and
got up without alcohol. And in my friend's case
above stated, if anything was any aid to nature, it
was the rubbing to excite the circulation to the
surface, and the patient got well in spite of the
obstruction of the alcohol. Another case : A lady
had been long in a debilitated condition; had
been "taking everything," as the saying is—quinine, and all the other approved "building up"
medicines, and all to no purpose. Finally she
abandoned all other medicines and went down to a
little ale, and then she immediately improved and
got well. Now the secret of this cure is very
plain. The abandonment of the more powerful
drugs is what did it; and without the ale she

would have done still better. But the ale was so slight a damage that the remaining vitality was able to overcome it and restore the patient, too, immediately.

A BEER ARGUMENT.

A very curious argument was lately promulgated by a distinguished professor in a medical college and published in a paper of large circulation, in favor of the use of *fermented* alcoholic liquors, as medicine and as beverage.

He says that there are two kinds of alcohol— fermented alcohol and distilled alcohol. He does not tell us what the difference is, only that there is a scientific, a very important, a fundamental difference between fermented and distilled liquors, and that fermentation is the work of Omnipotence, and distillation is the work of man or the devil; *ergo* fermented liquors are good for people to drink ; that is, as he says, while " a man can get foolish on it, he is not very likely to get very drunk ;" but distilled liquor "is the poison ; this is what does the harm."

He tells us also that God makes the fermented liquors, and we are enjoined by the Bible to use all things in moderation ; therefore we must use fermented liquors.

And in illustration of his theory he says that nitrogen, pure, is poisonous. It is death to breathe it for a short time. But mixed with oxygen in atmospheric air it is necessary to life. And so, alcohol, in a concentrated—distilled—state, is poisonous, while in a diluted state—fermented liquors—it is useful and necessary. And, "all milk has sugar in it; and in the milk it is useful; God put it there for a purpose. But if we were to take the sugar out of the milk, by a process analogous to distillation, and feed our children on that, they would die in three weeks' time. So it is when we take the alcohol out of the wine or cider, and mix it with something else to give it a flavor—juniper berries or the like; taken out of the article in which God put it, and used alone, it becomes destructive." But for the high source of these theories, they would seem to be too obviously unsound to require any notice. But great names are something in a bad cause, and so I will briefly review them.

His first proposition reverses all the science and all the experience of the world as to the nature of alcohol. It is produced by the vinous fermentation and in no other way. There is no difference between alcohol in any fermented mass and alcohol after it is distilled. The process of distillation does not make any chemical or scientific changes in alcohol—always previously produced by the vinous fermentation—and no change whatever, save in concentration, and separation from the coarser matter of the fermented mass. Distillation is simply the conversion of the alcohol existing in fermented liquors into vapor, driving it off and condensing it into liquid. That is all. There is nothing chemical, nothing mysterious about it. Take a pint of wine; distill the alcohol out of it, and then we call the alcohol part of it brandy. That brandy contains exactly the same alcohol that the wine did. It contains the same constituent elements, and in the same proportions. It contains exactly the same poison that the pint of wine did —no more, no less. Let a man drink all of that brandy, and it will have exactly the same drunk-making power, and the same poisoning power upon him that a pint of that same kind of wine would have; no more, no less. No chemist or well informed physician, except the said Professor will dispute this.

And then he is mistaken about the vinous fermentation being the work of Omnipotence. If a drop of alcohol was ever produced by the natural decay of any fruits, I am sure that no fermented alcoholic liquor was ever produced so that it could be gathered up. Vinous fermentation is the work of Omnipotence, it is true, under certain conditions that must be provided by man; *i. e.* there must be a weak solution of saccharine matter, air, and a certain degree of heat. With them provided by man, Omnipotence does the rest; just as in distilling. Given, a fermented liquor, a certain degree of heat, and an apparatus to catch the product, and then Omnipotence does the distilling. It drives off the concentrated liquor from the diluted mass. So that the process of distillation is about the same work of Omnipotence as is that of fermentation. To produce any tangible result they both require the aid of man.

And then the learned Professor's argument that fermented liquors should be used because God made them—if it were true that He does make them—is too thin. Suppose that God does make fermented liquors, in fruits or otherwise, He does also make the rattlesnake's virus, the saliva of the mad dog, the upas tree, and a thousand other things in vegetable, animal and mineral kingdoms, that are deleterious to human life, and which nobody would think of using because God makes them!

Secondly : this illustration of nitrogen is not in point. There is no analogy between the two cases. It is not any poison in pure nitrogen that will kill by breathing it. It is the want of oxygen that kills. Put a man in a vacuum and he will die just as quickly as he would in nitrogen gas, and certainly there is no poison in vacuum. And so, by excluding oxygen from the lungs in any other way, as by water, by a cord around the neck, or otherwise, death ensues in a very few minutes, not from any poison, but from the absence of oxygen in the lungs. To compare these processes with concentrated and diluted poison is only sophistry. If a man breathe pure nitrogen he excludes another gas that is indispensable to life—that is what kills. If a man takes pure alcohol, or diluted alcohol, into the stomach, he does not thereby exclude anything that is necessary to life. He may have all other needful things, and the alcohol may kill him; and in any event it poisons him. And then, supposing that nitrogen were a poison, and that by diluting it, it is rendered inert not only, but useful and necessary, as the doctor says; to say that all other poisons are rendered useful by dilution because that one is, is presuming a good deal upon the reader's gullibility. Arsenic, strychnine, or any other poison except alcohol, is not rendered inert by mere dilution; and it requires a vast amount of cheek in any man, however eminent, to ask the people to ignore their own senses, and reverse their previous modes of thinking, by believing that the poison of alcohol is extinguished by mere dilution, without a why or a wherefore, save that a learned doctor says so, and supports his say so by the fact that nitrogen gas alone will not support life, while a mixture of that and oxygen will!

Thirdly: This milk argument, that a child can live on milk, but on sugar of milk alone it would starve for want of suitable nourishment; therefore the poison of alcohol is extinguished by mere dilution needs no answer.

VI.

CONCLUSION.

The conclusion of the whole matter is that there is no really medical science authorizing the use of alcohol in any case whatever—medical science is entirely the other way.

And yet the great multitude of doctors go on with their alcoholic medication—alcoholizing sick people to keep them up, as they call it, and we often hear of dying patients being kept alive for days by alcoholic stimulants! And all this without any scientific pathological reason, and against the facts well established by all anti-alcoholic practitioners; all this without a why or a wherefore only that their books contain the prescriptions, and they are sustained by such

QUEER ARGUMENT

as was used a few years ago by Professor Alonzó Clark, of the New York College of Physicians and Surgeons, who stated, in a lecture to his medical class, that brandy had been the means of saving the lives of many typhus fever patients, and that without it they surely would have died. After the lecture he was asked if he had ever treated his patients any other way. He said "No." He was then asked if he had ever known any fever patients treated without stimulants, by others. He replied that he never had; but he knew they would die if they did not have the brandy.

That is all that is to be said on that side. All their patients are alcoholized. Some of them get well; *ergo* the alcohol cures them. How do they know? I say they get well in spite of the alcohol,

and the alcohol kills many of those that die, and
the facts are abundant to prove it.

COMMON SENSE.

Now let us take this matter in a common-
sense way, and see if we cannot get to the
bottom of the subject. What is death? It is
simply the stoppage of the action of the organs of
the body that constitutes life. And what stops
such action? The complete exhaustion of the forces
of the system that keeps it going, and which we call
vitality. Now I would like to know how alcohol
can keep a patient alive ; keep him up, etc., when
it *diminishes the vitality*, with all other bad effects
that medical science convicts it of. It is a fallacy
—a dangerous fallacy—a murderous fallacy.

WHY IT IS KEPT UP.

Why will the doctors keep up such a practice?
Dr. Edmunds tells us why, as follows :

" There is one difficulty I have in this matter, and
that is that unfortunately the weight of opinion in
the medical profession, I am afraid, appears to be in
favor of using these things as beverages. Well, medical opinion may be resolved into two elements—
elements which any person whose brains are properly
constructed can appraise : first, medical dogma ; and,
secondly, medical science. Now, medical science has
its well-defined scientific facts, and the inferences
which logically attach to those facts. Medical dogma
is something else. What is the history of medical
dogma ? Thirty years ago the fathers of the very
men who now prescribe brandy, and wine, and ale for
almost all the diseases to which we are liable, prescribed what ?' Not brandy, nor wine, nor ale, but
mercury, bleeding, and starving ; and when the old
woman said she would not be able to stand it, and the

doctor replied that he would not take the responsibility of the result of her refusing his prescription, she said she would take the responsibility, and she is a fine old woman now, but would not have been if she had yielded to the persuasions of these eminent gentlemen. They believed conscientiously in this mode of practice. Do not imagine that I am suggesting that the old gentlemen whose pictures we have seen of bleeding their patients had any intention to kill them. There is, however, no doubt about this fact: that they did kill nine patients for every one that they cured. I think you will find that medical dogma is a curse to mankind and a delusion to the profession.

* * * * * *

"As a student in olden time, I dare say I have killed scores of little children by the old-fashioned treatment of tartar emetic and leeching when they had a little cold on their chest. It is quite natural that the young ones should be influenced by the weight of opinion of their elders. Many medical men really have no well-defined belief, but they have seen the old gentlemen from whom they learned their profession do things in a certain way, and they remember what has been taught them at the hospital, and they continue to do the same way without thinking of the matter. You will do them a great deal of good if you follow them up and question them. Ask them why they order you spirit, what is it to do? If you ask your doctor questions, you very often do him service; you call his attention to this matter. My attention was called by a rough-handed total abstainer. I ordered him stout. I said, 'You must take a little beer.' He sat down in my dining-room and said, 'Doctor, I am sure you have a reason for everything. If you can show me it is good for me, I will take it; I have taken nothing for a dozen years, and I am a great deal better without it. What do you think it will do for me?' I had never been cornered in my life in that way. I really found I had no answer; and so you will find your doctors will have no answers for such questions. When they appeal to experience, resting it upon medical dogma, recollect the facts with regard to medical dogma—that medical dogma, as such has never been anything but a delusion and a snare."

WHAT THE TROUBLE IS.

The trouble is that the average doctor does not discriminate between medical dogma and medical science. He sees something written down in a medical book, and he takes that for medical science, whether founded on any ascertained medical facts or not. The old practice of "mercury, bleeding and starving," was not founded on any ascertained facts of curative power—there were no such facts, and so it was not science. And so now; the books are full of alcoholic prescriptions, without any established facts as to their modus operandi in curing; so that it is not science—it is medical dogma —somebody's mere opinions, with nothing to sustain them ; and the ordinary physicians pursue the alcoholic practice because they find it in the books, without further question.

MEDICAL SCIENCE.

But by the discoveries of the most eminent physicians and physiologists of Europe and America, in recent years, we now have a medical science in respect to alcoholic medication.

For example: when a medical writer recommends alcohol to build up an exhausted patient, without founding that prescription on any known fact showing *how* it will build him up, that is not science. But when Dr. Edmunds, or Richardson, tells us that alcohol will not build up the patient, but will be sure to further exhaust him, because of the well-established facts that it is not food in any sense, does not impart heat, and does not in any way increase muscular power, but does really expend and waste the remaining vitality of the patient, more or less, by the abnormal action of all the vital organs to expel the alcohol; and so of all other well-established manifestations of the injurious effects of alcohol, as medicine or otherwise; this is medical science. And this is what the doctors ought to be studying, instead of the medical dogmas of twenty years ago. They ought to keep up with the march of medical science.

NOT FOR TEMPERANCE ONLY.

There are a good many anti-alcoholic medication temperance people who are such merely for the sake of temperance. They believe alcohol to be good for medicine, but not indispensable, because substitutes can be had. And some go so far that when told by their physician that they must die unless they take alcohol, they say they will die then, and die sober. But they do not always die in such cases. But all advanced scientific thinkers on this subject go against it *for the sake of the sick*, as well as for the temperance cause; go against it for its intrinsic and universal badness; go against it because it is murderous *per se*, especially upon sick people; go against it because it is always injurious upon sick or well people, and never useful.

And this theory is sustained by all the science that appertains to the effects of alcohol upon the human machine, as heretofore set out in these papers. And not only so, but the scientific theory is fully sustained in practice. The anti-alcoholic practice does save life, while the opposite does kill; *i. e.* it clearly so appears wherever it has been tried. It is to be admitted that it is difficult to know to a dead certainty what cures a sick man if he gets well, or what kills him if he dies. Take a patient run down with fever; he is alcoholized, and dies. We cannot know for certain whether the alcohol or the disease killed him; or if he gets well we cannot know whether the alcohol cured him or he got well in spite of it. That is to say, we cannot know how this is by an individual case, only as we apply the science of the matter to it, as before stated.

But when we have the testimony of reliable physicians who have had long experience in the alcoholic practice, and also in the opposite practice—hundreds of cases in each—in all kinds of fevers and other diseases, in which alcohol is considered to be especially indispensable—when we have the testimony of such men, that in the former practice they always lost a considerable proportion of their cases, and in the latter they never lose a case when called in reasonable time; if there is anything in the practical application of scientific theory, the proof is as clear as experience can be that alcohol is always bad.

It is entirely clear, therefore, that when temperance doctors and temperance patients reject alco-

hol as medicine, they should not do it with excuses; not merely because it propagates intemperance, and thus does more harm than good ; but
for that and more ; because it always helps to kill
sick people and never helps to cure.

The general adoption of this true temperance
platform would *save thousands of lives* that alcoholic medicine is all the time killing, and start the
temperance cause in a career of advancement that
it never can hope for otherwise.

PART THIRD.

ESSAYS ON LABOR, CAPITAL, MONEY AND WEALTH.

I.—THE TIMES OF 1873–1878.

Contraction not the cause— The cause of the trouble— Useless palliatives— The remedy—Strikes —No class in fault—Lions in the way—Unequal production— The remedy will apply itself— The proof.

1.—CONTRACTION NOT THE CAUSE.

The purpose of these little essays upon the philosophy of the subjects named above is to correct, as sententiously as I can, some of the erroneous theories that always prevail, more or less, with working men, and have obtained especial prominence since 1873.

The substance of this number was written early in 1878—the darkest time of the panic—and I introduce it here as preliminary to the specific discussion of my subjects. I present it as it was written—applicable to that time, as the most eligible way to enforce the economic truths involved.

The greenback inflation philosophy is held out to the people as a panacea for all the financial, industrial and business troubles that the country has been afflicted with for these four years. With a great deal of flourish and superficial reasoning, it is alleged that the panic that broke upon us in 1873 was caused by a contraction of the currency— the lack of sufficient circulating medium to transact the business of the country ; and so it is argued that the cure can only be by supplying that deficiency ; whereas the amount of circulating money of the country was greater in 1873–4 than in the prosperous years of 1870, 1871, and 1872, or any previous year.

I take the following figures from statements made by ex-Speaker Grow to the New York *Tribune*, Jan. 12, 1878 :

The entire circulation was, in

1870.	$681,983,110
1871.	714,260,507
1872.	734,557,162
1873.	746,100,224
1874.	758,139,653

Mr. Grow speaks from the official records; and I think these figures have never been disputed, only in this way : The conversion of the 7-30 bonds and other interest bearing securities into 5-20s is alleged to be a contraction of the currency—counting those securities as circulating money—and so a great contraction is figured out : a proposition that only needs to be stated to refute itself; for if the first named securities were circulating money, the 5-20s into which they were converted are also.

Taking Mr. Grow's figures for true, then, it will be seen at a glance that it is not any lack of money that has caused our troubles. And I propose to show what the real trouble has been.

2—THE CAUSE OF THE TROUBLE.

I think it is evident enough to the most superficial observer that the war of the rebellion, somehow, created the disturbance in the economic relations of the country that superinduced the industrial and business depressions commencing in 1873, and continuing with increasing intensity up to the present time. Let us see if we can ascertain *how*.

For four years all the available energies of the country, on one side and the other, were employed in war, war upon our own soil. A million of able-bodied men, more or less, were engaged in the consumption of the current products of industry, as well as large amounts of fixed capital, and producing no material values. After the temporary industrial depression, caused by the change from peace to war, in 1861, and after the ingenious financial processes of the government had supplied abundant pecuniary means to pay for all the expenses of war, as well as a sound and satisfactory currency for the people, sufficient in volume to carry on the extraordinary amount of business incident to a gigantic war, all the then existing manufacturing and mining industries found themselves fully and profitably employed. And not only so, but the demand was for more and more; giving full employment and high wages to all species of labor,

18

high prices for all the products of agriculture, and large profits to all industrial enterprises.

Those were what we call good times. I think they were really good times to the masses of the people, for everybody could have employment at high rates, not only in money price, but as measured by the necessaries and comforts of life, irrespective of inflated currency and speculative times The provident classes could accumulate largely, the improvident could expend freely upon luxuries, and altogether things went on swimmingly, on the high pressure principle, to the end of the war.

The close of the war in 1865 involved great changes in the manufacturing industries of the country, but no diminution of them, for the time being. The diversion of manufacturing from the production of the material of war to that of commodities adapted to time of peace, was easy. The inordinate demand for all commodities during the war had kept the markets always comparatively bare, and prices high, so that at the change all existing industries kept along in full and profitable employment, and no relapse was caused by the great change from war to peace.

But then, the consumptions of war having ceased, and that large class of consumers having become producers—a large share of them in manufacturing and mining industries, increasing their volume correspondingly—the looked for crash after the war not having come—the usual concomitant of a long course of prosperity, *i. e.* speculation, over-trading, general extravagance, inflated prices, etc., ensued. In fact the people—business men, manufacturers, mechanics, laborers, mining operators, miners, professional men, all, all became intoxicated with the prosperity of the times, and were blind to the fact that that state of things was some time to have an end. The great profits of all manufacturing and mining industries had multiplied those enterprises to an unprecedented extent; everybody forgetting that any of those prospering pursuits could be overdone; forgetting that too much coal, and iron, and cloth, and the hundreds of other products of factories could be produced and put upon the market. For the time being too many working men could not be obtained at mines, at factories, in cities and towns, and on railroads; for the intoxication of inordinate prosperity—whether real or fictitious, it matters not to this discussion—stimulated every variety of industrial enterprise—railroad building, and public and private improvements of every description, as well as the ordinary manufacturing and mining operations.

3.—USELESS PALLIATIVES.

Such an inordinate rush of those industries could not but outrun the current demand for their products. But it went on, year after year, with increasing accumulations of stock, bolstered up with all the expedients that could be devised to ward off the inevitable economical effect of glutted markets, until 1873, when the comparatively trifling event of the failure of a banking house, which had partaken largely of the general speculative mania of the times, pierced the economic bubble that was ready to break on the slightest disturbance in the general monetary affairs of the country. And then, not to be taught by the plainest indications of the pressure of economic law upon the overcrowded industries, and the speculative business of the country, and under the fallacy that the then existing trouble was owing to collateral and transient causes only, and not to the vital fact of the vast overproduction of the manufacturing and mining industries, all the ingenuity and wisdom of the country was for years exhausted to keep all the factories, and mills, and shops, and mines, and railroads, and all their employes in full employment, rather than diminish any of those pursuits, in the vain hope that the same prosperous times were to be restored by a continuance of the same industrial policy that had destroyed them—by the continuous production of so vast quantities of commodities not wanted. In the *vain* hope, I say, for the laws of trade are inexorable. They will have their sway in spite of all expedients that may obstruct them temporarily. An overproduction in any department of industry must break itself down. It has.

And now, here we are, after more than four years of pressure of economic law, pressing harder and harder, flatter and flatter, until the reaction from the unnatural business and industrial activity is complete; yea and more, for as is usual in such times of revulsion, the stagnation and the shrinkage of values have gone beyond the normal standard; and we are told that there are three millions of unemployed working men in the country, for whom it is gravely proposed, by some process of legislation, or some legerdemain of finance, to create employment in the same vocations that they have been forced out of as aforesaid—in the production of commodities that there is no market for, and cannot be. It cannot be done.

4.—THE REMEDY.

And is there no remedy? Is there no work for those people? In this great boasted asylum for the oppressed of all nations, is there a necessity for three millions, or for any other number of willing men to be out of work? Is there such a thing in the philosophy of life as a general overproduction that starves people? Is there any law in nature by which, without any pressure of population upon the limit of the land, there is not work for everybody to do whereby to procure the necessaries of life? Let us see. By the foregoing it is clear that there has been an *unequal* production—too many men employed in everything else but agriculture, and too few in this. The reaction has thrown those surplus men out of employment and it is impossible to devise any way to give them employment in those pursuits, because it is impossible for three men to get full work and good wages to do the work of two.

But while there is no remedy in any inflation scheme, or in any other process to create employment in contravention of the laws of supply and demand, in our vast area of fertile unoccupied lands, always inviting the hand of labor, always offering remunerative employment for indefinite numbers of working men, we have the ready remedy. And until all our vacant lands are occupied and cultivated to the extent of their food producing power, there will always be something for everybody to do, not only for our present population, but for the surplus industrious and worthy population of other lands. There is room for all.

Oh, that is pretty hard, we are told. Poor laboring people cannot get there and get started. Very well, I am not making the law, but only stating it, when I say that some of them *must* go upon land and get their bread and butter out of the soil, or starve. That's the way God has fixed the laws by which these matters *must* be governed. He has spread out, within our reach, His vast expanses of fat lands and invites the needy to go up and take them. They can if they will, and there is no other way to solve this labor problem.

In this great country of unoccupied fertile land, awaiting the hand of industry to produce abundant independence to millions of happy homes, there is not the slightest need, for some hundreds of years yet, of any pressure of labor upon the hired labor market so as to depress wages below a liberal rate. The trouble is in the prevailing passion of young men—old men too—to press upon railroads and towns and cities to sell themselves for hire, instead of scattering out upon the broad expanses of God's green earth and cultivating the soil.

5.—STRIKES.

And in such a time as this, finding the wages too low, and when an abundance of idle men are ready to take the places of the present hired workmen, in all branches of industry, they expect to remedy the trouble by combinations and strikes! As if employers of labor had made all the trouble and could be compelled to cure it; when the fact is that they have suffered no less severely than have the working men. No class of people is exempt. Men who were rich a few years ago find themselves poor to-day—thousands of them. Business men, employers of working men, capitalists, corporations large and small all suffer more or less, unequally it may be, but all are reached by the common malady. Many go under, others struggle along and pull through by the hardest. And it is by all this that the pressure reaches the working men. Many a manufacturing firm, with the hard earnings of a lifetime involved and risked in the carrying of their business successfully through these times, with orders and work running down to the most meagre dimensions, and the prices down to rates unprecedented; many a man of that description who has for many a year given work to numerous working men, would be happy to exchange places with his cheapest mechanic, with work and wages provided for him, and relieved from the care and tribulation, the anxious days and the sleepless nights that such business involves in such times as these. And these are the men that are supposed to be oppressing labor.

I do not say that a peaceful, quiet strike is always reprehensible. A suspension of work, either individually or in masses, is sometimes the means of enforcing the laws of supply and demand when wages become too low. When a hundred hired men think their wages too low, let them quit, if they please, and quietly wait. If the employer cannot supply their places at the old rate, he must come up to such price as he can hire for. But if he can supply their places at his price, then it is clear that they are mistaken. They are asking too much. The only thing for them to do is to leave entirely or go back for the old wages; for they cannot possibly have any claims for more than he can hire as good men for. The employer has no claim on them for their work, and they have no claim upon him for the employment. All rights and claims in this behalf depend entirely upon contract, as hereafter stated.

It is clear, therefore, that hired working-men on

a strike have no right to interfere with any other
men who desire to work for such wages as they can
get, or to meddle with their late employer's business in any way, except by quietly leaving him;
and that any combinations, strikes, or violence of
any kind cannot force wages beyond the regular,
natural, general rate as governed by supply and demand. And that rate may always be known by
what another set of men can be hired for.

6.—NO PARTICULAR CLASS IN FAULT.

For all this general calamity, I do not see that
anybody is in fault. If it is the fault of any it is
the fault of all. It is the effect of inexorable
economic laws upon the facts of our national life
for the last seventeen years, which we have tried
in vain to ignore and evade. It is the inevitable
depression after extraordinary abnormal national
exertion.

The only sensible way to deal with this great
problem of the times, is to accept the situation as
we find it, and address ourselves to the rational
remedy; to accept the fact that in every part of
the country people are out of work and looking
starvation in the face, because their particular
trades are overdone, and not for any other reason;
and the only possible remedy is to equalize the
labor and productions of the country by the idle
people scattering away upon land and cultivating
the soil; and idle men, and other working men had

much better accept these solid facts of the situation than to longer listen to political demagogues
and office seekers.

7. But to all this we are answered that there are
very large

LIONS IN THE WAY.

They tell us that "This is pretty hard. There
are great difficulties in the way of a change of occupation and of location. It costs something; and
most of idle people have little or nothing to defray
such expenses with, or to buy land with, or to live
on while raising a crop," etc., etc. All of which is
true. And when I am asked how these changes
are to be made, how poor idle people are to be
transferred to farm labor, I freely admit that I
don't know. But all this does not alter *the facts
of the situation.* It does not extinguish the solid
fact that that is the only way to solve the labor
problem and that it is a perfect philosophical and
practical solution of it, however hard and difficult
it may be. It does not alter the fact that idle people *must* go into farm labor, or remain out of employment. It does not justify the idle hungry
people in lingering around factories, and shops,
and towns, and railroads, and mines, and clamor-
ing against employers of labor, and capital, and government, and listening to political aspirants who
promise them that voting certain tickets, will, in
some mysterious way, bring relief for all their
complaints—set them to work where there is no

work for them to do—set people to hiring working men to manufacture goods that there is no market for—employ the superabundance of labor in the same channels that it has been thrown out of because of the superabundance and for no other reason.

Yes, the situation is a hard one, and the remedy is difficult. There is no disputing that. It is not agreeable to change occupation, but it can be done. We see it done, very commonly, in the best of times. There is a repugnance to going from a shop, or from any town employment, to a farm; but I cannot understand why. To me a well-improved nice little farm seems the nearest thing to a paradise that can be had in this world. To own such a property is a laudable ambition for a young man; and any industrious enterprising young man can achieve all that if he will.

Nobody disputes the efficiency of farm labor to solve the great labor problem, but there are very large lions in the way. Oh dear, poor people cannot go to the west; as if there were no land this side of a couple of thousand miles towards the setting sun.

The west is a good place to go to, irrespective of any necessity, at any time, of relieving the labor market of an abnormal pressure upon it, by diverting a portion of the hired labor of the country to self-employing farm labor; a good place for young men to go to, to lay the foundation of future competence for themselves and their families. Going west is not a good thing to do for the purpose of getting a living by doing nothing ; but those who accept the necessity of hard work as the foundation for prosperity, can find in the cultivation of the soil, as they go along, compensation, in the necessaries of life, equal to the meagre and uncertain wages of the hireling, and in a course of years find themselves the owners of homesteads to make themselves comfortably independent. I know whereof I write in this behalf, for I have seen it done.

But for all this it is not necessary to go west very far. There is land enough in Steuben county to be bought on credit, or to be had to work for hire, or on shares, or for rent, for every idle man and boy in the county to make a living on, to the great advantage of the county in general, in the improvement of its idle lands. And so as to the entire State of New York. She has idle lands enough to give employment and a good living for all her idle people. But I am asked how these poor people are to live while clearing a patch of ground and making a crop of potatoes and other food? I will answer by asking how they are to live for the same length of time without doing that or any other work ?

In my travels, as I look upon the bountiful crops that pervade the country, and upon the idle lands in every square mile of territory, that would be like fruitful and responsive to the hand of labor, I cannot avoid the thought that it is an insult to a bountiful Providence to prate of enforced idleness of working men, and of starvation.

8.—NOT OVER–PRODUCTION BUT UNEQUAL PRODUCTION.

We hear a good deal about over-production. I think a general over-production is impossible. Equalize the productions of the country, by transferring the surplus manufacturing and mining labor to agriculture, and then the productions of all cannot be too much.

In times such as we have had, too many factories and shops, and collieries, and stores, and houses, can be built; they have been; and too much coal, and iron, and most other manufactured goods have been produced; but if, instead of producing such surpluses, a suitable proportion of the working men had been drawn off into agricultural pursuits, at the proper time, it is self-evident that there would have been no surplus of anything, and nobody out of employment, and the more they could all produce the richer all would be; at least none could work themselves out of a job or out of food and raiment.

Whenever any number of men find themselves out of work and cannot find any body to hire them, or when there are two men ready for every day's work that is offered, it is self-evident that their particular trade is over-done, and the only remedy is for half of them to take themselves out of the market, and go somewhere upon land, be their own employers, and build up for themselves homes where they can always produce their own bread and butter, despite railroad companies or other employers of labor. And then the other half will have no trouble in getting satisfactory wages. It is idle to think of a superabundance of hired labor getting higher wages by any human contrivances. In all the history of the world it never has been done. It never will be.

9.—THE REMEDY WILL APPLY ITSELF.

Such is the remedy for the industrial and business troubles of these times. And this remedy will eventually apply itself. The same economic law that has forced these people out of their former employment will somehow conduct them to the only vocation open to them; for large masses of men will not always rely on intangible and false political theories to give them bread and butter, while abundance of fat soils are awaiting their coming to make for themselves independent homes, to be their own employers, and to solve the labor problem for themselves and for the workingmen left behind. Disabuse the working men everywhere of the false political theories from which they are expecting relief , and educate them in the laws of nature that God has fixed upon us to govern this problem of labor, and the end of these troubles will quickly be reached.

10.—THE PROOF.

And now, August, 1879, it is gratifying to see a complete verification of the general theory of this paper, in the following, taken from a late daily paper :

"There is a growing tendency to take up and occupy new farming lands in the west. For the year ending July 16,000,000 acres of Government lands were taken up by homestead entries alone, and at least 14,-000,000 acres of new lands were sold to settlers during the same period. Half a million people settled upon the new lands in the year 1878. These are figures that incontestably prove the steadily growing importance of the Great West. They tell of a race of strong, hardy people who are emigrating to these lands and wresting from the soil its abundant wealth. The West is no place for sluggards. The man who goes there must go with the determination to work, and if he carries out his determination he will become wealthy and prosperous, for the West is a bounteous mistress to those who wed her properly."

II.

THE LABOR PROBLEM.

The hardship of labor—Capital and labor and the rights of each—Corporations—The laws of supply and demand must govern—Capital and labor not antagonistic—Self-imposed hardships—Inequalities—Governmental interference—Hours of labor—What capital is and how it oppresses labor—Prison labor—Chinese labor.

1.—THE HARDSHIP OF LABOR.

We hear a great deal about the hardships of laboring people, the oppressions of capital upon them—in the unjust apportionment between capital and labor of the values of the productions of the country. " Capital robs labor of its rights," is a very common hue and cry. And it is not uncommon to hear and read eloquent harangues on the hardship—and sometimes it is almost called injustice—of labor *per se ;* as if it were so repulsive, so severe, and so unadapted to the constitution of man ; as if God made such a mistake when He fixed things so " we must work for our bread," that the laboring man is really to be commiserated, and there ought to be some way to relieve him from his hard lot.

But what is called labor in this behalf is limited to physical employments only. We hear nothing of the hardships of the multitudes of people, not called laborers, who work more hours every day than any hired "laborers," and in pursuits more exhausting to the human machine, and more fatal to life, than physical labor. The wailings are all for the one division of the labor of the world.

On this phase of the subject there is not much to be said. Discussion cannot change the matter much. After all that can be said or done, the same necessity for labor remains, and we cannot help it. And to complain of the hardship of labor, *per se,* is to quarrel with Providence.

But God has not fixed things so very badly after all. To a healthy, vigorous man, and *woman* too, with souls in them, fit to live in this beautiful

world, willing to accept this place of probation
as they find it, any necessary labor is *not* a
hardship. The spirit and ambition to do something and be somebody—to do something for
the world for the privilege of living in it, to do
something for themselves, not only for current
needs, but for declining years, to do something to
make the world the better for their having lived in
it—makes labor easy, makes *hard* work easy. I
know about this. I have been there. Many years
of my life were spent in what is called hard work,
and I know how it feels. I have no bad report to
make of work. When I was working in a blacksmith shop fourteen hours a day, steadily, year
after year, I did not think it was hard. It was not
a hardship. When I was working on a farm, chopping timber, clearing land, and doing all the brunt
of farm labor as it was done forty years ago, with
physical exhaustion, more or less, every day, it
was easy. I do not say that I took to that labor
for its own sake. I do not think that labor is ever
intrinsically attractive to any man or woman; but
for its results it is quite endurable; yes, it can be
made enjoyable; not only for its personal compensation, but for the satisfaction of doing a good
thing—producing values out of nothing. A mechanic puts up a good piece of work, of any kind,
that will be of utility, or productive of utilities,
perhaps, to multiply and accumulate indefinitely.
If he is a real man—ambitious, well-disposed, right
19

thinking, he takes a pride and an enjoyment in such work that largely counteracts the repulsiveness of the labor itself. It is the listless, insipid, inefficient, time-serving, hand-to-mouth class of people—those who think that the world is greatly favored by their presence in it, and that the world owes them a living, and therefore drift along determined to do just as little as possible towards making their own living—it is this class who always have a quarrel with labor.

2.—CAPITAL AND LABOR, AND THE RIGHTS OF EACH.

What are the rights of labor, and what the rights of capital, in their necessary connection in the production of values?   And how are those rights to be secured, respectively?   What are the equities between the parties?   What the equitable wages of labor, and what the equities on the other side?   These are questions that periodically agitate this country from one end to the other.

I do not see how there can be any inherent rights on one side or the other. All the rights that can possibly exist in this behalf are created by contract.   No man has any *right* to work for any other man, or any company of men, only by the consent of the other party; and then he has no *right* to any particular rate of wages, only by agreement; exactly as the employer has no right to any man's labor only by his consent, and then only at wages that the man agrees to; so that the right of labor is to make the best bargain it can, the whole world to make it in, and to receive the price agreed on, exactly as it is the right of a farmer to sell his wheat for all he can, and to get his pay for it. And the right of the employer is to buy his labor as cheaply as he can, and to get good, honest service for the money agreed on, just as the miller or the consumer has the right to buy the farmer's wheat as cheaply as he can, and to get what he contracts for. That is all there is of it. And so long as the parties are free to contract and to execute, there cannot be any oppression or any wrong on one side or the other. And this " contest between capital and labor"—all the clamor as to the " rights of labor"—involves the principle that employers are to be coerced, by some power other than of the laws of trade and legitimate business principles, to make contracts against their will. If they should ask the benefit of that rule to be applied to laborers we would call it slavery.

3.—CORPORATIONS.

Nor can I see how the workmen of any corporation can have any *grievances* against their employers, as it respects the rate of wages. I once applied to a rich corporation for employment as a blacksmith. I wanted a dollar a day and board. The manager replied that there was a great difference in men, but he could get plenty of blacksmiths for $16 or $18 a month. I did not think that I had any grievance against that company, but I went to work at something else. I did not think of such a thing as taking forcible possession of their shop and compelling them to pay my price, as many working men have since done in respect to that same company's property. I cannot understand the grievances of those men unless the company were slaves, and bound to employ that particular set of men at their own price.

But corporations are fearful monsters. They oppress labor somehow, and are the source of pretty much all the poverty and distress that working people are afflicted with, as well as various other damages to all the world.

Let us see. What is a corporation? Simply an association of men organized for the purpose of massing together money sufficient to carry on enterprises of public utility that cannot be done by individuals, and with the same powers that individuals have for the like purposes. That is about all. They have no power over laborers, or poor people, that every man does not have. There are many living men who remember when a corporation had not made this Erie railroad. Will any labor reformer say how that corporation has ever oppressed any laborer? Have not its employes always worked for it of their own free choice? And have not all other vocations been open to them the same as before the railroad was thought of? Are they not just as free to go where they please as before?

I remember very well when the Lackawana valley, where I was born, with all her mineral wealth, now of world-wide notoriety, was locked in, hope-lessly locked in, as it seemed to us then, from the outside world. And when we consider that but for corporations that valley must ever have remained undeveloped, and when we see the great population and thrift of that locality now, and consider the untold benefits to every part of the country from the acquisition of the Lackawana coal; and all this the fruits of innumerable millions of corporate cap-ital; corporations with no more power to oppress or injure anybody than has every farmer in the land, this hue and cry against corporations seems to be the silliest of bosh.

And then, corporations are monopolies, and so they oppress laborers. It would seem that the au-thors of this phase of the clamor do not know what a monopoly is. The idea that the thousands of corporations who hire men—railroad companies, coal companies, and all the various manufacturing companies—are monopolies in respect to their deal-ings with hired laborers, is supremely ridiculous. Some thousands of corporate entities, in all branches of industry, scattered all over the coun-try, and in competition with each other and with the rest of the world in the hiring of labor; and they are monopolies for oppressing labor. There is no possibility for any such monopoly, until all employers combine and are directed by a single authority, which is simply impossible. And a principal charge against the railroad companies has been that they are *not a monopoly*, that is, that by their ruinous competition with each other they have crippled themselves so that they have to reduce wages.

No; in this great country, with its multifarious business and labor interests, and with its great expanse of fertile and uncultivated lands, there cannot be a monopoly for any permanent oppression on one side or the other. The laws of trade will prevail in the main, in hiring labor as in all other matters of traffic. The great coal combination ruled the price of coal for a season, at the cost of consumers, and labor unions kept up the price of labor meanwhile, but they both broke down; and the war of 1877, instead of being primarily between capital and labor, was the culmination of the war between both of these and the inexorable laws of political economy—a futile resistance to the laws that Nature's God has fixed over us. Both parties suffered the penalty of violated law. It is the inevitable reaction from unnatural prices.

4.—THE LAWS OF SUPPLY AND DEMAND MUST GOVERN.

The upshot of the whole matter is that there is a natural and inexorable law of trade—the law of supply and demand—that does, and always must, in general, govern the price of hired labor, just as it does that of everything else that is bought and sold. That law cannot be extinguished by any devices of man. Any artificial obstructions to its supremacy can only be ephemeral.

Whenever the remuneration of hired labor is too low, it is the laborers' own fault. They make it so by overstocking the market. And the ever ready relief is for a suitable portion to retire from the competition, and go out upon land and till the soil, as set out in my last paper.

When wages become too low, if the working men, instead of organizing strikes and mobs to compel employers to pay wages higher than plenty of men can be had for, would organize to diminish the supply of labor in the market, by sending a part of it out upon the land, to be their own employers, we would hear no more of the antagonisms of labor and capital.

Young men, when your wages get too low go somewhere and buy a piece of land to make yourself a farm of, on credit if need be, or rent it, pitch into it for your life-work, and the great problem of capital and labor with you will be solved. You may be your own capitalist, as well as a laborer.

5.—CAPITAL AND LABOR NOT ANTAGONISTIC.

It is also generally understood that capital and labor are mutually antagonistic. They are antagonistic just as the farmer and the miller who buys his wheat are antagonistic—the one wants to sell as dearly as he can, and the other wants to buy as cheaply as he can; or as the merchant and his customers are antagonistic—the former wants to sell his goods as high as he can, and the latter wants to buy as low as he can. This kind of antagonism exists between all the different classes of people and all individuals who deal with each other in all the relations of life in civilized society, and is no more reprehensible between employers of labor and laborers than elsewhere. But I deny that there is any other antagonism between capital and labor. Every employer *must* get his labor at the current rates—as cheaply as others—or he must fail; he cannot compete with those who get it cheaper. But it is not especially the interest of the employers of labor, as a class, that the current rate of wages shall be low. The wages enter into the price of the productions, and so there cannot be any antagonism between capital and labor as to what the current rate of wages shall be. It is just as profitable to the employer that it shall be high as low. And more than this, the interests of capital and labor are *mutual;* exactly as all other varied interests, as they are intermingled in society, are mutual. The farmer wants the mechanics and all other vocations in his vicinity to prosper, so that he can have ready markets at home at good prices, for his produce; and the mechanics and manufacturers want the farmers to prosper so they can buy what they need of manufactured goods. And so capital, employing labor, wants labor prosperous, intelligent and contented, so as to be skillful, efficient and reliable ; while laborers' true interests are that employers shall prosper, so as to enlarge their business and increase the demand for and wages of labor.

But from all this it is clear that an employer—an individual or a company—cannot enter into what is called the equities between capital and labor—to fix wages according to what may be deemed necessary for the respectable support of laborers and their families, any more than a miller can pay $2 a bushel for wheat when the current price is only $1 —upon the ground that the farmer's family cannot be respectably supported at a less price. Such a process in any business, is sure to terminate in bankruptcy. No ; each side must be for itself in this behalf, and not for the other. The employer who hires men for *their* benefit, and adjusts their wages to their *needs*, irrespective of what they earn at the current rates, is sure to fail, and his men must come to the common standard at last. Business cannot be done on charitable or benevolent principles.

Such in brief, are the inexorable laws by which hired labor is and must be governed. Whatever of hardship there is in this, is not the fault of any employing class.

6.—SELF-IMPOSED HARDSHIPS.

" In the sweat of thy face shalt thou eat bread." And this is what's the matter. Some people hate to work for their bread. But, accepting the neces-

sity of so doing, the tendency is to work just as
little as possible for it. This is the reason why
there are so many poor, unprofitable hirelings, and
why the few good ones are usually the successful
men. And then there is the disposition to squan-
der our earnings upon unnecessary indulgences, instead of saving a portion of them, all along, for a
wet day or for old age, which I think is the principal cause of the hardship of the natural laws of
trade upon laboring men. Whatever hardship
there is in continuous labor itself must be endured.
There is no remedy. As to the incidental hardships
complained of, I think usually they are self-imposed
as aforesaid ; for I have seen men working for a
long course of years at the lowest wages, support-
ing their families comfortably, always above board,
accumulating something all the time, and never
complaining of hardship. And I have always
noticed that the improvident class of people—
those who expend all their income, be it more or
less,—are always in a fret about the hardships of
labor and the hardness of the times. The times
are ever hard. The times are out of joint. The
present time is always especially the worst. In
days of yore the times were better. And they are
looking for great things in the times of the future,
to cure their own deficiencies. Young man, never
depend on the times to make you, but make the
times for yourself. Cheerfully accept the times as
you find them, and make the most of them, and

you will never have any reason to croak of the times.

7.—INEQUALITIES.

And there are inequalities in men, involving more of hardship upon some than others. Some have to sweat more for their bread than others. One man has twice the physical power of another —can do twice the work of the other. He can earn, and is entitled to, twice the wages, or can earn the same wages in half the time. A man has the natural aptitude and the practical experience for difficult and valuable workmanship. An employer can afford to pay him four times the wages of a common laborer. He is entitled to it, and no one has any right to object. If a lawyer can make himself worth to a client a hundred dollars for a day's work, he is as well entitled to that as the wood-chopper is to the price that he agrees to work for. When Jenny Lind could draw such audiences that Barnum could afford to pay her a thousand dollars a night, she was as well entitled to that sum as the blacksmith is to the day's wages that he works for. If a railroad president can make his services so necessary and valuable to the company that they can afford to pay him twenty-five, thirty, or forty thousand dollars a year, that is his honest money just the same as the wages of brakemen, firemen and engineers are theirs, and they have no reason to complain of it as long as they get what they agree to work for. And yet we hear a good deal of public clamor because railroad officials are paid too much and engineers and brakemen too little. These inequalities are inherent in our nature. Their results are unavoidable, and it is useless for any body to fret over it. But in individual cases they can be modified to great advantage. Industry, enterprise, push and integrity can overcome great natural disabilities, while the opposite qualities may practically extinguish the most brilliant powers. Many a man of medium natural endowments has risen to the higher vocations of life by the mere force of vigorous work and determination ; while stronger men stay at the bottom for want of such application.

8.—GOVERNMENTAL INTERFERENCE.

There is always more or less demand that the government shall, somehow, aid the hired laborers of the country to get higher prices for their labor than they are able to get in the natural way.

There is a good deal of truth in the old Democratic maxim that " the world is governed too much." Aside from the protection to life and property, ordinarily there is very little that the government can do for the people ; especially as to business, etc., the best that it can do for them usually, is to let them alone.

The time has been when governments undertook the impossibility of regulating the prices of commodities, but it is now too late in the day for any intelligent writer to insist that any governmental power—however absolute—and despotic—can effectually repeal or nullify the laws of trade that God has fixed upon us, and make any legal prices of goods or labor effectual between man and man. And yet this is what is expected to be done in some indirect way, which must always be equally futile.

I think all accredited writers on political economy and on government are now agreed that all that any government can possibly do for the benefit of labor—unless it be to tax the property of the country for the benefit of laborers—is to extend its protection to employer and laborer in their freedom to make their own bargains, to enforce them and then to let the matter alone to regulate itself. Wealth cannot be produced by legal enactment, and government has no mysterious power to regulate its production and distribution. It is a consumer only. Its legitimate duties are very few and simple, and they do not consist in providing employment for labor, or interfering in any way between employer and employe; and unless other classes are to be taxed, directly or indirectly, for the benefit of laborers—which would be legalized robbery—it is difficult to see what the government can do more than to give its protection to all classes alike, in "life, liberty and the pursuit of happiness." And yet we have more or less of attempts indirectly to enact by law larger pay to the laboring class.

9.—HOURS OF LABOR.

For instance : it is fondly imagined that the legal restriction of the hours of a day's work will give the laborer the price of ten hours' work for eight hours' work. A man's wages must always be, in the long run, governed by the amount and value of his productions. If one man does twice the labor of another his wages will be twice as much, and *vice versa*. And unless eight hours' work will, in general, produce as much value as ten hours, it is impossible for a laborer to get as much pay for eight hours as for ten. To illustrate : Suppose a man, instead of working at one trade and exchanging that work for all other productions that he wants, should work alternately, say at cultivating the soil to produce his food, and making cloth and shoes, and all other commodities that he needs. He works twelve hours a day. Now a law is enacted that eight hours shall be a day's work. Will that law enable him to produce as much for himself in eight hours as he could in twelve ? Now what we call the division of labor—one man working at one particular trade so as to be more efficient, and selling that labor for all other things that he wants —does not change the inexorable law that in the production of values a man cannot have any more than he produces, save by some species of rapacity and wrong. Although the division of labor, and the buying and selling of labor, and the exchange of commodities, mystifies the subject to common comprehension, yet it is easy enough to see that taking the aggregate of all the laborers, and the employers, and the capital that is at the bottom of all production, eight hours of work cannot produce as much as ten or twelve, and by whatever rate the distribution of the value of the products is made among the different parties, the share of each must be proportionate to the production; so that a general reduction of the hours of labor is a reduction of the income of all and not of the capitalist merely. And equally ineffectual are all other devices by which legislative demagogues make capital in assuming to control the relations between capital and labor

These public clamors seem to contemplate some process by which the unequal accumulation of wealth is to be prevented. In this country, with no laws of primogeniture, with no entailed estates, no land monopoly, with the notorious fact that usually no large estates are sustained beyond the second generation, it is difficult to see what labor reform would have in this respect unless it be the abrogation of the right of property itself. This is what they mean, to some extent at least, if they mean anything beyond demagogism.

10.—WHAT CAPITAL IS AND HOW IT OPPRESSES LABOR.

To come down to the initial facts of the right of property and the accumulation of wealth : A man goes out upon a spot of earth, builds him a habitation, subdues and cultivates the ground, and makes it to "blossom as the rose." In his lifetime of vigor he toils and accumulates value in that land, in that it has been made capable of producing all that its owner needs and more, without his personal toil. His house is all that is to be desired for his comfortable, and perhaps elegant, accommodation ; his barns are ample, and altogether it is an attractive and luxurious home. It is a machine that will care for its maker all along the down hill side of life. It is his. No other man shall come and drive him away and enjoy the luxurious fruits of that homestead. This is the right of property. This is the accumulation of wealth, and all there is about it. Whatever other forms human exertion takes for individual life-work, it all comes down to this at last ; industry, self-denial and economy are the only sources of accumulated wealth. That farm is what we call capital. That man is one of these hated capitalists. He is an employer of labor, lives at his ease and fattens on the labor of others, as they call it. He may trade his farm for railroad stock, and then he will be a part of a wicked corporation. In either case he is an oppressor of labor, if he hires men for what they are worth in the labor market. Or he may trade his farm for government securities, and then he will be a bloated bondholder, and have nothing to do but to cut his coupons, to the great oppression of the poor !

Another man comes along, as gray-haired as the

owner of that home. He has been a life-long worker, but he has enjoyed all the fruits of his labor as he went along—if it is enjoyment to dissipate all that is earned through all the years of vigorous manhood, with the certainty of the distresses of poverty in old age—he has no farm or other resources to recline upon. He is a reviler of the wealthy and a hater of mammon. He thinks he has the right to breathe the free air of Heaven, to walk the green earth and to partake of its fruits. He thinks he has about as good a right to that man's farm as he whom the law calls its owner—or at least to half of it; for has he not done as much work through life as the other? And when he fails to overcome the prejudices of the law against his theory, and the necessity of labor still stares him in the face, he is sure that labor has lost all its rights, and there ought to be some way to compel that rich farmer to pay him more wages than he can hire as good a man for. Such is labor reform, and such the reasons for it. It is simply the insane desire to get some of the wicked wealth that somebody else has earned and saved. That is all.

11.—PRISON LABOR.

Shall there be any labor carried on in the prisons so as to bring such labor into competition with honest free labor?

I think that question is about tantamount to this: Shall the plow come into competition with honest human muscle in digging up the earth? Or

20

shall the water-wheel come into competition with the tread-mill? Or shall the steam engine come into competition with horse-power and human hands? Or shall the spinning jenny come into competition with deft human spinners? Or shall the cotton gin come into competition with human cotton pickers? Or shall the printing press come into competition with scribes? Or shall the thousands of other labor-saving machines be allowed to come into competition with the honest hand-labor that they have superseded?

There always has been more or less of opposition to the introduction of labor-saving machines, upon the ground that they tend to the injury of the laboring people. But looking back over the ages, and looking over the world's condition to-day, with the efficiency of human labor increased a hundred fold by labor-saving machines, there never was a time when there was not something somewhere, for everybody to do to procure the materials of living, and there never can be such a time until the pressure of population, all over the earth, shall be beyond the earth's food-producing power. And it may be added, that the condition of all classes of people, and civilization itself, have always kept pace with the improved methods of labor.

Well, what of it? What has all that to do with the question of prison labor? It has everything to do with it. If somebody should invent a machine by which one horse could manufacture all the boots and shoes that Steuben and Chemung counties could consume, merely with a boy to feed the materials into the hopper, there would at once go up a clamor that all the shoemakers in two counties were to be thrown out of work, and added to the army of tramps, and the machine must be put down. I shall not argue the propriety of that machine further than to say that the temporary incovenience to the shoemakers, of being thrown out of employment, (and it would only be temporary, for they could find something else to do) would be for the permanent advantage of everybody that wears boots or shoes in these counties, in getting them cheaper.

Well, we have a machine at Elmira that will do just that. It can make all the boots and shoes that two counties can wear out, without any cost for labor; and there is a great clamor because the State proposes to use it and throw some shoemakers out of employment. That is to say : there are some hundreds of prisoners in the Elmira prison who are to be fed and clothed by the State ; and the question is raised whether they are to work or not. Being thus on the hands of the State to be supported anyhow, as between working and not working, their work, if they are to be set to work—will cost nothing. It is practically a machine that will do the work of that number of men for nothing. Suppose they are set at boot and shoe making, and suppose that all the prisons in the State should do the same.   The State could just as well afford to give all that *work* to the buyers of boots and shoes, in the price of the goods, as to let the prisoners remain idle.   Then every body who would buy any of those goods would profit by that new machine, so to speak ; or in other words, by that prison work, in contradistinction to the barbarous policy of killing off prisoners by enforced idleness.

But the honest shoemakers will then be out of employment, we are told.   Be it so.   If boot and shoe making is the best thing for prisoners to do, and if the prisons of this State can do all the needed work in that line in the State, then let all other boot and shoe makers be out of that particular kind of work.   They have no patent on it and no claim upon the State to protect them in it at the expense of every body else.   When you talk of the rights of honest working men in this behalf, it is merely a question between one class of working men and all other working men ; the question whether *all* working men shall pay a higher price for boots and shoes, for the purpose of keeping the boot and shoe makers in work out of prison.

And at the worst this can only be a temporary disadvantage to the shoe makers ; for, as we have already seen, there is something else for them to do ; and it is a clear gain to the whole community, to the value of that prison work, that it be utilized.

Nor does it matter how it is utilized—whether the State sells it out by the day's work to contracting manufacturers for what it is worth, (and it must eventually bring all it is worth if this system is adopted) or carries on the work and sells the goods for what they are worth ; in either case it benefits all the tax payers ; or whether the goods are manufactured by the State and sold to the people at prices regardless of the labor in making them. In any phase that we place it in, the people would be benefited by that prison labor to the extent of its value.

On the whole the question is : shall the whole people of the State be taxed to support her criminals in idleness for the purpose of giving employment to free working men in doing the work that the prisoners would do for the benefit of the State for nothing, upon the fundamental fallacy that there is only a limited amount of work in the world to do, that a portion of the people must necessarily be out of employment, that labor in prisons must rob somebody else of just so much labor to do, and that honest laborers are better entitled to the work than criminals. It is a false philosophy, based upon ignorance of the economic laws that govern the production of values ; its tendency is only to block all progress and improvement ; its spirit is degeneracy and barbarism.

12.—CHINESE LABOR.

The same principles as before stated apply to the

question of Chinese labor. John Chinaman is objected to because he works too cheaply. A queer objection truly, to any person who will take the trouble to think on the subject at all. It is contrary to the fundamental principle of political economy that the easier and more cheaply all the wants of civilized society can be procured, the better for the race. While the natural tendency of our nature is to do as little work as possible and get as much for it as we can, this objection to the Chinese assumes that the true policy for mankind is to do as much work as possible and get as little for it as we can.

I think it is self-evident that if a machine could be invented, or a race of men found that would do all the labor that is needed in all this country for nothing, it would be a pretty good thing for everybody—at least it would be so accepted by those who hate to work for their living so badly. It would be pretty nearly a paradise for everybody but those free laborers or that machine. Then if the Chinese will come here and do certain kinds of work for one-half of the price that it has been costing, thus cheapening the products to that extent, that will be a general benefit to that extent, notwithstanding the temporary damage to those workmen thrown out of employment thereby—temporary only because it is not a question of just so much work to do and who shall do it, but there is and always will be work enough for all, as before shown in these papers. I think this is about all there is of the Chinese labor question.

III.

MONEY—WHAT IT IS.

Money must cost all it is worth—Authorities— Money not a mystery—Fiat money—Legal tender paper.

1.—MONEY MUST COST ALL IT IS WORTH.

The theory that there can be any process by which money in abundance can be produced easily, cheaply, without much labor of any kind, is a very taking one. This is quite natural. Money is a good thing for every body to have, for the purpose of supplying their daily wants. But the idea that it is any better to have money *cheap* instead of *dear*, is a fallacy. Money must cost all it is worth, if obtained honestly. To make it cheaply obtainable is to lessen its value, to diminish its purchasing power. When all can buy cheaply, it must be sold cheaply, so that the cheap money will not make our labor any more productive of what we buy with our money. If by any change in the matter of money, dollars should be made twice as plenty as now, so as to be obtained twice as easily, so that people would give twice as many of them for a day's work, the workingman would also have to give twice as many of them for whatever he buys.

Neither would that process facilitate manufacturing or other business enterprises, for it would take twice the number of dollars to do the same work or business as before. So that, really, the only difference between cheap money and dear money is that we have to be encumbered with more of it in one case than in the other to do the same amount of business.

Money, as money, being the mere medium of exchange, it must cost, it always will cost individuals, in all legitimate transactions, all that the commodities are worth that it will buy—as much labor as those commodities cost in labor. And it is really no difference what the volume of the money is, in the matter of exchanges; no matter whether a bushel of wheat or a day's work sells for one ounce of silver, or ten ounces.

Before the invention of money, commerce and trade were of the crudest description. The inconvenience and great labor of direct barter of commodities led to the invention of money; in other words, the adoption of something that by common consent would be received by everybody in exchange for their particular products that they have to sell. Of course it was indispensable that that thing to be called money, and to be used as money, should have an intrinsic value. It must be worth as much as the things that are to be exchanged for it; for a chip could not be made to pass, by common consent, for a bushel of wheat, or a bit of common stone for an ox, or a bit of sheet iron for

a plow, or a piece of paper for a house.   In the
early ages of money, such a way of making money
was not thought of; and in later times all the
plausible inventions for making money out of nothing have failed.

In the early ages many different kinds of property were used as money—as a medium of exchange—but for centuries gold and silver have
been adopted by common consent as the principal
materials for money. The reason for the choice
will be quite obvious when we consider their peculiar characteristics, which are indispensable in the
material for money :

1. Their value is less fluctuating than that of
any other commodities; principally for the reason
that their volume cannot be suddenly increased or
diminished, and that their cost of production is
tolerably uniform ;

2. They are in demand everywhere, irrespective
of their monetary character, so that there never
has been any trouble about the universality of
their adoption as the material for money ;

3. Their value is great in small bulk ;

4. They are easily divisible without waste, im-
pressible, attractive, and practically indestructible,
and everywhere and always of uniform quality.

In consequence of these qualities, these metals
came to be used as money, independent of the enactments of any government, or any coinage stamp.
Their value is intrinsic, and they seem to be the

natural money of the world. Whether in the form of money or not, they are always salable in all countries at about their coin value.

2.—AUTHORITIES.

Professor Perry, a standard authority on Political economy, says:

"Government indeed coins them for the use of the people; but coinage is nothing in the world but a public attest to the quantity and quality of the metal contained in the coin." * * * "The value of coined money regulates itself on just the same principles as wheat regulates itself, and governments are as powerless to alter the one as the other. Indeed, the coining of either metal, by itself, is a matter of quantity and quality alone, and not a matter of value at all; the United States say by law that a gold dollar shall consist of 25 and 4-5 grains Troy, of which nine parts shall be pure, and one part alloy, but of the value of this dollar thus coined the law says nothing. It can say nothing. The coin is publicly attested, so heavy, so fine, and thereafter it takes its chance as to value. All governments have now learned, after oft repeated and always vain trials to regulate the value of their coin, that all they can do is to regulate the amount and fineness of the metals contained in them."—*Perry's Political Economy*, pp. 261-2.

"Gold and silver, as money, have value in the same sense and for the same reason as any other productive instrument."—*id* 251.

"Money makes no alteration in any law of value, but merely substitutes for convenience sake in every transaction in which it plays a part, a universal for a specific purchasing power."—*id* 231.

"In one word, value in the form of money is in a more available shape for general purchasing, than value in any other form. It is different from other commodities in just one respect, namely, while they have the power of buying some sorts of things from some persons, it has the power, derived from the usages of society, to buy all sorts of things from all persons."—*id* 232.

"In 1834, the gold eagle of the United States was reduced in weight from 270 to 258 grains, and the alloy increased to one part in ten, from one part in twelve. This was taking out more than six parts of gold out of every 100 parts, in all the gold coins of the country. Yet the coins bore the same name as before. As a medium, their purchasing power was diminished more than six per centum." * * * "If for any reason an ounce of gold will buy less of other things than formerly, the coins cut from that gold will buy less than formerly." * * * "When the current dollar sinks to one-half, or rises to twice its purchasing power, we call it a dollar all the while."—*id* 244-5.

I next quote a few passages from Prof. Wayland's Political Economy:

"We do not use them (gold and silver) as a circulating medium because we see a stamp upon them, nor because government has made them a legal tender, but because we know that they represent a given amount of value, and we therefore know that we can exchange them for the same amount of value, whenever we please. If a bushel of wheat sells for a dollar, we know that it costs as much labor to produce a dollar at the mine and bring it to us, as to produce a bushel of wheat and bring it to us."—*p* 199

"The cost or price of the money employed in every exchange, is equal to the cost or price of the article which is exchanged for it. If a barrel of flour in Lima be exchanged for ten ounces of silver, the cost of producing the flour, and of transporting it to Lima, is equal to the cost of producing the silver and transporting it to the same place. If a barrel of flour in New York, be exchanged for seven ounces of silver, the cost and transportation of the one at the place of exchange, is equal to that of the other." * * "That this is so is evident from the fact, that if the cost of the precious metals change, their changeable value varies, like that of any other product. Thus, if new and richer mines are opened, so that the cost of producing the precious metals is reduced, the price of the precious metals falls. In such a case we receive more silver for a day's work, for a bushel of wheat, for a pound of wool, or for any other product." * * "If the cost of producing an ounce of silver is increased, while that of producing a bushel of wheat remains the same, we shall receive less silver in exchange for a bushel of wheat.   That is, in exchanging products for the precious metals, as for anything else, *we exchange on the principle of labor for labor.*"—*pp* 201-2.

"We see, then, that the exchangeable value of money is not derived from its shape or color, from the stamp of the mint, or from the enactments of the government; but that, like everything else, it is based upon the cost of its production, varying slightly, and for short periods, like everything else, with the accidental fluctuations of supply and demand.   And hence, the reason why a man exchanges a bushel of wheat for two ounces of silver, and a yard of broadcloth for six ounces, is that it costs as much labor and capital to produce the one at the place of exchange, as the other."—*p* 203.

On this phase of the subject I might quote, also, to the same effect as the foregoing, from Say, Chalmers and Smith, all accredited writers on Political Economy.   In fact, it is the unanimous voice of all respectable writers on the subject.

3.—MONEY NOT A MYSTERY.

The sum total of it all is, then, that there is nothing mysterious, or very complicated, or puzzling about this money question.   Any body can understand it to its foundation; as follows:

Money is simply a product of labor, subject to exchange for other products, precisely the same as are other products exchangeable for each other; with the additional quality that it has a universal demand because it is the medium for the exchange of all other commodities; and it is, and always must be, worth the same as any commodities for which it is exchanged; and with one more quality:

that being the medium of exchange, it is necessarily used as a *measure* of value. Without some common measure for all values, exchanges would be very difficult and troublesome, in the simple matter of reckoning or comparison. It might be easy to compare a few products with each other for the purpose of exchange; for instance, a day's work with wheat, or potatoes with iron; but to come to the multitudinous mercantile exchanges, such as buttons for coal, paper for rice, coffee for combs, watches for hats, books for shoes, it would be practically impossible to have any intelligible system of exchanges. But all products can easily be measured by one; especially the one that is used for money. A dollar is so much gold or silver. Every other product can be compared to that and its value estimated in dollars and fractions of a dollar, and then the comparative value of any one product with that of any other is easily ascertained and exchanges readily made, whether money is used or not. This is what is meant by measure of value.

Such is money—its constitution, character and uses, and all there is of them.

4.—FIAT MONEY.

It is proper to remark here, however, that it is in the power of government, when not constitutionally restricted, to give a certain currency to substitutes for money, beyond the intrinsic or representative value, by *fiat.*

Our legal-tender act was of that character. Through all the fluctuations in the market value, in gold, of the legal-tender notes—from 35 cents on the dollar up to par—they were always worth 100 cents for the purpose of paying debts contracted prior to the passage of that act, on a gold basis and payable in gold. But that the *fiat* of the government did not create any appreciable value in the notes is shown by the fact that for any other purpose than paying such debts their value fluctuated according to the fluctuations in the chances of the war and the probability of their redemption in gold.

That legal-tender process was simply a forced loan. The government said to all creditors, substantially, "whenever any money payments are made to you on debts, you shall lend us that money, *i. e.* you shall take our greenback notes that we have put upon the market for that purpose; and we pledge the nation to redeem those notes some time."

Such was the law; and then all debts contracted for dollars when dollars meant gold dollars, were at once payable in greenbacks worth 35 cents or any other price as it happened. It is clear, therefore, that legal tender did not make those notes worth 100 cents in gold, but simply compelled the creditor to cancel a gold dollar of debt for 35 cents, or whatever the price of greenbacks might be in the market.

This operated as the grossest injustice between debtor and creditor. The debtor having had gold value for the debt that he owed, was enabled by this law to pay it with 35 cents; for the nominal prices of whatever he produced to buy greenbacks with, having advanced as the real value of the greenback had gone below gold, it is clear that he only paid 35 cents in full for a dollar of debt.

Such a despotic interference with private rights is tolerable only under the sheerest necessity, and for the preservation of the government itself, as in our case. And for any other purpose there is no power in this government to make such a law.

5.—THE DEGRADING OF COIN.

Of the same general character is the degrading of coins from ahigher to a lower standard. Under the fallacy that the government stamp was what made the money, governments have assumed to increase the circulating medium by increasing the nominal value of coins—diminishing the weight and calling them by the same name.

The British pound sterling was originally a pound —Troy weight—of silver. What is now called a pound sterling is about one-third of that quantity of silver. The French *livre* of Charlemagne contained 12 ounces of fine silver. At the era of the French Revolution the *livre* weighed only one-sixth of an ounce.

These great reductions in the size of coins have been effected by a succession of changes, under the idea that the *fiat* of government would make the small coin worth as much as the larger.

" The public authority persuaded itself that it could raise or depress the value of money at pleasure ; and that on every exchange of goods for money, the value of the goods adjusted itself to the imaginary value which it pleased the authority to affix to it, and not to the value naturally attached to the agent of exchange, money, by the conflicting influence of demand and supply.

" Thus when Philip I, of France, adulterated the *livre* of Charlemagne, containing 12 oz. of fine silver, and mixed with its a third part alloy, but still continued to call it a *livre*, though containing but 8 oz. of fine silver, he was nevertheless persuaded that his adulterated *livre* was worth quite as much as the *livre* of his predecessors. Yet it really was worth one-third less than the *livre* of Charlemagne. A *livre* in coin would purchase but two-thirds of what it had done before. However, the creditors of the monarch, and of individuals, got paid but two-thirds of their just claims; land owners received from their tenants but two-thirds of their former revenue, till the renewal of leases placed matters on a more equitable footing. Abundance of injustice was committed and authorized ; but after all it was impossible to make 8 oz. of silver equal to 12."—*Say's Polit. Econ.*, p. 235.

All such schemes for raising the value of money always have been, and always must be futile. Their only effect has been legalized fraud and plunder. There is no power in any government—there never was and never will be—to make one ounce of fine silver worth a much as two ounces. And when a law says that a creditor shall receive in full for a debt payable in pounds or livres, or dollars, coins of such denominations containing less of the precious metal than the pounds, or livres, or dollars contained when the debt was contracted, such law is simply a fraud—a repudiation of part of the debt. That is all.

In this country at least, as before intimated, such a law could not be sustained in the courts. And yet it is gravely proposed not to scale down the coins merely, but to create a national money without any intrinsic value whatever, and never redeemable in money of intrinsic value—to create money indefinitely, out of nothing, by the fiat of the government, and make it a legal tender for the payment of all debts, public and private!

IV.

MONEY—WHAT IT IS NOT.

Paper substitutes for money — The greenback scheme—Real money a legal tender naturally— Legal tender restriction necessary— A double standard impossible— The true theory of coinage adopted— The retrograde in coinage.

1.—PAPER SUBSTITUTES FOR MONEY.

Having explained what money really is, upon principle, and facts, and scientific authorities, I may as well explain how it is not, and cannot be, what a certain school of philosophers claim for it.

I can well remember my first ideas of paper money when a very small boy. A bank note seemed to me to be a wonderful thing. The paper was peculiar and rich—the pictures beautiful, and

21

I thought those qualities were what constituted its value. I thought that a bank, by procuring that kind of paper, and printing that kind of pictures, could manufacture good money indefinitely, and without any other condition. I presume children of four or five years of age have similar ideas now. There are some men who seem to be exactly where I was then. They think that good money can be manufactured in any quantity by a mere print on pieces of paper.

Having seen that money is, and must be, a product of labor, costing its possessor the same that any other product that it is exchanged for costs its possessor, we are now led to the consideration of what is called

" PAPER MONEY."

In this discussion it is not necessary to consider the expediency or inexpediency of banks and paper money, but, recognizing them as we find them, I propose merely to explain their bearing upon the main subject in hand.

Really there is no money but coin. All so-called paper money is only the representative of actual money, so far as there is any money value in it. We call it money, because it passes from hand to hand, fulfilling the office of money. It is con-venient to call it so, and it is just as well. But that it is not money at all, is evident on its face. Take a dollar greenback. It does not pretend to be a dollar, but only a promise to pay a dollar.

What is the dollar that it promises to pay? Not another greenback, surely, but a dollar in coin. And so of all bank notes. They are not dollars, and do not pretend to be. And the legal tender quality of the greenback does not alter the case. That does not make it a dollar. A dollar is a certain quantity of gold or silver. The legal tender law does not change the quality of the dollar at all, but merely says to every creditor: " You shall take those promises for your debts and trust the United States to pay you the actual dollars that your debtor owes you." In other words, the government, by her sovereign authority, and under the inexorable necessity of war, said to her people : " you shall permit us to collect your debts, and you shall loan to us the avails thereof, and take our promise to pay you your dollars at a future time, and you shall run the risk of our ability and willingness to redeem that promise at some time in the future." That is all the money quality there is in the greenback. It is the medium of a forced loan, merely. And there can be no possible excuse, save the necessity of war, for the issue of such paper, and none for maintaining it in forced circulation after the necessity is past.

Paper money, then, has no value in itself, and it cannot be endowed with any such value by any ingenuity or scheme of law. Whatever of exchangeable value it has is in consequence of the money that it represents, or purports to represent—the promise to pay money and the probability that the promise will some time be redeemed. This is exemplified by our greenbacks.   In the darkest period of the war they went down to about 35 cents on the dollar. And then, as the prospect of the final success of our army improved they appreciated, until at the close of the war they were worth about 66. Since then, under judicious legislation for the maintenance of the public credit, and the honest payment of all public debts, they continued to advance until they came up to par a short time before the day fixed by law for resumption.

This representative character of paper money is further proven by bank notes.   Our National bank notes are always at par with greenbacks, whether the bank breaks or not, because there is a security deposited that always ensures their redemption in greenbacks.   Under the old State bank system the notes of a bank would be at par one day and worthless the next; for the reason that it would just then become known that there was no money or other value in the vaults of the bank to redeem them.

So that, on the whole, paper cannot be made into actual money value; cannot be made into any exchangeable value, only as it represents something, somewhere, that is pledged to its redemption. And no human power can enforce the acceptance, as money, of anything devoid of value—intrinsic or representative.   If a government compel the people to accept such stuff in the payment of debts, it is simply legalized robbery, and not a payment at all.

2.—THE GREENBACK SCHEME.

And it is gravely proposed to make actual money dollars by printing on pieces of paper:

" This is one dollar United States legal tender lawful money always at par with gold."

And so for all other denominations ; $5s, $10s, $20s, $50s, $100s, $1000s, etc. And then enforce it upon the people as the actual money of the country, and keep it at par with gold by enacting that it shall always be par with gold and shall be a legal tender. And with this they propose to pay off all the National indebtedness—bonds, the present greenbacks, and all other obligations.

So far as the National debt is concerned, this scheme is repudiation, plain and simple; for it is impossible that that sort of stuff could be worth any more than waste paper by the pound. But as to the effect of so insane a project upon the business and labor of the country, imagination cannot conceive the disastrous effects of such a gigantic calamity upon all classes of the people.

This scheme is not entirely new. It has been tried repeatedly, though the present philosophers have improved upon all former experiments in irredeemable paper currency by excluding all pretense of redemption.

John Law's Royal Government Bank of France, in the year 1718, is an example of a great financial bubble of irredeemable so-called paper money, bolstered up with all the legal decrees and penalties that could be devised, paying off the National debt, and creating the wildest mania of speculation known to history, and finally collapsing in general ruin and distress. In four years, the said paper money came down to its real value—*nothing* —just what it was worth from the beginning. And this so-called money was gauranteed by the State, receivable in taxes, nominally redeemable in coin, and made a legal tender ; and at one time it actually bore ten per cent. premium over gold and silver. But it really represented no value ; and when this came to be known, it went to nothing.

And again in 1790, France tried another paper bubble to relieve herself from financial embarrassments, in the issue of her famous *assignats* to the amount of 45,500,000,000 francs, and nominally founded upon public lands. They were legal tender, the use of coin was prohibited, a maximum price in assignats for everything was fixed by law, heavy penalties, and at last death, were decreed against those who refused to receive them at par ; but all in vain. After an unnatural circulation of six years, with continual depreciation, their life went out entirely ; the fate of all paper currency not founded on sufficient money value. Prof. Perry says :

"The distress and consternation into which a country falls when its measure of value is disturbed and destroyed, as it was by the issue of the assignats, is past all power of description. There can be no doubt that these assignats caused more suffering in the French Revolution, a hundred fold, than the prisons and the guillotine."

Another notable example in point is our own Continental money, issued by the Continental Congress, from 1775 to 1779, to the amount of $200,000,000, which passed at par for a year or so after the first emission, but then began to depreciate, and in less than five years it went to nothing.

The difficulty in all these cases was not that the paper was not nominally redeemable, it had a promise to pay on its face ; but that the promise was exactly like the promise of a broken bank; there was nothing to redeem it with ; and being issued in such vast amounts, and so little value received for it, that it was really out of the question to afterwards make provision for its payment ; or at any rate it never was attempted ; so that their issue was practically equivalent to the issue of greenbacks now proposed, *i. e.*, without any promise or pretence of redemption ; a violation of a fundamental law of monetary science, that to maintain a paper currency in circulation, there must be real money at the bottom of it. It must be worth the money that it passes for, and value cannot be created by legal enactment. A law making power cannot make a scorpion into a codfish, a bundle of straw into a barrel of flour, or a piece of paper into a dollar. And it cannot enforce the exchange of anything whatever for more than it is worth.

The radical defect in the greenback theory is that they expect to create good money out of nothing, by law. It cannot be done. And the attempt to manufacture money in that way can only end in disaster to the country. Working men who have been captivated by this easy theory of wealth, would do well to stop and think, and apply their own common sense to this subject, before creating a whirlwind that will involve them, with all other business interests, in one common ruin. The real working men have nothing to gain, but everything to lose by such an overturning as the greenback agitation contemplates.

3.—REAL MONEY A LEGAL TENDER NATURALLY.

Usually it is not any special legal tender law that makes coins of the precious metals legal tender in the payment of debts. For instance, our government coins dollars of gold and silver; a contract is made to pay $100 on a certain day. On the day named the tender of a hundred of such dollars as were current when the contract was made, whether gold or silver, will be a legal tender in the absence of any legal tender law, just as a debt payable in wheat will be discharged by a tender of the wheat at the time and place agreed on.

4.—LEGAL TENDER RESTRICTION NECESSARY.

But with two or more metals coined into money by the government, it is the province of law to say which shall *not* be a general legal tender, and to what extent they may be; *i. e.* which shall be the regular paramount money of the country, to the end that the more desirable metal may not be demonetized by fluctuations in the market value of such metals; for

5.—A DOUBLE STANDARD IS IMPOSSIBLE.

It is an impossibility for two kinds of metal coins, called dollars for instance, to circulate as general money, side by side interchangeably; because of the fluctuations in the market value of such metals. The relatively cheaper metal; *i. e.* the coin that contains the least bullion value to the dollar, will always be the principal circulating medium. The other will retire, because it is worth more as bullion than as coin.

Our first national coinage of gold and silver— law of 1792—was made on the basis of the relative value of gold and silver being one to fifteen; which was supposed to be the true ratio at that time. But it was soon found that gold had been under valued. The gold eagles were worth more for exportation as bullion than for circulation at home; and up to the year 1834 American gold coin was not known in common use. Neither gold nor silver was in any degree demonetized by law, and so the cheaper coin was used and the dearer pushed aside.

In 1834 Congress deemed it expedient to change

the coinage of gold so as to bring it into general circulation; and accordingly the gold eagle was reduced from 270 to 258 grains in weight, with an increase of alloy from one-twelfth to one-tenth of the weight of the coin; thus increasing the nominal value of gold, in relation to silver, more than six per cent. This proved to be an over valuation of gold, and the silver soon began to slip away, and gold supplied the general circulation.

6.—THE TRUE THEORY OF COINAGE ADOPTED.

Finally, after some further tinkering, the government having learned the simple economic fact that gold and silver cannot long remain of one relative value to each other, and therefore they cannot both be kept in general circulation as money, in 1853 Congress adopted the very sensible plan of making gold the paramount money, with silver as subsidiary and fractional merely; this by reducing the weight of the half dollar and its sub-divisions so that their nominal value should be considerably above their real value as compared with gold coins —thus preventing their exportation—and by limiting the legal tender quality of silver to sums not exceeding $5. The silver dollars had long been out of circulation on account of their under valuation, and they were nominally demonetized in 1873.

7.—THE RETROGRADE IN COINAGE.

Thus the matter stood until the recent great fall

in the value of silver occurred; when the inflation spirit of the country took a craze over silver money, which culminated in the foolish Bland silvel bill of 1878, providing for the coinage of two millions of full legal tender silver dollars per month, indefinitely, intrinsically worth about eighty-seven cents in gold per dollar. This would inevitably degrade the currency at the rate of about thirteen per cent., and drive all gold out of circulation, were it not for the provisions of the law that the government shall coin them on its own account—buying the bullion at the market price, and selling the dollars at their nominal coin value, in gold or its equivalent, which keeps them chiefly hoarded in the treasury, as there is no demand for them at that price. What are forced out in payments by the government, find their way back by payments to the government. The fact that they cannot be had for less than 100 cents, when only worth 87 cents, keeps them in the government vaults. There is no speculation in them, even to pay debts with.

On the whole the Bland silver bill is a humiliating abortion; a piece of magnificent pettifoggery, without a bit of statesmanship or financial skill. It assumes to do impossible things—to legislate money into the pockets of one set of men without taking it out of the pockets of another set; to make 87 cents' worth of silver worth 100 cents; to make and maintain a double standard of money; in a word, to abolish the inexorable laws of trade.

No, it cannot be done. You might as well try to make two yard sticks, of unequal lengths, to measure the same. The only way to get the 87 cent dollar into general circulation is to sell them cheaper, so that there will be a speculation in them in the payment of debts. If the government is prepared for such fraud as that, and for the retirement of gold from our currency, that is the way to do it; provided that the legal tender clause, requiring the creditor to take a cheaper dollar than he contracted for, will stand the test of the courts.

But the honest and sensible way is to back out from that grand mistake, melt up the fictitious dollars into bullion, and go back to the law of 1853; for at this day and age of the world gold is the natural legitimate money, with silver as fractional money, for change and small transactions, overvalued sufficiently to keep it in circulation, and regulated by convertibility into gold at the treasury on demand. This, with a base metal coinage of the smallest coins, also convertible, as aforesaid, with limited legal tender to all the fractional coins, is the perfection of metallic money. And without National Banking system, founded on such metallic money, we will have the most perfect currency that the world has ever seen.

V.

MONEY—INFLATION NOT BENEFICIAL TO INDUSTRY.

(Written in 1878, before the revival of business.)

Cheap money not desirable—Authorities—Facts of the case— The practical proof.   ·

1.—CHEAP MONEY NOT DESIRABLE.

The inflation of the currency is advocated chiefly for the purpose of benefiting industry; as if a redundant currency were any the better for the industries of the country.

In my first number of this series, I demonstrated, from reliable statistics, that the panic, commencing in 1873, was not caused by any deficiency of circulating medium, and consequently there is no reason to suppose that inflation can cure it.

In my third and fourth numbers I have shown that the project of irredeemable paper, if adopted, would extinguish all reliable currency, and be destructive of all the interests of the country. But now let us suppose the project to be to inflate the currency on a substantial basis ; *i. e.*, to make and put into circulation a large addition of *good* paper money, representing real money. I have already tried to show that good money cannot be cheap. It must cost all it is worth; *i. e.*, all it will sell for. And I beg the reader to bear this in mind all along, as an essential factor in this exposition. Money cannot be cheap in the sense that wheat, or other consumable products, are cheap. With a large wheat crop, wheat may fall from $2 to $1 per bushel, and we will then get our bread for one-half the labor as before the fall. That wheat is really cheaper to us because we supply our want of bread at half the cost of labor that it cost before. But, if by any means, money becomes so plentiful as to be procured with half the labor as formerly, that is none the better for us, for we only want the money as a medinm of exchange for other things, and not to consume, as with wheat. If we buy it with half the labor as before, we must sell it at the same rate. When we buy it cheap, we must sell it cheap, so that the larger sum is really worth no more to us than the smaller sum was before the change. Suppose wheat to be $1 a bushel, and labor $1 a day. And suppose money to be made cheaper, as they call it, by inflation, so that a bushel of wheat buys $2, and a day's labor buys $2. The working man does not want the money to make bread of, or to consume in any way, but to buy a bushel of wheat with, and the $2 are worth no more to him than the $1 was before the change. He will get just the same quantity of wheat for his day's work as before; and so with all other commodities that any boly wants to buy. In other words, while money can be intrinsically cheap as a commodity of exchangeable value, it cannot be cheap as a matter of money, because it is the mere medium or tool to facilitate the exchange of other values, and not the *object* or *end* of the exchange.   Whether intrinsically cheap or dear it cannot affect the relative prices of the real objects of exchange for which it is the implement or tool.   It cannot enable the working man to get any more bread for his day's work, or the farmer to get any more work for his bushel of wheat.   If cheap money were the ultimate object of desire, the iron money oi Lycurgus would be a good thing. A farmer would get about a wagon load of money for a wagon load of wheat, and a watch maker would get a couple of wagon loads for a watch. Or, still better, give us the irredeemable greenback now proposed, and we would get a wagon load of it for a wagon load of waste paper.   And if *quantities* of money would make us rich, we could all get rich quite easily.

Now, to apply these principles of economic law to any industrial enterprises : take any manufacturing firm in Corning ; suppose that in the present state of the currency they cannot raise sufficient money to carry on the work that they can get to do ; and suppose the currency now to be inflated —made cheap—so that two dollars can be got at the same cost of labor, as one heretofore.   The wages of labor, all materials, all the means of living, etc., will cost twice as much as before, so that the work that could be done for $1,000 heretofore will require an outlay of $2,000, and if the firm was not able to carry on their work before the inflation, for the want of money, they will be equally unable afterwards. The fact is that if there is, at this time, any deficiency of money anywhere for needed industrial enterprise, it is because the parties have not the means to buy it with, and not that the money cannot be had on suitable security ; and such infirmity cannot be cured by inflation or any other legislation. It is self-evident that if the currency were to be inflated as aforesaid, so as to require $2,000 to do what $1,000 is now doing, the $2,000 would not be any easier attainable than $1,000 now. For it is not to be supposed that the government, or any money lenders, are to hand this money around to people without just as good security for payment as is required now ; and property holders will not then be any more eager to endorse $2,000 notes than $1,000 notes now.

2.—AUTHORITIES.

In proof of these theories of money, I quote from Say's *Political Economy:* "Money is a commodity whose value is determined by the same general laws as that of all other commodities ; that is to say, rises and falls in proportion to the relative demand and supply" *p.* 226. (That is to say, all other commodities fluctuate in money price as money fluctuates as aforesaid.)

" No government has the power of increasing the total National money otherwise than nominally. The increased quantity of the whole reduces the value of every part; and *vice versa*" *p.* 227.

" The value of money, like that of everything else,

is always in the direct ratio to the demand, and in the inverse ratio to the supply," *p.* 231.

I next quote a passage from Wayland's *Political Economy :*

" To accomplish a given amount of exchange, a certain value in money is required, and in ordinary times, this value always exists. And, the exchanges remaining the same, we cannot employ for this purpose, more than this amount of value. If a quantity equal to one thousand ounces of silver, or of one thousand bushels of wheat, be required to perform the exchanges of a certain community, we cannot employ more than this amount of value. If we increase the quantity, we shall only decrease the value proportionally. If such a country be insulated from other countries, and we introduce into its circulation one thousand additional ounces of silver, equal to one thousand additional bushels of wheat, the value of the whole two thousand will be just equal to that of the one thousand ounces before; that is, the (gross) *value* will not alter. If, on the other hand, from such a country thus insulated, we remove half the circulating medium, the remaining half will accomplish the purpose of the whole: that is, it will double in value" *p.* 209.

Next from Prof. Perry's *Political Economy :*

" Money is a medium of exchange; and the question arises how much of it is wanted? Clearly only so much as will serve the purposes which such a medium is fitted to subserve ; there should be enough fairly to mediate between the services actually ready to be exchanged then and there, and also enough fairly to call out other services, proper and profitable in the then circumstances of society, and whose only obstacle to a profitable exchange then and there, is the lack of a facilitating medium. All increase of money beyond this point, which the very nature of money itself makes out as the boundary, leads to a diminution in value of every part of it, to a consequent disturbance of all existing money contracts, to a universal rise of prices which are illusory and gainless, to unsteadiness and derangement in all legitimate business," *p.* 239.

22

From all which good and standard authorities in economic science, my theory is abundantly made out that it is not lack of money that has been the matter with the labor interests of the country.

3.—THE FACTS OF THE CASE.

And then, furthermore, without regard to philosophic principles, to come right down to substantial facts; the depression of industries and business is notoriously *not* caused by any scarcity of money. Go to any suspended manufactory of any kind, or any one that has curtailed its operations, and inquire into the cause; and it will be found, uniformly, that it is not the inability to get money to run it, but the inability to sell its productions. Go into a town where building is suspended, and you will find that new houses are not wanted, and not that there is any lack of money to build them. There are too many houses already. The coal combination, formed to limit the production of coal, is not made for the want of money to run the collieries to their full capacity, but for the want of market for all the coal that they can produce.

4.—MONEY CANNOT DO IT.

Money cannot set people to work where there is not something to do to produce something that somebody wants to buy. Offer a Corning manufacturer $10,000 at one per cent. interest and he would not take it to invest in manufacturing something that he cannot sell. Every Corning manufacturing firm could double up their working force in a week if they could get the work to do. And so it is every where. It is not the lack of money, but the lack of orders for work, that is the matter. I am credibly informed that a large Elmira manufacturer is to-day, borrowing all the money he wants at *four per cent.* interest.

With any amount of idle money, nobody can afford to manufacture goods that will not sell, or build houses that are not wanted.

And the lack of buyers sufficient to keep all the factories and all the working men in full work was not caused by deficiency of money; for the deficiency of markets commenced, not in 1873 when the bubble broke, but years before that, in the time of the highest prosperity, when every body was employed at the highest wages, and everything was going on swimmingly, when stocks began to accumulate beyond the wants of the country by reason of the super-abundance of industrial enterprises other than in agriculture, as set out at large in my first number.

On the whole, therefore, it is entirely clear,

1st. That the fundamental idea of irredeemable paper would be legalized robbery simply, so far as legal enactments should enforce any circulation of such worthless stuff, and fraught only with disaster to all the interests of the country;

2nd. That there is and has been no deficiency of

circulating medium for all purposes of all the productive and commercial interests of the country; consequently,

3rd. That there is no occasion for any inflation of *good* money for the benefit of any industrial interests; and finally,

4th. That the idea that the working men of the country can possibly be identified, in interest, with these wild money theories, in any way, shape or manner, is a delusion and a snare.

Workingmen, the economic doctrines that I have laid down for your instruction in these papers, are the laws that the experience of all ages of the world has demonstrated to be correct. They have been jotted down by the ablest experts from age to age. You have them as the concentrated wisdom of the world, and not as theories of mine. They are the laws that God has fixed over us, and not human expedients or human power can repeal them. Study them well, and let your life be guided by them, in your work and in your politics, instead of vainly attempting to resist them, and all will be well.

5.—THE PRACTICAL PROOF.

And now, August, 1879, it may be added that the general revival of the industries and business of the country, under resumption of specie payments, is practical proof of the foregoing theories, written in the darkest time of the panic. And yet the clamor for inflation goes on.

VI.

MONEY—GOVERNMENT BANKING VS. NATIONAL BANKS.

*How and why the National Banks were instituted
—A great hit—Easier elasticity suggested—Substitution of Greenbacks for National Bank
Notes—Double interest—Government business
for profit—The other side considered.*

1.—HOW AND WHY THE NATIONAL BANKS WERE INSTITUTED.

There is a moderate grade of greenback money-
men, who do not believe in the wild theories of the
irredeemable paper inflationists, but do believe in
abolishing the National banks and issuing greenbacks to supply the country with all needful
paper circulating medium in place of the present
National bank notes; that is to say, as I suppose,
to issue *good* greenbacks, redeemable in money,
and not an irredeemable paper to be called absolute money, to be endowed with inherent value by
calling it value, as the boy said when his father
asked him how many legs the calf would have, calling the tail one ; " five, father." " Oh, no, my son,
only four, for calling the tail a leg does not make
it a leg." And so this moderate sentiment does
not propose to create good dollars by merely calling valueless things dollars, but to issue a currency
exchangeable for dollars.

Preliminary to the discussion of this subject, I

will state briefly the origin of the National banks. The government was fighting for existence. Its credit was exhausted and it had to fight on credit or go down. The experience of the world had demonstrated that it could not go through by merely printing stuff called money. $2,500,000,000 of mere government currency would not have been worth anything. By the great skill of Secretary Chase a combination of government legal tenders, long bonds, and National banks was made, the National credit was restored and sustained and we went through. That is to say : legal tenders were issued to a moderate amount, bonds were issued for the residue of our needs ; and to float the whole the National banks were invented, founded on both legal tenders and the bonds, in order to put the wealth of the country to the bottom of it all—to make it for the money interest of the country to own National bank stock, and for the interest of the National banks to sell the bonds, and to keep them up, and finally for the interest of every body to carry the war through and keep all the government obligations good. Altogether it was a wonderful invention,—never surpassed in the history of the world. It almost did the economic impossibility of making good money out of nothing by legislation.

2.—THE NATIONAL BANKS A GRAND HIT.

But that great scheme of finance was based upon

promises to pay, and sustained by maintaining the ability and willingness of the government to pay, and not by the *fiat* of law. And beyond its grand success as a war measure, it was a great hit on banking *per se*. It is the most successful and valuable system of paper money that ever was invented. Let any business man refer back to the days of State bank currency, with all its inequalities, annoyances, uncertainties, hazards and actual losses—which I need not describe in detail—and compare it with this system of sound, stable, uniform currency, every bill of it, from any quarter of the Union, equal to gold everywhere in the Union, as it is now, a currency which has never cheated a holder a dollar in the sixteen years of its existence; and he will appreciate the value of National Banks, and the ease and cheapness with which the financial part of any business is now conducted. But the younger portion of business men never can really understand this unless the insanity of the times should revive the State bank system.

3.—EASIER ELASTICITY SUGGESTED.

So long as we are to have paper money at all, there never can be much improvement on this National banking system. With direct convertibility into coin, and a slight amendment, for easier elasticity, it will be a perfect paper money banking system. This improvement, for which I am indebted to Quincy W. Wellington, Esq., a shrewd

and far-seeing banker of Corning, is as follows:
For instance : A national banker in Minnesota
wants an extra fifty thousand dollars to lend to
his customers for forty days, to move the crops of
the locality. He has his four per cent. bonds to
deposit for that amount of currency. He only
wants it for forty days, and then he will want to
exchange back for the bonds, for he cannot afford
to keep idle currency. Well, all this can be done
under present laws ; but with only one office and
depository for this business for the whole country
it takes too long to make such transfers. When
an emergency occurs a banker wants such a conversion made in twenty-four hours instead of a delay of many days as now. The change proposed
is to establish a depository at every considerable
commercial centre throughout the country for the
exchange and transfer of bonds and National Bank
currency, as aforesaid ; so that any amount of National currency can be commanded for any and
every possible need of industry and business on
the shortest possible notice, for a longer or shorter
time, and to be retired speedily when no longer
needed.

With such an amendment to the law the world
has never seen a paper currency system to compare with what our National Banks will be.

And when inflation of the currency is demanded,
sufficient for the wants of business, as the saying
is, this National Banking system does just that

exactly. With the creation of this Bank paper free, save only that it shall be made secure, and with freedom to retire it too, there cannot be a monetary system more perfectly adapted to the wants of business. It will always supply the exact amount of currency needed. The self-interest of capitalists will regulate it.

4.—SUBSTITUTION OF GREENBACKS FOR NATIONAL BANK NOTES.

Now to return to the main question in hand—the question whether this banking system should be continued. With a good deal of pertinacity this plausible theory is urged : The National bank notes are secured by deposits of United States bonds, and issued on their credit, the bank drawing interest on the bonds, and also lending out, upon interest, the notes that thus represent the said bonds, and enabling the banker to realize a double interest on the capital. And why not—they ask—issue an amount of greenbacks equal to the National bank notes, surrender to the banks their bonds, retire their notes, and then, with the said greenbacks, buy their value in bonds, and burn them, and let the greenbacks go into circulation and save the interest now being paid to the banks on said bonds?

Now, superficially, that looks like a good thing to do. But I think it lands us right into the labyrinths of the insane theories of creating values and paying debts by hocus pocus, or of repudiation,

which ever you please to call it. The bonds proposed to be retired are a fair and honest debt that
must be paid; and the only way to get rid of the
interest is to pay them up when payable, or buy
them up in the market—mind that I am now argu-
ing on the theory of honesty and not that of any
repudiation scheme. Now, if we could pay up by
issuing greenbacks to buy the bonds with, without
incurring another debt, that would certainly be
very nice; but the payment would only be like the
man who gave his note for a store debt, saying:
"there, that debt is paid." The exchange of greenbacks for bonds is only an exchange of one form of
debt for another, and not a payment, exactly as in
the case of giving a note for a debt previously existing.

" Admitting all that to be so, greenbacks do not
bear interest, and by exchanging a non-interest
bearing security for interest bearing bonds, we
will surely save the interest," we are told.

Let us see about that. That theory pre-supposes
that the matter is to be ended when the greenbacks
are issued and the exchange is made; that the
greenbacks will then take care of themselves, circulate as money indefinitely, without any further
trouble, or volition, or expense by the government;
that the debt will then be paid and the transaction
ended. Don't you see that this is the exact theory
of the wildest of *fiat* moneyism—that the greenbacks are to be absolute perpetual money, never

subject to redemption? And the greenbacks that we are considering, as substitutes for National bank notes, are to be promises to pay, and redeemable.

We may assume, then, that the greenbacks proposed to be exchanged for the National bank notes must be equal to those now in circulation; *i. e.*, payable in specie on demand, and by such exchange the government simply resolves itself into a bank of issue, with all that that implies. It must keep up the credit of its bills by promptly redeeming them on demand; to this end it must keep open banking houses at all commercial centres, and keep sufficient amounts of coin at all times for that purpose. What amount of coin in proportion to the bills issued this would require I do not know; but whatever it is it must be procured by incurring interest paying debt or taken from current revenues which might otherwise go to extinguish interest paying debt. In either case that must be an offset, so far as it goes, against the interest saved by the issue of the bills. And I do not know how much the expense of this system of banking would be, in the way of all the high-priced men, and the palatial appliances supposed to be necessary in high-toned banking; which must also be an offset against the interest as aforesaid.

5.—DOUBLE INTEREST.

Now let us go back to the National banks.

They tell us, with ever so much holy horror, that the National banks draw interest on the bonds upon which their notes are issued, and also upon their notes when they lend them out in their business, so that they get double interest on their capital. This is nothing new. Probably there never was a bank of issue in this country that did not have a similar privilege. The old-fashioned State chartered banks were allowed to issue and lend out three or four times the amount of bills that they were required to keep of specie in their vaults. The improved New York system, by which bonds and mortgages and public stocks were made a basis of security for bank bills, was identical in this respect with the National banks. The banks received interest on the securities and also on their notes based upon them. And it may be remarked that without some such advantage as this no banks of issue would ever be instituted; for nobody would be fool enough to incur the expense of a bank for the purpose of issuing bills to the mere amount of capital invested, with no other profit on the issue than the interest on such amount. It is easy enough, and much cheaper, to get that interest without a bank.

6.—GOVERNMENT BUSINESS FOR PROFIT.

Returning to the question of government banking : it is to be observed, further, that in this project the government cannot lend out its notes and receive interest on them, as the banks do, because they are to be exchanged for the bonds on which the interest is to be saved by the process, so that that interest is all the profit that can accrue from the issue of the notes, to offset against the interest on the hoard of coin necessary for creditable and successful banking, and all the other expenses before alluded to. The bills redeemed in the regular course of business would have to be re-issued for the purpose of keeping up the coin reserve somehow and not lent out upon interest.

This matter then resolves itself into a question of the government's going into business for profit —to *earn* the money wherewith to pay the interest on some $350,000,000 of bonds, and not a mere swapping of government circulating notes for that amount of bonds. And when we come to that, I need not say that it is at least problematical whether that business would produce any net profit or not—whether we would save any interest after all. And if it is to be the policy of the government to embark in business for the purpose of earning money, banking is not any more suitable enterprise for the government to make money at than merchandise, or manufacturing, or agriculture, or house building, or any other productive enterprises.

I will drop this subject here, for it is not necessary to make an argument to prove that such business is not what governments are for.

7.—THE OTHER SIDE CONSIDERED.

Some otherwise very sound men on the money

question and on National finance, do not like to be convinced that the government cannot as well as not profit largely by substituting greenbacks for the National Bank currency; *i. e.* by saving the interest on a corresponding amount of bonds.

To begin at the bottom of the subject, then, the first point of argument of the other side is that the notes are to be based upon the credit of the government; that credit is based upon the entire property of the nation—not only that belonging, technically, to the government, but all taxable property of all the people; so that the security for a government paper circulating medium, is of the amplest kind, and such paper will always be accepted by the people, irrespective of its payment or any provision for payment.

Now, to go down to the very elementary principles of business, without puzzling over any mysteries of finance or banking, it may be stated as a sound proposition that no business whatever, public or private—individuals, corporations, or governments—can be sustained continuously, for any great length of time, upon credit and security without payment. How long will a man's credit last if he never pays? And what is the security for but for compulsory payment? In fact, security, apart from a provision for payment, is an impossibility. The idea is nonsense.

A business man takes a customer's note, with ample real estate or other security. When it becomes due, the creditor, if not pressed himself, will perhaps waive immediate payment, for the debtor's accommodation; but if the latter should claim that he need not pay at all, for the reason that the debt is secured, he would soon find that the security does not take the place of payment. It cannot answer the purposes of the creditor, in paying his debts, or in making his investments. It is of no possible use only in view of payment. Payment is the fundamental factor of all business · and when we are told that the government can issue $350,000,000, or so of greenbacks and keep them afloat continuously without payment, the very groundwork of all sound business principles is ignored. The fact that bank creditors are all sure to want their money when the security fails, but do not all want it so long as the security is good so that they can get it when they do want it, is not a solution of the difficulty of doing business without paying. The creditor of a bank cannot be satisfied whether he *needs* his money at once or not, until assured that the bank is *ready* to pay. Security without paying cannot be satisfactory to the creditor, and cannot sustain the credit of the bank. And in the case of the government it is an entire fallacy. There can be no property security for the payment of any government debt. When you talk about the property of the nation being security for a government paper circulation, or for anything else, it must be borne in mind that that security all depends on the *willingness* of the powers that be to pay ; for the government cannot be sued and a debt collected against her will, as in the case of individuals.

And then, secondly, this matter of *payment* involves the necessity of *values* to pay with. If I owe a debt, I cannot extinguish that debt, honestly, without passing to my creditor some valuable thing corresponding with the amount of the debt—equal to the value of the things that the debt was contracted for.

And thirdly, values cannot be produced by any financial legerdemain. I cannot extinguish my debt by giving my note. There is no inherent value in that, more than in any other piece of paper. If there be any exchangeable value in it, on account of which my creditor will take it, for the time, he takes it only as an evidence of debt, and the representative of valuable things that he supposes I will be possessed of when the note becomes due, and out of which he expects to get good and honest value for the debt. I cannot create values by merely saying that worthless things are worth a bushel of potatoes, a bushel of wheat, a dollar, or a thousand dollars. Calling a calf's tail a leg cannot make it a leg.

In these respects the government has no mysterious power more than an individual has. Whatever its needs are, in the way of values, it must give values for, if it is to maintain its reputation as an honest government. It can acquire such values by exercising its power of taxation in various ways, and I do not say it cannot acquire them by engaging in agriculture or merchandise, or banking; but it cannot *create* them by the word of its power, any more than I can. It cannot create a bushel of wheat by saying that chips are wheat. It cannot create a dollar by printing on a piece of paper that "this is a dollar," or by printing or writing a promise to pay a dollar. All the value there is in this is the dollar that it is supposed to represent and that is to be paid for it some time.

The fatal fallacy of this phase of greenbackism is that the issue of greenbacks to supersede the National bank currency can somehow be made to operate as a payment of an equal amount of bonds; whereas the controlling facts are that the bonds are an honest debt incurred for honest value, and can be extinguished, honestly, only by rendering equal value; that until so extinguished the interest must be paid in value; that such values cannot be created by law, but the government can only procure them by taxation or by earning them somehow; that the exchange of greenbacks for bonds is not an extinction of the debt, but the creation of a new liability in the shape of circulating notes payable on demand in coin, if honest greenbacks, which are to be kept afloat precisely as bank notes are kept afloat—by payment on demand, and re-issue, and by all the ordinary appliances of banks of issue. In a word the government is to be a vast bank of issue, furnishing the country with its paper circulating medium, precisely as any other bank or banks would furnish it; *i. e.*, by a continuous business, just begun when the notes are put into circulation. This is the service by which the interest on the bonds is to be saved—precisely the same that any bank of issue performs to earn money for its stockholders ; and it amounts to just this : that the government goes into the banking business to earn money to pay the interest on a portion of its bonds ; or, if you like it any better, performs a service to the public, and incurs expenses, in lieu of paying said interest ; no matter which we call it.

And now, in conclusion, without raising the question of the expediency of the government's embarking in speculation or business enterprises of any kind for profit, in view of what we have seen in these five or six years especially, and what we always see more or less of—the wholesale robberies of the largest money institutions by trusted agents, even where under the interested eyes of their owners; and of the innumerable failures of such institutions everywhere, by various causes, who can say that it is not cheaper to tax the people to pay the interest on $350,000,000 of bonds than to tax them to pay the expenses, and the stealings, and the losses that are inevitable in such a gigantic system of government banking, without the self-interest of an owner any where as a regulator.

And then when we consider the instability of a currency issued by a single great government bank, manipulated by politicians in Congress, fluctuating as political administration fluctuates, and not regulated in any respect by the real needs of business, as it could not be then, with the resulting instability of money values, the damage of such a currency to the whole country, in comparison to the present system, would be incalculable.

VII.

THE BONDS AND BONDHOLDERS.

What the bonds were for—The bargain—The greenback claim—The tax question—Clamors answered.

I have no vindication to make for the bondholders. They do not need any. This chapter is written for the instruction of that class of people who have been deluded by the clamors of demagogues against the government bonds and their owners.

This denunciation of the bonds and bondholders implies that the bondholder is a public enemy, and the bonds his weapons by which he has all along been destroying the prosperity of the people.

Why? What crime are these bonds and their owners tainted with? Let us see.

1.—WHAT THE BONDS WERE FOR.

The Nation was in a deadly war for its life—the most gigantic war of modern times. The struggle was a doubtful one. As in all great wars, the government was compelled to fight the battle out on its credit. The alternative was upon us to borrow money to prosecute the war and maintain the Union, or give up the contest and let the Union go. Then, as now, there was a clamor, long and loud, against Government bonds and against greenbacks too, not however, that the takers were bloated then, or would be, from any profits to be derived from investments in their government to aid in saving its life-blood from running out; not that they were to derive any advantage whatever from the hated bonds; but that the bonds were worthless and the buyers were fools for buying them at any price. Yes, I remember those times, and I remember who it was that led that factious opposition to the bonds, and the greenbacks, and all other successful financial measures. It was not those who were aiding in any way to suppress the rebellion. Their efforts were unceasing to prevent men of money from buying the bonds; not that they suggested any better way to provide the sinews of war, but because *there was no other way,* and to defeat the sale of bonds would be to assure the success of the rebellion.   Such was the origin of the war upon the bonds.

But they failed.   The mass of Northern capitalists—large and small, Republican and Democratic—put their faith in their government, and so they took the risk and advanced the money on the government's promises, and the Union was saved. Such is the crime that the original bondholders were guilty of.   But we are told, with ever so much holy horror, that the bonds were bought with greenbacks, which were at a large discount at the time, and so the holders are profiting by the necessities of the government, if they are to be paid in coin.

Now the question is : must this great government of the United States, this government of forty millions of people, after the successful resistance to the serried hosts of the enemy that for four bitter years battled to crush it out, after fourteen years, since then, of honest faith to every obligation, and thus maintaining a public credit never surpassed, under similar circumstances, since governments and wars were invented, is there any necessity now, for this government and this people to *plead baby* upon their contracts of indebtedness by which all that was done, by which we live and have a being as a nation to-day ?

2.—THE BARGAIN.

Was there anything unfair in the bargain ?   Let us see.   The Nation was in deadly peril.   It had the patriotic men to fight the battle out.   It was on its knees to the money world—to the Shylocks, if you please, and it is a good thing that there were Shylocks then—on its knees for money, *money*, MONEY. It had naught to offer for it but its pledge of honor that never had been forfeited, its pledge that if not overpowered by the enemy the paper promises would be redeemed. The bond buyers took the risk—the risk of rebel success and national bankruptcy, and also the risk of subsequent dishonesty and repudiation.

For all that risk, and for their money, did the money lenders get too good a bargain? In the first place the chances were about even that they would lose it all by the failure of our arms. And now let us see what the bonds cost them—say they were all rich money lenders, if you please. " Oh they paid for them in greenbacks at par; and greenbacks were a good deal below par," we are told. Yes, they paid in greenbacks, but what did the greenbacks cost them? When the greenbacks were issued the Shylocks had their money invested somewhere, for it is not supposable that they were keeping it idle. Somebody owed it to them in coin. Then the government stepped in with its legal tender law, and said to them: " Mr. Shylock, you shall take these greenbacks for all debts owing to you at par. We know that your contracts call for gold, or silver, but our national necessity and the laws of war are higher laws than money contracts, and we have been compelled to issue these paper promises to raise supplies for our starving soldiers, and to pay their wages, and to procure other indispensable material of war; and to give them currency it was necessary to give them this legal tender character."

And thus it was that rich men with money owing to them, profited by buying bonds with greenbacks. However much the greenbacks depreciated in *purchasing* power they never depreciated at all in *debt paying* power. Debts contracted on a gold basis were always receivable in greenbacks, so that the bonds originally purchased by the rich actually cost dollar for dollar in gold; and if eventually paid in gold, principal and interest, the buyers will come out exactly even—*all the risk thrown in.*

And now, on looking back over all those transactions, in those dark and gloomy and doubtful years, and entering into the spirit and feeling of those times, so nearly as now we can, as they were upon all true and loyal manhood all through those bloody days, and considering the money cost of those bonds, it is easy to see that it was patriotism more than business and money making principles, that incited their purchase. Yea, well do I remember how it was understood, all through the war, that the money men were risking their money for their country, even as the patriotic young men risked their lives. And therefore, beyond the exact terms of the money contract, we owe to

every man, woman, and child, Democrat and Republican, who then invested any amount of money
in those bonds, a debt of gratitude for their indispensable aid in saving their country. It required
patriotic money as well as patriotic muscle to put
down that rebellion, and there was patriotism
enough in the money of the country to take its
share in the work, in spite of all the assurances
of the other side that the money would be lost.

Such is the advantage that the loyal capitalists
of the country took of the necessities of their
country. Such is the way that they speculated.

3.—THE GREENBACK CLAIM.

And now (Oct., 1879), as to the claim of a political party, not yet quite dead, that the bonds were
originally and are now payable in greenbacks, and
should be paid by an issue of greenbacks for that
purpose at once. It is alleged that the contract
somehow implied such payment as that. Let us
see. It is not necessary to recite the various laws
under which the bonds were issued ; but what do
the bonds call for? The government reached out
after the money of the people, by all possible
agencies, saying to them, "bring us your money,
or whatever we have compelled you to take for
money for the time being, and in twenty, forty, or
fifty years, we will repay you in *dollars*, with in
terest, and your claim upon us shall not be taxable.
Whereupon the bargain was consummated by the
delivery of the money, and the issue of the various

promises to pay *dollars*. That is a fair and honest bargain by competent parties; and there is nothing in any law contrary to it. The holder of a bond is entitled to receive just what it calls for, and when it calls for it. Every honest man of any party will agree to this. Then what is the dollar that is meant when it is said, "the United States will pay one hundred dollars?" What is a dollar? A promise to pay a dollar cannot be a dollar; and so the present greenback, being a promise to pay a dollar, is not the dollar that it promises to pay. The greenback promise to pay a dollar cannot mean to repay another greenback. That would be nonsense; for why change at all, if the change is for another just like the first; and then it is clear that the promise on the bond to pay a hundred dollars does not mean to pay $100 in another promise to pay $100. Who would take a note of the best man in Corning payable in a year in another note payable at his option? And who would have advanced money to the government and taken bonds payable in twenty or fifty years in other promises to pay, with no assurance or pledge that the lender should ever get the *dollars*? Nobody. The money of the country was willing to trust the government and risk its *ability* to pay, but it never would have accepted less than the faith of the nation that good actual dollars would be paid. Or at least it did not take anything less than that. The pledge is to pay *dollars*, and a dollar is a certain quantity of gold or silver, as I have shown in a previous paper. There is no precedent of the treasury, and nothing in the transaction itself, or in the law, to warrant the assumption that the promise in the bonds contemplated anything but coin.

Much more preposterous is the idea that the bargain of the government with the bondtakers contemplated payment in stuff to be called dollars, to be invented afterwards, to be legislated into dollars out of nothing, without any intrinsic value, and without as much as a promise to pay dollars or any other value; stuff that never was known in the history of the world to be used as money, that cannot have any attribute of money, and cannot be used as money, and its only effect, if attempted, would be to repudiate the indebtedness.

4.—THE TAX QUESTION.

The non-taxability of the bonds is held up as a considerable oppression upon the poor working men—non-property holders. The total fallacy of that hue and cry will be apparent from the single fact that the non-property holder is not taxed a cent the more, directly or indirectly, by reason that the bonds are not taxed, so that it makes no difference whatever to him whether they are taxed or not. In proof of this it is only necessary to bear in mind the fact that the taxes that the said bonds would be liable to if they had not been made exempt from taxation, are State, county, and municipal direct

taxes upon the property of the country, and not
taxes upon poverty or indirect taxes upon consumption.   So that whether such exemption be
right or wrong, it is not a question between labor
and capital, or between wealth and poverty, but
simply between property holders themselves.

And it is not a question between *large* property
holders and *small* ones—not between wealthy people and those of small means ; for the bonds are
not owned exclusively by the rich any more than
is other property. While some industrious, thrifty
people own small amounts of real estate or other
taxable property, others own small amounts of
government bonds—even as low as fifty dollars.
Bondholding is not a class privilege. Whatever of
advantage there may be in it is accessible to every
person who can raise as much as fifty dollars.

But let us see exactly how it is between bondholders and other property holders—how it was at
first and how it is now. I have shown how the
bonds were created, what for, and what the bargain
was. It is not to be denied that the bonding
scheme intended to make the terms so that the
money holders of the country could afford to buy
them—so far as it was in power of the government
to do so. And the exemption from taxation was
one of the conditions of the bargain—then supposed to be a necessary condition to induce the
people to buy them. Or at any rate, if it is now
supposed that the bargain was especially a good

one for the buyers, the chance was open to everybody who had any money or property. They were not offered to a selected class of Shylocks who were to have the exclusive privilege of being bloated bondholders. All kinds of property were then saleable at high prices for money, and any man, woman or child who had any kind of property had the privilege of buying the bonds—everybody at the same price—and reap all the advantages of exemption from taxation, gold interest, gold principal and all, exactly according to the terms held out. That is the way it was in the beginning, and anybody can see that the bond buyers then had no advantage over those who did not buy them.

How is it now? We have seen that in view of the great risk that the bond buyers were taking during the war, the bargain was not especially a good one for them. Even the most astute Shylock could not know whether the bonds would be worth anything in the future or not. But the war terminated in our favor, the risk of loss is over, (except the risk of this greenback scheme of repudiation;) the bonds are worth their face and more; it has resulted in a good bargain for the original takers or any who took them before the war was over. Those who were patriotic enough to buy at the hazard have profited by it. Those who thus bought and have kept them are fully entitled to all the gains that the terms of the bonds gives them; those who have sold are entitled to all the profit that they realized—entitled to all that exactly as the farmer is entitled to the market price for his wheat, or the working man to his day's wages.

And now how stands the matter? The bonds have assumed their level of value, so to speak, in the markets of the world, the same as any other property, in view of all the advantages attached to them. Non-taxability, gold interest, etc., all go to make up their value in the market. The present holders, mostly, are second-hand purchasers, and not original takers. These have sold and made the profits of the rise. Those have bought at what the property is worth with all its advantages, and with the risk eliminated from the bargain. It is always in the market for sale and accessible to all, at the market price. There is no exclusive and privileged class of bondholders. The bonds are an established property accessible to everybody, exactly as in any other property; and the rich greenbacker who thinks it is more profitable property to own than any other, has just the same opportunity to own it as others; the poorer greenbacker has exactly the same chance according to his means. If it is more profitable to hold a few hundred dollars in bonds than in a house and lot, or in a mortgage, or any other species of property, it is his privilege to own the bonds. And as to those who own nothing and pay no taxes, I cannot see that they are affected in one way or the other by this bond tax question.

And whatever advantage the exemption may be to the bondholder now, when we consider that the taxpayer, large or small, as a constituent of the government, and a part of the contracting power, received a full equivalent in advance for this additional tax that he is paying now, in the bargain, in the dark days of the rebellion, when the money was borrowed, in the price received, or the rate of interest, just as the seller of a farm would get a better price by agreeing to pay the taxes upon it for a series of years; when all this is considered it is easy enough to see that this feature of the bond transaction, instead of being a great wrong, has really been as advantageous to the government and to the taxpayers as any other of the measures by which we have been saved a country.

5.—CLAMORS ANSWERED.

All the clamors about the bonds being an invention for the benefit of money men, and all the criticisms as to the processes through which they originated, are conclusively answered by the unquestionable facts that somehow they represent the solid values received by the government of somebody and consumed in the war for the salvation of the government, and that in all the history of the world no war of equal magnitude was ever prosecuted more successfully as it respects its financial department, or more economically in that department where the expense of it was honestly paid.

Reader, there are many burdens to be borne in this life, of which the payment of honest indebtedness is supposed to be one; but when we have had the value for it, it ought not to be esteemed a burden at all. Whatever of burden this public debt may be, we cannot afford to do less than to redeem the national pledges to the letter and in the spirit of the contract; for with nations as with individuals, honesty is always the best policy, whether we have any conscience in it or not.

I close this chapter with a quotation from President Washington:

"There is no truth more thoroughly established, than that there exists in the economy and course of nature, an indissoluble union between virtue and happiness, between duty and advantage, between the genuine maxims of an honest and magnanimous policy and the solid rewards of public prosperity and felicity."

VIII.

WEALTH AND ITS USES.

Communism—How wealth is produced—Interest on capital—What the use of money is worth— Inflation cannot reduce interest—Concluding address to workiny men—Conclusion.

1.—COMMUNISM.

I do not suppose it is necessary to discuss the question of the right of property. I shall not make an argument to prove that where we see two young men start out in life together, with equal opportunities, working in the same shop it may be, or in a store, or on farms, or in any other occupation, no matter what; one economizes and saves every dollar of his earnings not necessary for his comfortable support, working on from year to year, and putting his money where it will earn him something all along, until, in a course of years he finds himself the owner of a few thousands of dollars worth of honest property; while the other has expended all his earnings as he went along; so that one is comfortably above board, and the other penniless; I say I shall not make any argument to prove that such inequality of property is not any fault or any wrong on the part of that successful man, or any fault or short-coming on the part of the government, or of any body else but that spendthrift man himself, or that there is not or cannot be any cure for such a state of things otherwise than for every body to save a part of their earnings and put it to use for their future benefit. It is not necessary to argue this; but I do say that the lives of those two men, thus briefly pointed out, represent, respectively, the fundamental factors of the wealth and the poverty of the world, with all that each implies.

The fact is not to be disguised that there is extant in this country more or less of the spirit of French and German communism; arraying the poor against the rich, not only, but arraying the shiftless, dissipated, unworthy, slumocracy against all property holders, large and small; teaching that accumulated wealth is accumulated wickedness, that the money lords should be crushed out somehow, that interest on money beyond one or two per cent. per annum is especially unjust and oppressive, and on the whole, that the property holders are the cause of all the poverty and destitution in the land ; by all of which, thousands of well-disposed people are dangerously deluded.

And so I deem it appropriate to conclude this book with a little chapter on the fundamental facts of the creation and use of wealth.

2.—HOW WEALTH IS PRODUCED.

A young man goes into the wilderness to make himself a home and a living for himself and family. He chops down the trees of the forest, subdues the ground and cultivates it, persevering, year after year, in his vigorous industry and self-denying economy, until, at the end of twenty years, he finds himself the possessor of a farm of a hundred acres, in a high state of cultivation, with an ample and luxurious habitation, with fruits and meadows, and all desirable stock and implements for large and almost spontaneous production of many of the necessaries and luxuries of life. It is a living for himself and his family. He has paid the price of that land as it was in a state of nature. He has made the improvements. It is his, and it is as nearly a paradise as this world's goods can make.

24

He may do with it as he will. He may continue to occupy it and work it with his own hands, or hire others to work it for him, or rent it for a share of the products, or for money rent, or sell it for money, or for a mortgage, or give it away. Whatever he does with it nobody is injured by it. There is not a respectable working man so ignorant and so reckless as not to admit all this to be so. This is wealth.

3.—INTEREST ON CAPITAL.

Now, as old age begins to creep along upon this man, he thinks he can afford to take the world easier. A young man comes along, starting out in life with his bare hands, to hew his way through the world. And on looking that farm over, he sees that he can better afford to take it, with the stock and implements, all ready at hand for the easy production of large values, and give the owner a considerable share of the produce, or pay him a money rent, than to start in the forest as that owner did. And so they strike a bargain; the young man takes the farm, with the stock and tools, and the old man retires. Or the young man buys it all, and gives a bond and mortgage at such price, and with such interest annually as he finds, on a fair computation of the income of the property, that he can better afford to pay than to commence life in any other way. In either case the old man lives in idleness, if he so chooses, on the income from that property. And that old man is called a pauper, living upon the labor of the young man. This is interest of money eating up one-half or three-quarters of the earnings of industry. This is capital oppressing labor. This is the rich robbing the poor. That old man has no right to live in idleness, with that young man to bring his bread and butter to him. He has no right to any of the corn that the young man raises by his honest toil, or to interest money wrung from the sweat of his brow. All this is sought to be abolished somehow,

I will not argue the merits of this process. This practical illustration of the production and enjoyment of property in its simplest form is sufficient. Anybody can understand it. And this illustration will apply to all other phases of interest or rent paying, for they are both substantially one; they are both compensation for the use of values previously produced by labor, and generally used for the production of other values and indispensable for their profitable production. It matters not whether such borrowed values are taken in the shape of money, farms, shops, tools, or what not, or whether the borrower deals directly with the man who actually made them, or earned them, the same principle is at the bottom of it all. They have cost the labor of somebody, the use of them is worth something, and the borrower can better afford to pay what he agrees to pay for their use than to go without them, or wait till he can produce them himself; it is the better for him that somebody has accumulated them; and the more of them in the market for hire the cheaper will be the interest or rent, as we shall see further on.

To go back to our farmer illustration. In course of time the old farmer dies, and that interest paying fund of his falls into the hands of an only son, who is now quite rich, and with reasonable prudence is able to live a life of idleness. What difference does that make to the young man who pays that interest? If he was not impoverished or injured by paying the old man for the use of the property, he surely will not be by paying to the son. If as industrious and economical as the old man was, he will own the whole in due time; if not it is a good thing for him to have the use by paying for it, so long as he can do no better. So that the accumulation of property and the paying for its use, by borrowers, cannot possibly be any injury to any body. Of course people sometimes make mistakes in this, as in any other matters of business, and lose money by borrowing; but in general it is to be supposed that every man knows his own business, and what is for his own interest, and will not borrow capital when not profitable to him, any more than he will buy a horse or a steam engine when not profitable. And so this matter will always regulate itself; when borrowed capital is likely to be injurious to borrowers they will let it alone. The remedy is always in their own hands. There cannot possibly be any power in wealth to oppress them in this matter of interest. They can always be just as independent of the money power, as they call it, as if all wealth were extinguished and we were to begin down on the plane of barbarism. Everybody is free to begin there who wishes to, and the wealth of other people need not hurt them at all. They have only to let it alone.

4.—WHAT THE USE OF MONEY IS WORTH.

But the *rates* of interest are too high, we are told, and we are entertained with elaborate figure work to show how many days' labor are expended to pay the interest on borrowed capital; but they forget to estimate how many more days' work every borrower would have to do than now were it not for the help that the borrowed tools gives him.

As to the price for the use of a farm, or for the money to buy it with, or for a shop and tools, or the money to buy them with, or for any other form of hired capital—all resolving themselves substantially into interest of money—it is safe enough for every man to make his own bargains, precisely the same as in any matter of traffic. As we have heretofore seen, no man will pay interest when he cannot afford it, and the same rule will apply to the rates; and if the individual interest payers profit by paying interest, the country at large cannot lose by it, whatever the rates may be.

The real intrinsic value of the use of capital cannot be ascertained with much precision. It is always much more than its exchangeable value, or the interest paid for it. The real value to the borrower is what he can produce with it, in excess of what he could produce without it.

To put this matter in the clearest light, to show what the use of capital is worth—imagine a man going out upon a prairie to make his living, with nothing but his naked hands to do it with, and no way of getting any implements but to borrow two dollars to buy a spade and a hoe. A man comes along and offers to lend him $2 and there is no other person who will do it. What can he afford to pay for the use of $2 for a year rather than do without it? We cannot know exactly but it is surely within bounds to say that he can better afford to pay $5 as interest, or two hundred and fifty per cent., than to dig up the soil with his hands and such natural aids as he can find. There is, then, a real intrinsic value in the use of $2, of not less than $5 for one year.

Then the next year the capitalist comes along again and offers to lend this farmer $100 to buy a mule and a plow. With these aids he can produce about ten times as much as before. Now, it would be quite a moderate estimate to say that he can better afford to pay fifty per cent. interest for that $100 for a year than to do without the mule and plow.

But no such prices are paid for the use of money. Why? Because there is so much capital accumulated, beyond the immediate wants of its owners, and seeking investment for hire, that the competition brings the price down vastly below the intrinsic value.

For further illustration : It is not to be presumed that our young farmer first alluded to would agree to pay rent or interest on that farm that would not leave him the better for it. And exactly so with all other phases of interest or rent. Brick Pomeroy can better afford to pay large interest on the capital required to print his pestilent papers to the best advantage than to print them on the old ramage press of fifty years ago. Our merchants can better afford to pay three or four hundred dollars a year for a good store room than to put their goods into slab shanties. A young beginner can better afford to pay a high rate of interest on money to buy horses and plows, and mowing machines, and other improved implements than to dig up his soil with a spade, and cut his crops with a jack-knife, etc. And exactly so with all other phases of labor and business. It is clearly the better for the poor beginners that somebody has accumulated wealth to lend to them on interest, or rent, or whatever you please to call it, at such rates as they can agree upon. The money paid for the use of capital is just as advantageous to the payer as is that paid by the farmer for his seed wheat, by the blacksmith for his iron, or the shoemaker for his leather. And if the receiver of interest lives in idleness it is none the worse for the working men.   If one-half of the working men could at once be transformed into millionaires, the wages of the other half would not be any the less, surely.   It would be just as sensible to clamor against merchants' bills, doctors' bills, mechanics' bills, and working men's wages, as against the payment of interest on borrowed capital.

5.—INFLATION WILL NOT REDUCE INTEREST

But the greenback policy—inflation—making money plenty and cheap—will reduce the *rates* of interest, we are told.   This is another of the wild fallacies of uniformed teachers.   I have demonstrated in a previous paper how it is that the value of money always diminishes as its volume increases, so that with an inflation of the currency the quantity of money required to do any business is increased in proportion to the increase of currency.

Now suppose the currency to be doubled with good money.   As it will then require twice as much money to do the work and business of the country as before, the demand for money to loan will be double what it was before.   There will be twice the amount of money in the hands of lenders to lend, and twice as much wanted by borrowers ; so that the rate of interest must remain exactly the same, for the reason that the relative supply and demand remain the same.

The rate of interest is governed by the amount of real capital—wealth—that is in the market for hire ; and this does not depend on the quantity of circulating medium. This may be doubled without increasing the real wealth of the community at all. But it does depend on the improved farms, the buildings, and property of all kinds that is in excess of the immediate wants of their owners. The more of all this the lower is the rate of interest, or rent. Referring again to the farmer illustration: when the young man comes along to hire that farm, if there should be two such properties for rent, and only one applicant, the rate would be low ; but if only one farm and two applicants the rent would be higher ; so that the more property unemployed by the owners, the more people able to live upon the income of their property, the more wealth in proportion to the number of people who work for their living and hire money or property, the lower the rate of interest. Accordingly it is notorious that in the older settled and richer portions of our country the rate of interest is lower than in the newer localities where less of wealth is accumulated.

For authority on this point I will here quote from " Say's Political Economy :"

" The more abundant is the disposable capital, in proportion to the multiplicity of its employments, the lower will the interest of borrowed capital fall. With regard to the supply of disposable capital, that must depend on the quantum of previous savings."—*Page* 349.

" Capital, at the moment of lending, commonly assumes the form of money ; whence it has been inferred that abundance of money is the same thing as abundance of capital; and, consequently, that abundance of money is what lowers the rate of interest. The fact is, that abundance or scarcity of money, or its substitute, whatever it may be, no more affects the rate of interest, than abundance or scarcity of cinnamon, of wheat, or of silk."—*Page 350.*

"The glut or scarcity of the commodity lent only affects its relative price to other commodities, and has no influence whatever on the rate of interest, upon its advance or loan. Thus, when silver money lost three-fourths of its former relative value, although four times as much of it was necessary to pass a loan of the same extent of capital, the rate of interest remained unaltered. The quantity of specie or money in the market, might increase ten fold without multiplying the quantity of disposable, or circulation capital."—*p.* 353.

It is quite clear therefore, that interest paying is not oppressive, *per se*, to any body, that the rate of interest will always regulate itself justly by the laws of supply and demand, exactly as the prices of corn or other commodities adjust themselves, and that the accumulation of capital by some people, and lending it to others for hire, is indispensable to any progress or improvement, nay to civilization itself; for it is self-evident that nobody would care to accumulate any values for others to use if no compensation could be had for their use.

6.—CONCLUDING ADDRESS TO WORKING MEN.

Now, in conclusion, a further word to working men. Nothing can be more senseless than for you to set up antagonism to wealth. Every one of you can accumulate some of it if you will; if you will not, your interest is identical with that of the wealth that runs the industries where you expect always to get a livelihood.   But the theory seems to be : extinguish the money lords, crush out the men who own anything, then the working men will have plenty of work, big wages, short hours, cheap goods ; in other words, universal luxury flowing to them with very little effort.   It is a fallacy, a fraud upon honest working men.   It cannot be done. Working men in good positions would do much better for themselves by extra exertions to promote their employers' interests than by engaging in these crusades to pull them down.

There is no necessary antagonism between labor and capital—between the working man and the man that hires him.   There is no antagonism between them, only the common self-interests of the race that is indispensable to its self-preservation and the perpetuity—the selfishness that properly in. cites every one to take care of his or her own in terests; that impels the farmer to sell his products as high as he and can buy his necessaries as cheaply as he can, and the merchant to buy his goods as cheaply, and sell them as dearly as he can, and the manufacturer to buy his labor and materials as cheaply as he can, and the working man to work as little and get as much pay for it as he can, and the man of money to get all for his money that he can. There is no more antagonism between a rich man and a laborer, than between the merchant and his customer, or between the farmer and the blacksmith.   And then, when we come to the question of the wealth that runs industrial enterprises, and the muscle that does the work, as a matter of class interest, the interest of the one is eminently identical with that of the other; evidently so to all who will take the trouble to think. Every working man knows that the wealth that builds the shops and the machinery, and implements for manufacturing enterprises, and buys the materials, and pays the wages, is only accumulated labor—labor performed by somebody, and in this country more usually by the owners of it, who are the owners of such enterprises; and when not so it is procured upon their credit. And without such accumulated labor—wealth—there would be no hiring of labor, and no manufacturing labor done in any other way. In fact the accumulation of capital is the fundamental factor of civilization.

And then it follows: that the essential interest of working men requires,

1st, That somebody should accumulate capital, and the more of it the better, for the more the capital the more and the greater variety of industries;

2nd, That such capital shall be invested in industrial enterprises to the greatest possible extent;

3rd, That such industries shall be profitable to their owners; for otherwise they cannot continue to exist: and consequently,

4th, That working men, everywhere, should strive, in all ways, to promote the success of their employers, instead of engaging in a factious opposition to them, as a class, political or otherwise.

7.—CONCLUSION.

In conclusion of the whole matter of this book, reader, in my studies of the many topics herein discussed, and in writing down my conclusions, with my own experience and observation where applicable, and in presenting them in this form, if I have succeeded in imparting to you any instruction by which you will be made the better—more prosperous, more happy through life, my object is accomplished.

FINIS.